MURDER UNTIMELY

ANITA WALLER

Print ISBN 978-1-913419-00-4

For Doris Lester, it had been a difficult night of dreams, not all good, and to make matters worse, around twelve inches of snow had fallen during the dark hours; expected according to the weather forecast, but not really believed.

Doris had known before she'd even put a foot out of bed. There had been that curious stillness that comes with snowfall, that odd white glow permeating into the room.

And then had come the phone call from granddaughter Mouse, sounding far too awake to be true. 'Nan, don't even think about driving in. That little thing you call a car will turn into a sledge if you try to drive down that steep hill from the cottage. Will you be able to walk down to the main road? I'll collect you from there.'

'Of course, but maybe we should think about having another day off...?'

'Not a chance,' Mouse laughed. 'I can't wait to get back in that office. Do you realise the twenty-third of December to the second of January is nine whole days of inactivity? We have stuff to do. I've already been down and put on the heating, so, as planned, we're back today.'

'We're not going sledging then?'

'You're too old. Now, get your breakfast and give me a ring when you're ten minutes away from setting off. And take care.'

'What about Kat?'

'Already spoken to her. She took Martha to Nanny Enid's last night, so she says she'll walk down.'

'Okay,' Doris said, abandoning all hopes of a day beside her roaring fire with a book. 'And take care, there's some proper numpties driving around Derbyshire these days. They get a four-by-four and think they're invincible.'

'We are,' Mouse said with a laugh.

Doris disconnected and wandered around trying to get her brain into gear – working with Kat Rowe and Mouse for the past year following what she thought of as her own annus horribilis when her granddaughter had been shot, had taken ten years off her, given Doris some of her youth back. Except at eight o'clock on a snowy morning.

The three of them had bonded to such an extent that even Kat now called her Nan, and the closeness had tightened with the shooting of Kat's husband, Leon. The forming of Connection, their investigation agency, had brought something good out of something bad, and today was going to be a good day. It hadn't been anticipated, but an agreement had been reached.

The toaster popped, and Doris smiled as she walked towards it. A bit of snow wasn't going to stop their plans – not according to Mouse, anyway.

Mouse collected Doris an hour later, and drove with the considerable skill and care required on that whiteout of a day. The journey to Eyam hadn't been easy; Kat had already arrived, having taken the easy method of walking.

Mouse was excited. Today was Nan's first day as a partner in the business, and the meeting was to determine how they could reconfigure the layout of the office premises to give Doris a consulting room of her own, and still leave a reception area.

They would then bring in builders and work from Mouse's flat above the office until the construction and redecoration was finished. Today was discussion day. A bit of snow – well, okay, Mouse conceded to herself, twelve inches or so – wasn't going to bring Connection to a snow-bound halt.

Kat opened the door for them and they stamped around outside, trying to remove the unwelcome white stuff from their boots before trailing it into the office.

'Morning,' Kat said with a smile. Her own cheeks were still rosy from the walk down through the village. 'Hot chocolate?'

They nodded, and Kat went into her own office to prepare the drinks while Mouse and Doris took off their many layers of clothes.

'Let's live in Derbyshire,' Mouse grumbled as she walked through. 'It's a lovely place, very picturesque, we'll like it there. Which plank said all of that without thinking about mountains of snow?'

'You did, my love,' Doris said.

'Did I?'

'You did indeed. It was about the point where you saw this flat with the shop underneath.'

'Is it always this bad, Kat?' Mouse asked.

'This isn't bad,' Kat responded. 'Things are still getting through, so at least we're not at the stage where we're cut off from the rest of the world. I imagine Buxton is wiped out; they always get more snow than us.'

'Then let's hope any business we may pick up from the Buxton area is confined to the summer.' Mouse stood in the doorway of her office, took off her bobble hat and launched it towards her coat stand. It landed on the windowsill and she sighed. One day...

On the top of her filing cabinet stood two large rolls of paper, and she gathered them up before going into Kat's office. The bigger desk in there would come in handy on this most auspicious day.

Hot chocolates were handed around, and Mouse rolled out the first of the two papers, laying it on the desk and commandeering staplers and pen tubs to hold down the four corners.

'Okay,' she said, 'this is what I've spent Christmas doing. This is our space as it is now. The measurements are as exact as I can get them, and I think you'll see just how much space we're wasting by having such a big reception area. We can easily fit three offices in here, and still have a small reception. I don't think we need to move the shop door, because the third office would be at the same side of this space as Kat's. If we move Kat's door up towards my office by around a metre, the wall for the third office space can start here.' She leaned across and drew a small mark.

Kat and Doris stared at the complex drawing.

'You've spent Christmas doing this?' Doris asked.

'Not all Christmas, but some of it.' There was a faint blush of colour suddenly apparent on Mouse's face.

Neither Kat nor Doris made any comment about what she was probably doing when she wasn't drawing on the sheets of paper.

Mouse removed the staplers and pens holding down the corners and rolled the paper up. 'This,' she said with a flourish, 'is the plan if we agree to put the third office next to Kat's.' Mouse repeated the anchoring procedure for the corners, and they all leaned over.

'This is the sensible way. It means the only alteration to the existing layout as far as Kat and I are concerned is that the office door will have to be removed and repositioned in the end of her wall. It will give you more space inside your office, Kat, because you'll have the additional length of wall. I have no idea why we put the door there in the first place, it doesn't make any sense, but we did. The other alternative, which will be much more costly, is to rip everything out and start from scratch. It will also delay our getting back in here. Thoughts?' She sat down, sipping at her drink.

'Firstly, I'm impressed,' Doris said. 'I'm assuming this new office will be clad to match the rest? And what about the reception desk?'

'I think we can cut the existing one down, and spin it around so that the receptionist is facing the door, rather than the main window. It will be more welcoming.'

'Have you shown these to anyone?' Kat asked.

'Only Joel.'

'That's answered what would have been my second question,' Kat laughed, 'but I meant had you shown them to a builder.'

The faint blush that had died down now appeared as definite rosy cheeks. 'Walked straight into that, didn't I. I've asked that builder from the top end of the village how quickly he could do it if we were to approach him, and he says building work is dead after Christmas, so he could start next week. Stefan Patmore.'

Kat nodded. 'He's good. We had him for loads of stuff when we first moved in. I'm more than happy with him taking this on. You okay with this layout, Nan?'

'I'm amazed at it. A bit overwhelmed, really. You must have started on this as soon as I agreed to be a partner, Mouse.'

'No, before.'

'But you didn't know I would say yes...'

'Nan,' Kat spoke gently, 'it wasn't a request that you would formally join us in the business, it was more an instruction. So when this snow goes you need to be out there choosing a desk. All the paperwork should be back from the solicitors by the tenth of January, and then we're good to go. There is one other thing we need to give some attention though. We won't have a receptionist.'

'School leaver?' Mouse asked.

'Mouse, it's early January. Kids leave school in the summer.' Nan frowned, giving thought to the issue. 'We could approach a recruitment agency.'

'Or we could stick a notice on the Co-op noticeboard with the job details and a contact phone number, stressing that local people will be given primary consideration,' practical Kat said. 'Put an age range of sixteen to eighteen, saying that full training will be given, and I bet we get a few applicants.'

'See,' Mouse said, 'I knew we had Kat for a reason. Why didn't we think of that, Nan?'

'I didn't because I'm still trying to get my head around me starting a new job at my age,' Doris said. 'But of course Kat is right. We want somebody local, not somebody who lives in Sheffield and wouldn't be able to get here when it snows. When are we talking to the builder?'

'I said I'd ring him as soon as we'd had the talk, and he'll come down to see us straight away.' She picked up the phone. 'Okay to do it?'

'Fine by me.'

'And me.'

Stefan agreed that it was fine by him too. He pored over the drawings, scratched his head a couple of times, double-checked a measurement for the reception area and said it was good to go.

'I'll source the materials this week, but I think you should consider a vertical blind for this big window. Whoever is sitting at that reception desk is going to be in full view of everybody outside. With vertical blinds they can see out without feeling quite so exposed. Previously the desk was set back and that wouldn't have been an issue.'

Doris quickly nodded her agreement. 'You're right. I was always aware of being on show, even though there was a desk between me and the window, so it will be much more uncomfortable with the desk right by it. You can organise that for us as well?'

'I can, and I would recommend a cream colour. It won't take away your light, and it will blend well with the office walls. If you're all in agreement…?'

'We are,' Mouse said.

'Then thank you. I'll source the materials when I get home, cost it and speak to you tomorrow with the quote. It won't be cheap because you can't go cheap, you're a class outfit, and there is an extra suggestion I want to make. In this new office, the way you've drawn it, the new part, Mrs Lester's area, doesn't have any natural light. I'm proposing we take that side wall only so far up the main window, create a window sill and put a smaller version of the vertical blind in that. That way there will be natural light, and Mrs Lester will be able to see outside. From the pavement it will simply look like two windows, a large shop one, and a smaller office one.'

Mouse smiled at Stefan. 'You're saying, politely, that I'll never be an architect? You're right, of course. I hadn't thought that one through fully, had I?'

He headed for the door. 'I'll get back to you sometime tomorrow, ladies. I have to tell you though, that if you expand the workforce any more, you'll have to move. You can't squeeze another office in this building.'

He took the two drawings with him, and set off to walk back up the hill, leaving his three new customers to sit down with a thud around Kat's desk.

'Do we want other quotes?' Mouse asked.

'I don't think so,' Doris said slowly, thoughtfully. 'Kat recommends him, which is good enough for me, and he's giving me a window. And he's local, which is something I think is important.

I've written out a job advert for the receptionist, so I'll take it across to the Co-op and put it on their noticeboard. Okay by you two?'

They agreed, and Kat stood to wash out the four cups. 'Then let's go home. There's nobody about, we've done what needed to be done, and it's started snowing again.'

'Nan, are you staying at mine?' Mouse looked concerned. 'If this carries on, you'll be stuck at the top of that hill. I'd rather you be here with me.'

Doris held up her bag. 'Book and knickers in here, already thought this one through, my lovely. Are you cooking our evening meal?'

2

For most of the three weeks that it took for the alterations to be completed, Kat, Mouse and Doris worked in Mouse's flat. They had received three responses to their receptionist advertisement, two girls and a boy, and had scheduled them for the Thursday of the third week, hoping that most of the noise would have stopped by then, and finishing touches would be underway.

They had initially decided that only one of them would do the interviewing; it would keep any feelings of intimidation at bay. It was only after considerable thought that they decided all three needed to be there. If any of the applicants felt put off by three ladies sitting at the other side of a desk, they wouldn't be up to the job anyway.

The first interviewee was a seventeen-year-old girl who had no confidence at all. She was competent on a computer to school level, but hadn't continued with education after leaving at sixteen, and had no plans to do so. They thanked her and said they would let her know by the end of the day.

The second applicant was completely the opposite; bright,

bubbly and a true chatterbox. With jet-black spiky hair, and an overuse of make-up, she looked horrified at the idea that she might have to tone it down, but assured them that she would do so if she was lucky enough to get the position. She left and blew all three of them a kiss as she walked out the door.

Doris slumped onto the desk. 'Don't they get any training in schools these days about interview protocols? She was lovely, a tremendous personality, but she'd drive us mad within a week. And slowly that make-up and spiky hair would come back. I'm sorry, but my vote is a no.'

'Mine too,' Kat agreed. 'She talks too much. And from the way she spoke, she would be relying on her mum to bring her into work every day. I'm sure her mum will want that.'

'I really liked her as a person, I like people to be different, but not our receptionist.' Mouse stood up. 'We've half an hour before our young man arrives. Coffee?'

Luke Taylor arrived two minutes early, and shook hands with all three of them. He was tall, with dark curly hair and deep brown eyes; his smile lit up the eyes.

He sat down and waited.

'Luke, thank you for coming,' Mouse said. 'Impressive exam results. You didn't want to stay on at school?'

'No. And that's for several reasons. I didn't know what I wanted to do. I've been earning money by working in a restaurant at night, washing pots, helping with prep, that sort of thing, and I couldn't face staying on at school. I think working has made me grow up. Apart from all that, if you don't know what you want to do for a career, how do you decide what A level subjects you want to take?'

Kat glanced to the next point. 'You're a driver?'

He nodded. 'I am. Mum taught me how to make a car move and stop by letting me drive around cemeteries and other such places, and we used to go to a driver-training centre about once a month, from me being sixteen. She paid for an intensive week for my seventeenth birthday, and I passed first time. I've now got Mum's cast-off Citroen, and she's bought a new one.'

'You didn't drive here today?' She had seen him walking down the road.

'No, I wanted to walk. I thought it would calm me down, but more than that I wanted to see how long it would take me. Six and a half minutes.'

'What made you apply, Luke?'

He paused for a moment, as if gathering his thoughts into a coherent mass. 'I said I didn't know what career I wanted, but I also knew that one day I would know. And then I did. Your advertisement said receptionist, and full training given. I am hoping that training is in investigative work, and not just reception, because your card was like a lightning bolt. I am quite happy to sit at that desk, but I now know what I need to learn, and it's not History and Geography. I don't know if I'm explaining this very well, but I feel this is so right for me.'

'Don't worry,' Doris smiled, 'you're explaining it very well. Luke, we're obviously an equal opportunities employer, and will facilitate anything that an employee would want to tackle. How do you see equality?'

He looked puzzled. 'That's a difficult one to answer because equal means equal. I'll try to explain.' Again he gathered his thoughts. 'I've kept in touch with most of my friends from school, lads and girls. Some went on to college, some started jobs, some are in sixth form. All of that is irrelevant. They're just friends. Wayne, my best friend, has parents who came here from Jamaica. He's not my Jamaican friend. He's my friend. I have a close friend called Lily, she's my friend but not my girlfriend. That's really the only way I can explain it. If we're alive, we're equal.'

'Thank you, Luke. If we were to offer you the position, when are you available to start?'

'Now.'

'What about your restaurant job?'

'I'll give them a week's notice. I can combine the two for a week. I won't leave them in the lurch.'

Kat stood. 'Just one final question, Luke, and then we'd like you to wait outside in reception for a few minutes. Will that be okay?'

'Yes, of course.'

'Okay, and this is the biggy. You'll be working with three women. We have frequent visits from two police officers, both women. You will be surrounded and overwhelmed by women. Can you handle it?'

He laughed. 'Mrs Rowe, I live with two younger sisters, a mum, a nan, and a dog called Daisy. Even the fish is called Esmerelda although I don't know what its sex is. I haven't had a dad since I was about eight, so in answer to your question, being around ladies doesn't bother me at all.'

'Thank you, Luke. Please wait in reception.'

They turned to one another and all three said, 'Yes.'

And so began a new era in the Connection saga.

Luke started work on the Monday morning, looking just as smart as he had for the interview.

His first day was spent in Doris's office, where they went through his training requirements, what he wanted from the job, and what courses he would be happy to take.

'We have all taken online courses over the last couple of years, and have our own certificates in our offices, but collectively it's a pretty impressive bunch. They are timed courses – when you've passed one section, you're sent the following part, so it makes it learning that stays in the brain. Primarily you're our meet and greet person, and that could continue for some time, but occasionally we get surveillance jobs in, or jobs that require interviewing people, but you won't be thrown into that. Kat is our most skilful negotiator, and she'll see to your training in people management.'

'Thank you, Mrs Lester. I'm happy to take whatever courses I can, and I'm sure you'll guide me through which ones I need at what times. And I'm sorry, but I can't call you Doris. It will have to be Mrs Lester. You're like my nan, and I could never in a million years call her Geraldine. I'm okay with Kat and Beth, but not you.'

There was a hint of redness in his cheeks, and Doris laughed. 'Call me whatever you want, Luke. I answer to most things. The girls, you may have noticed, call me Nan, even though Kat is no relation to me. Beth, of course, is my granddaughter. Just wait until the day comes when she gives you permission to call her Mouse, then you'll know you're a proper friend. And on that day, you can start to call me Nan. Deal?'

'Deal,' he agreed. 'My mum knows Kat, thinks she's awesome. Erm... I thought I'd better tell you that because of everything that happened with her husband. Mum told me the story. She goes to Kat's church.'

'Luke, everybody around here knows what happened with Leon Rowe – don't let it worry you. Kat has got over it, and is now with a lovely man. You'll meet him eventually; he pops in if he's working around here. Actually, I'd better fill you in on our police friends. DI Carl Heaton is Kat's fiancé, and we work closely with DI Tessa Marsden, and her DS, Hannah Granger. They pop in every so often for coffee and doughnuts and a natter, usually a brainstorming session when a case is slowing down. In addition to all of these we have Martha, Kat's baby, nearly one now, and sometimes Kat brings her in just so that she can spend some precious time with her. Everybody other than these people tend to be clients. We get a lot of people who ring us first, so it would be unusual to have someone walk in without an appointment. Now, let's discuss IT. I assume you're pretty smart with it?'

'I think so. I can usually work out any issues, and I like computer work.'

'Then here's something you need to know. In amongst all these certificates there's one for the level of IT I have achieved. It's high. It's the same in Beth's office. It's not the same in Kat's office.'

'She doesn't like computer work?'

'She's scared of it. At least once a week she complains the Internet is broken, and she's broken it. She has no confidence in her abilities, although the Kat of a couple of years ago isn't the same person who is here now. I've trained her bit by bit, and she can handle most things, but occasionally stuff does go wrong. You need to know this so you can sort her out. She preaches most Sundays in front of a large congregation, can stand up and talk to any size audience – she's an amazing woman. But she would happily live without her laptop. That is why we log all appointments on to the computer, but also keep a physical diary so that Kat can just open it to the correct date and see what's in for that day.'

'No problem. My head's buzzing with all of this. My mum was going to throw me out onto the streets yesterday afternoon, I was bouncing.'

Doris nodded, and slowly turned towards him. 'Occasionally, Luke, it can be quite dangerous. We started the business initially because Beth was shot down the side of the old Rowe pharmacy across the road. We ended up staying with Kat for a while, and our friendship grew, but guns and knives have featured in our investigations. It's not all about being nice to people and helping them, we always have to be aware of dangerous situations. Obviously we will never knowingly place you in danger, but we will always make you aware.'

'And I didn't think today could get any better,' he said with a laugh. They both heard the security buzzer, and Luke stood. 'Yes,' he said, 'my first visitor.'

3

The snow fell again on ground that had started to revert to its usual green around three o'clock that morning, and by five, the body that had been propped up against a tree began to seriously resemble a snowman. The wind had caused the snow to drift, and almost all of the slumped shape was no longer visible under its mantle of white. Only the shoes, sticking out of the blinding whiteness, indicated that maybe a snowman hadn't been built in the early hours of the morning.

Harry Hardy, feeling aware of his fifty-eight years, walked the grounds of Chatsworth every morning for a couple of hours, just looking, before heading into the kitchens for breakfast. Her ladyship insisted they all have breakfast, especially in the winter months. He spotted the snowman and wondered who the bloody hell had been out so early making one, but then saw the shoes pointing towards the sky. He stared at the mound of snow for a minute or so, then climbed the small incline towards it. He took one look and knew he wasn't going to get his breakfast that day. He took out his walkie-talkie and pressed speak.

'Harry?'

'Frank, we've got a problem.' Frank would know it would be a problem; Harry rarely used his walkie-talkie, preferring to sort any issues out there and then.

'You need help, Harry?'

'Police help. There's a body. I've touched nowt,' Harry said, 'but I can see the shoes, and they look like ladies boots to me.'

'Where are you?'

'B road. Just past the cattle grid, heading towards the house. That little copse of trees, set up from the road. She's leaning against a tree.'

'You okay?'

'Aye, I'll be fine. I'll stay here, but I reckon we'll not have visitors this early, especially with all this snow. It'll only be staff arriving.'

'I'll call you back. Over and out.'

Harry waited, staring at the snowflakes increasing in intensity. If they didn't hurry, the boots would be covered soon. The wind had picked up, causing the flakes to whirl around and whipping up the snow already lying on the ground.

His receiver crackled and he heard Frank's voice. 'They'll be with you as quick as possible, Harry. I'm sending young Davy over with a thermos of coffee. Reckon you might need it.'

'Tell him to be careful, Frank. It's treacherous underfoot. You told His Grace?'

'Not yet. It's my next job. Your coffee comes first. Let me know when the police arrive. I'll be over to join you when they get there.'

'Thanks, Frank. Over and out.'

Harry stood a distance away from the body, his footsteps being filled in by the falling snow. He could see Davy in the distance and he waved.

Davy made it without slipping, and handed over a carrier bag. 'There's a bacon sandwich for each for us, and two flasks of coffee. Mr Norman says I've to stay with you, but he didn't want us getting cold.'

'Aye, he's a good boss. It could be a while; I should think the roads are pretty bad. Heaven only knows where the police are coming from, but there's not been a deal of traffic on the roads to open them up yet.' He checked his watch. 'Good lord, it's only half past seven. I feel as though I've done a full day's work already.'

Harry took a bite of his sandwich, already cooling in the bitter air.

Davy put his to his mouth, but then caught sight of the reason he was there, the body propped against the tree. 'Shit,' he said, and slowly put the sandwich back into the tinfoil it had just been in. 'You've not checked if it's actually dead?'

'No. She's dead. If she was alive the snow around her nose and mouth would have melted. Don't be scared, lad, she can't hurt you.' He could tell how uncomfortable Davy was. 'Let's have a drink of coffee, we need to warm up. We'll go higher and get out of this, we're right in the snowstorm here. It could be a long wait.'

They skirted the body and climbed slightly higher up the incline and into the shelter of the circle of trees. The snow wasn't so thick, and they cleared it from a tree stump, split the carrier bag and placed it over the top. 'That'll stop wet arses,' Harry said with a grin to the young lad, who was clearly uncomfortable with the situation. They faced the back of the tree where the body was, and Harry hoped Davy would be able to finish his breakfast and drink the coffee. It would make him feel better.

They chatted for nearly an hour, bacon sandwiches and coffee consumed in that time. It was a welcome sound when they heard sirens, and Harry spoke into his walkie-talkie again. 'They're here, Frank, just arriving. I'm going down to meet them on the road.'

DI Tessa Marsden was first out of the car, and walked across to the tall well-wrapped up man who appeared to have the situation under his control. A younger version of him stood by his side.

She held out her hand. 'DI Marsden,' she said, 'and the officer trying desperately to put on her wellingtons is DS Hannah Granger. We have other cars following, but it's a nightmare getting here. Please stay put, I need to check things out. You haven't touched the body?'

'No, ma'am,' Harry said. 'I walked up to it because at first I thought it was a snowman, but then I saw the boots. I realised if it is indeed a dead body, that accounted for no melted snow.'

Marsden nodded and walked up the incline. She kept the thought to herself, but it crossed her mind that if this were a living person, out of her head on alcohol or drugs, she'd kill her anyway, to pay her back for the bloody nightmare of a journey they'd just had. But she knew. She didn't need to bend down and feel for a pulse. The body was definitely dead.

Hannah joined her and they looked around. 'Crime scene tape around all the trees?' Hannah asked.

Tessa nodded. 'And down to the road, across it and I'd say about twenty yards the other side of the road. That's going to bugger up life a little bit for anybody using this road to go through Chatsworth to Rowsley, but it can't be helped.' She turned her head at the sound of further sirens, and walked down to the road to meet the rest of the team.

They immediately sealed off the area, and Harry and Davy were invited to sit in Tessa's car and get warm. She switched on the engine, gave them a smile, and said she would be back to talk to them shortly.

In the distance, Harry could see the stocky figure of Frank, with a second figure walking by his side. He glanced up at the incline towards Marsden and wondered whether to tell her or leave her to find out who the second man was; Davy seemed to read his mind. 'Don't tell her,' he laughed. 'Let's see how she handles it.'

The forensic team had erected a tent over the body, a tent that was already showing the beginning of a snow pile on its roof. Death was confirmed; a female, aged around forty, killed by a ligature that was still around her throat.

Tessa watched from the outside as flashes told her scene photographs were being taken, and when they stopped, she popped her head through the opening. 'Anything to give us a start?'

'Not yet. They'd be assumptions in this weather, and I don't do assumptions.' The man stood and turned towards Tessa. He took off a latex glove and shook her hand. 'Martin Robinson, started in the job yesterday and already we're in the presence of royalty.'

'Royalty?'

'Chatsworth, Duke of Devonshire and all that. My last job was inner city Birmingham, no royalty there.'

She smiled. 'Well, it's good to meet you. DI Tessa Marsden, and DS Hannah Granger, wherever she is, is my second in command. And I can't see the Duke getting himself involved in this.'

He flashed his dark brown eyes at her, and pulled on a fresh glove. 'PM tomorrow at nine. Will you be there, DI Marsden?' His smile dared her to say no, but that was never going to happen.

Oh most definitely, she wanted to say. 'Yes. I'll be there. Have you come across any sort of identification on her?'

'Nothing so far. I'll let you know if we do,' and he turned back to the cadaver, continuing the meticulous work he had already started. Marsden stood and watched him for a moment, then shook her head. Something to be appreciated at some other time, she thought, especially with a back view as good as the front one.

Hannah joined her and reported that all the crime scene tape was now up, diversion signs were being sorted, and the snow had temporarily stopped. She had initiated a search in the trees that formed a semi-circle behind the body, and the refreshments truck had arrived. 'I've told everybody they've to get a hot drink,' she said, almost belligerently, as if daring Tessa to disagree with her.

'Quite right. It's damn freezing. They'll work better if they don't feel frozen through to their bones.'

There was a shout from one of the PCs working in the trees and he came around towards Tessa and Hannah. 'Handbag, ma'am,' he said. 'I've left it in situ and warned the others not to tread on it. It's in deep snow.'

Tessa and Hannah followed him around to where he pointed, and Tessa knelt in the snow. She carefully scraped it clear, still leaving it where it was, then opened the front flap using her pen. It was a messenger style of bag; the front flap had a magnetic fastener, it simply went from back to front, clicked, and sat in place. It was made of fabric, now wet fabric. She teased out the purse and opened it. Inside were several cards, but only two with a name on them, a debit card and a credit card both for the use of Nicola Lynne Armstrong. Tessa took a quick photograph of them and put them back in the purse. It was as she replaced it in the bag that she found a letter to Nicola with an address in Baslow.

She photographed the envelope, then put it in an evidence bag. It was time to talk to the man who had found the body, and send him on his way to get warm in the magnificent great house that was Chatsworth. It currently was dominating a somewhat grey skyline, but looking just as impressive as it did in beautiful sunlight.

She marked the spot where the bag had been found, and bagged it up, then handed it to DC Ray Charlton for safekeeping.

'We'll go through it when we get back to headquarters,' Tessa said.

Tessa dropped down the hill, followed by Hannah. Suddenly she held out a hand as if in warning, and they stopped.

'Hannah, how many men are sitting in my car?'

'Four, boss.'

'That's what I thought. Any of them in uniform?'

'No, boss.'

'Well, that's a relief. I haven't got to bawl anybody out. Come on, let's go and find out what's going on. I need to get some sort of statement from… Harry… I think he's called that.'

They slid down the slope and walked across to the car, both of them feeling grateful for the wellingtons they routinely carried in the boot. All four doors opened at the same time and the men climbed out.

Harry Hardy moved towards Tessa, then stopped.

'DI Marsden, you met Davy earlier. This is my boss, Frank Norman, in charge of all the grounds staff here at Chatsworth, and this is his boss, His Grace the Duke of Devonshire.'

4

T essa didn't know whether to laugh or cry as she watched the four men trudging over the hill, back towards Chatsworth House. She had come so close to eyeing up the two men who had been in the back seat of her car, and simply saying, 'And you are?', so close…

Thank God Harry Hardy had been decent enough to jump in with introductions. The Duke explained that he had waited to speak to her, because he wanted to offer them space at Chatsworth if they needed an operations room. It was no difficulty for her to address him as Your Grace, and she had thanked him for his offer. She explained that it still had to be confirmed as a homicide, but if it proved to be the case, they would take him at his word, and move into whatever accommodation he could organise for them.

It was bitterly cold, and she watched as her team intermittently edged down towards the newly arrived refreshments truck, eager for a cup of anything hot that would warm their hands, and then the rest of them, as they drank. The notice, hastily scribbled, said VISITORS TOILETS OPEN AT THE BIG HOUSE, and was placed prominently in the window of the truck.

It soon occurred to everyone that it was quite a walk, and maybe they should limit their fluid intake. And peeing behind a tree in this locality could lead to them being arrested for murder.

The thoroughness of the search told them all that it was murder. So far nobody had said how she had died, but they were fingertipping as much as possible given the depth of the snow, and the area they had started to cover was all beginning to look like a grey smudgy blot on the pristine white landscape.

Eventually Martin Robinson gave the go-ahead for the body to be removed, allowing the inside of the tent to be searched.

'Congratulations, DI Marsden, you seemingly have yourself another murder. I heard on the grapevine on my first day that you'd just cleared up a couple of issues before Christmas.'

'My team did,' she said with a smile. 'I'm not Wonder Woman, I don't do these things on my own. We had two girls killed on the same night, both from Castleton. Unrelated crimes, but one was soon solved. The other was a bit more complicated. I have an address to start off the investigation with this one, but apart from her name that's all I have at the moment. I'll check in later and see if anyone's been reported missing.'

'You'll be at the post-mortem?'

'Definitely. It helps. Gives me a stronger link, call it empathy, to the victim.'

'And have they found anything, your team?'

'Only the handbag. It was some distance away from the body, and under deep snow, so I suspect she was killed before the snow started, about midnight according to His Grace...'

'His Grace? You saw our royalty? He's been here?'

'He was sitting on the back seat of my car,' she said ruefully. 'I was so close to demanding he get out, until the chap who found the body introduced us. The Duke's lovely, really down to earth, offered us a room in Chatsworth as headquarters for the investigation. That will be a help, because trailing out from Chesterfield every day for the entire team is a pain, especially in this weather.

Most of them live in Derbyshire, in one or other of the villages around here.'

He winked. 'Shouldn't worry, two days tops and you'll have it solved.'

'If only,' she said. 'Was there snow under the body?'

'None under where her bum was, but snow had drifted under and around her legs because they were slightly bent. She was definitely killed before it started, but I can't give you a precise time until we do the post-mortem.' He bent and picked up his case. 'It's been nice meeting you, DI Marsden.'

'Tessa,' she said, and returned his wink.

'You're flirting,' Hannah said. She appeared behind Tessa as she stood watching the tall man walk down to the road to get into his car.

'Never,' Tessa responded.

'Can I have him then?'

'Definitely not. I'm the boss, I get first dibs.'

Tessa was standing on the observation walkway when Martin Robinson waved to her to come down and join him in the autopsy room. Nicola Armstrong's body was covered with a sheet but the ligature was still around her neck, awaiting more detailed analysis before it was removed.

Tessa felt slightly sick at the thought of being up close and personal to the victim when Martin made the Y incision down her body; Tessa had been quite willing to stand on the walkway and observe.

He smiled at her as she entered the room. 'Good morning, DI Marsden. I thought you would be able to see better down here.'

She knew he was testing her.

'That's fine,' she said. 'I wouldn't have intruded, but thank you for the opportunity of seeing this at close quarters.'

He grinned. 'You're welcome. But if you're going to faint, can you make sure it's away from the autopsy table.'

'I'll try.' She said nothing further and waited patiently for him to start.

The ligature proved to be some brand of washing line, sold universally, and wasn't new. Martin confirmed it as cause of death, and estimated time of expiry to be between 22:03 and approximately midnight, when the snow began. 'She was definitely placed by the tree before the snow started, because there was no snow on the ground where she was sitting with her back to the tree.'

'22:03? That's very precise.' Tessa looked up from her notebook.

'Her mobile phone was in her jeans pocket. She made a phone call at 22:03. There has been no further activity on it overnight.' He passed the phone to Tessa, inside an evidence bag. 'It's okay,' he said. 'There's no passwords or fingerprint recognition on it, you can get straight into it. It's not exactly a state-of-the-art iPhone.'

'No,' she said, 'but the one inside her handbag is.'

The autopsy went smoothly enough, and her fingerprints proved beyond doubt that she was Nicola Lynne Armstrong. She had a conviction for shoplifting dating back twenty years, and her prints were on file. Tessa sat at her desk and quickly scanned through the details on the report.

Nicola's stomach contents showed that she hadn't eaten for a few hours, but the alcohol in her blood was high. Very high. It occurred to Tessa that maybe it was too high for Nicola to have been able to retaliate.

Tessa made a call. 'Martin… this alcohol level in Nicola's body. Would she have been able to fight back?'

'I doubt it. We got nothing from under her fingernails to indicate she might have struggled even a little. She had no weight on her, as you saw, a very slight lady. The alcohol at that level would render her able to walk but with a definite wobble, I would have thought.'

'That's what I figured. Just needed it confirming, thanks.'

'You're very welcome. Tessa…' he hesitated.

'Yes?'

'Oh, bugger it. Can I take you for a drink?'

'Yes.'

'Yes?'

'Yes. You want me to say it again?'

'No, I'm just a bit shocked you said it first time around. Tonight?'

'That would be lovely, unless I get tied up in this. I'll call you if it can't happen, okay?'

'Okay. My god, I love an organised efficient woman. I'll text you my mobile number.'

'You have mine?'

'Oh, I do. Made a point of getting it from the duty sergeant.'

Her laughter rang down the phone. It would be all around the police station in two days that Martin Robinson had asked for Tessa Marsden's phone number. 'Okay, Martin. You don't know what you've done, but I can handle it. I finish around six unless something crops up. That okay?'

'Definitely. I'll find your office.'

He put down the phone before she could say that wouldn't be advisable, and then she grinned. It would be good to see her team's faces when they realised what was happening.

She pulled Nicola's old mobile phone towards her, and woke

it up. Her own phone pinged with a message from Martin, as he sent her his number.

Nicola's phone told Tessa very little. There was only one number in the contacts list, the number Nicola had rung at just after ten o'clock the night she died. Tessa was undecided. Should she send it through for the experts to try to find out who it belonged to, or should she just ring the damn number and risk alerting the owner?

Her door opened and Hannah's smiling face appeared. 'Hey, that dishy pathologist asked for your phone number.'

Tessa heaved a huge sigh. It definitely hadn't taken two days. 'I know. He hadn't got it, and it's always possible he'll need it. Don't forget he's new here, he'll be getting everybody's mobile number.'

'He's not asked for mine.'

'I'll give it to him. Did you want something?'

'Yes. You recovered from the autopsy?'

'I have. As autopsies go, it wasn't too bad. I've been to worse. This was found in her jeans pocket.' She pushed the phone across to her DS.

'Anything helpful?' Hannah asked, as she picked it up.

'Not really. Only one number in it. I was just debating whether to ring it or not, or let the techy guys have it to try to trace that number. If I ring it and it's somebody we'd rather not alert to anything, we lose the element of surprise.'

'You're right. I say don't ring it yet, not till the techs have done their thing with it. Are you ready for going to that address in Baslow?'

Tessa stood. 'I am. Let's hope there's been some snow-clearing. We'll do the Baslow visit first, then head to Chatsworth, to the incident room.'

.   .   .

28

The drive to Baslow was easier than the day before and the landscape was breathtaking. Field after field was covered in deep snow, trees bent almost to the ground with the weight of it on their branches. The sun was shining but with no warmth in its rays, and it turned the air into a crisp end-of-the-nose-freezing blanket of coldness.

Hannah drove carefully. The road had been gritted but it was clear very little traffic had used it. She guessed most people were taking a snow day.

'I'd have liked a snow day today,' Hannah said, 'this is perfect sledging weather.'

'You go sledging?'

'I like to take my nieces. My sister hates the stuff, so I jumped at the chance. It's not often we get it like this though, there's usually just a couple of inches. I'm not going to be their favourite aunty if this lot goes before the weekend.' She slowed down for a sheep standing in the middle of the road. 'Shouldn't that be under cover somewhere?'

'I refuse to investigate a sheep in the middle of a Derbyshire road. If it's stupid enough to risk getting killed by standing there, then so be it,' Tessa said, while swivelling in her seat to look back at the animal, hoping it would continue its walk to the other side of the road.

The satnav told them they had arrived at their destination, and both women took a moment to look at the house. It was big, double fronted, with a bright red door situated centrally between the two large downstairs bay windows.

They got out of the car, and headed through the unmarked thick snow towards the front door.

5

Luke arrived at work with a shovel, and cleared the snow from outside the office. Doris handed him a pack of salt, and he scattered it around before heading back into the warmth.

All four of them stood looking out of the window, sipping hot chocolates, hands wrapped tightly around the warm mugs.

'I'll be quite annoyed if it snows again,' Luke said, casting his eyes skyward. 'Quite annoyed.'

'If it does,' Doris mused, 'our clients can take their chances. Luckily we have nobody booked in for today, so I've set up the entry-level course for you that we discussed. I suggest you crack on with that. It's a very flexible kind of job, anything can crop up at a minute's notice, so just go with it. Learn what you can from the courses, but I promise there will be hands-on stuff as well.'

'And I've got something for you,' Kat said. She disappeared into her office and returned with a fob.

Luke thanked her. 'What is it?'

'It's to get in here. If you arrive earlier than us I don't want you standing out in the cold.'

'Cool,' he said. 'I promise not to have any wild parties in here.'

'That's good,' Kat said, glancing around at the reception area that had shrunk considerably with the advent of Doris's office. 'It wouldn't be much of a party in this tiny space, and all the other offices are locked. The code for entering into the keypad to raise the shutters is 3162. They then rise automatically. You okay with that?'

Luke took a sip of his hot chocolate. 'I'm okay with everything. I'll be glad when Christmas is out of the way properly, and people start living again. We need clients. I'm a receptionist with nobody to receive,' he said with a laugh.

'See,' Doris said thoughtfully. 'See what Luke did then? He said people start living again. That's the attitude we want instead of all these dead bodies we end up being involved with. We need to make a notice for the window that says NO DEAD BODIES ALLOWED.'

Luke took a sip of his drink. 'Kat, is Mrs Lester always a spoilsport?'

Kat grinned at him. 'The problem with Nan is that she listens too much to DI Marsden. She always tells us not to find her any corpses, and we usually find her at least one. You ever seen a dead body, Luke?'

He shook his head before speaking. 'No, can't even say I've known anybody who died. My granddad passed just after I was born, so I didn't know him, and everybody else is still here. Thankfully,' he added. He didn't want anybody thinking he wanted to kill some random member of his family in order to see a body.

They took their drinks and disappeared into their offices, Mouse to have a conference call with Joel and one of the other partners, Kat to start on her sermon before switching her head around to Connection work, and Doris to check into her emails.

Mouse had been taken aback by the strength of her feelings that seemed to be developing for Joel Masters. From the first second she had been introduced to him when she had given a presentation at his company, the attraction had been there. Even seeing him from the distance of a conference call was a boost to her day, and emphasised to her just how special Christmas had been.

Luke clicked on the icon for the course Doris had arranged for him, and quickly read through the information pertaining to the qualification. It briefly occurred to him it was like being back at school, but lessons had never been like this. He sipped on his hot chocolate as the first page opened up for him. He smiled.

'I'm assuming that's her car,' Hannah said, as she knocked on the door of Nicola Armstrong's house in Baslow for the second time.

'Ring it in and get it checked once we get inside,' Tessa said. 'There's also no footprints apart from ours in this damn snow. It's a big house if it's for only one person. We'll give it a minute then go in.' She fished around in her bag for the set of keys found in the handbag discovered in Chatsworth's snow.

Hannah banged on the door for the third time, shouted 'Police!' through the letterbox, and inserted the key Tessa handed to her. They pushed against the bright red paintwork and the door swung open with a slight creak.

The hall was big, an enormously handsome jardinière taking up a section of it, complete with an aspidistra. The hall lights were lit, indicating that Nicola Armstrong had intended coming home the night of her death. The radiators were also on; definitely a welcoming house.

'Check upstairs, Hannah,' Marsden said, pulling latex gloves onto her cold hands.

Hannah pulled on her own gloves and climbed the stairs, not

touching the banister; she didn't want to smudge any fingerprints. She reached the top and turned to look back down the stairs and into the entrance hall. Marsden had disappeared, and nothing looked out of place.

The DS began by checking every room for occupation, but there was no sign of anyone, so she then became more methodical. The main bedroom was huge with built-in wardrobes along two walls, and an en suite. On the bed lay a pair of jeans and a thick woollen jumper, clearly discarded and looking out of place in the neatness of the rest of the room. The en suite revealed a bathroom cabinet with contraceptive tablets and sleeping pills, alongside aspirins, but nothing more revealing than that about the woman, showing very little of herself other than a tidiness and neatness.

Hannah walked around, observing. The real forensic work would start within the hour, as soon as they rang in to say this was definitely the victim's home. There was a picture on Nicola's bedside table, with a tall well-built man and a child, a boy of about five, with Nicola and the man both standing behind the boy, their hands on his shoulders. Hannah picked it up carefully, and removed the stand from the frame. Scribbled on the back of the photo it said, N A and D. Hannah photographed both sides and replaced it.

There were four more bedrooms, one clearly for a child. The others were tidy, but had no air of being lived in; guest bedrooms. One had an en suite, and the main bathroom served the other rooms.

The bathroom made Hannah gasp. She would kill for a place like this. It was huge and boasted a jacuzzi bath along with a shower cubicle that would comfortably take three people. Tiled floor to ceiling in white with occasional grey tiles added for effect, it was spotlessly clean. Other than normal bathroom toiletries, there was nothing in the wall cabinet, and she quietly closed the door behind her.

She headed back downstairs to find Tessa sitting at the kitchen table, going through some mail.

'It's mainly junk,' she said, waving a couple of envelopes around, 'but it confirms this is Nicola's house. Forensics will be here soon. We'll wait until they arrive then we'll head over to Chatsworth. We need to find some info on this woman, she must have a next of kin somewhere. Did you find anything that would help?' Tessa looked up at Hannah.

'Only this on the back of a photo,' Hannah said, and handed over her phone. Tessa looked and passed it back.

'That's helpful. Somewhere in her life is an A and a D. I wonder where the child is. Possibly with A? I'm guessing he's the male adult. Ever get the feeling this isn't going to be easy?'

Hannah laughed. 'You crease me up sometimes, boss. Are they ever easy? But we put Marnie Harrison away, didn't we? We'll sort this one, don't fret. It's massive upstairs. Master bedroom you could hold a ball in, three other large bedrooms and a child's. A bathroom that's out of this or any other world... you find anything else?'

'Not really. I'm a little surprised by that photograph. There are no pictures downstairs, and there are no toys. She seems obsessively tidy, and I would have said no children.'

They looked at each other and Tessa stood. 'Let's go look at this child's room before forensics get here and stop us going in.'

The room held a single bed with a duvet cover telling the world that the little boy loved Tatty Teddy. He had a toy box in one corner, also with a picture of the scruffy looking little bear painted on it and when they lifted the lid, a name was etched into the underside of it. Danny's toys.

Inside the box were many playthings, most in pristine condition. Hannah closed the lid with a little smile. 'Aw, kids are quite sweet, aren't they?'

Tessa's eyebrows headed for her hairline. 'Really?'

'Yeah, I mean… look at this.' She swept her arm around the room to indicate what she was talking about. 'And Martha, she's gorgeous.'

'They're all gorgeous when you can give them back to their owners.'

'I suppose you're right, but I love spending time with my nieces.' Hannah looked around the room once more. 'There's something wrong here though.' She frowned, trying to work something out.

'You think the child spends all his time in this room? There's no evidence of him downstairs.'

'No… it's… it's Tatty Teddy!' There was a touch of triumph in Hannah's voice. 'The rest of this house is bang on trend. It's smart, modern, up-to-date, and then we see Tatty Teddy. That would have been the thing to get about… ten years ago, I reckon. Now it would be George and his bloody dinosaur.'

'You reckon this room is a shrine? It's been kept exactly as it was ten years ago?'

'I think we need to look into it. We have to take Nicola's life apart. For a start we need to know how she can afford this house. Where does she work? Why has nobody reported her as missing? There are no men's clothes here despite that picture of A. Potentially the ex-husband, but why is he ex, and where is he now? And we desperately need a next of kin. If her name is out there, it may draw in information.' Hannah exuded triumph; the words had flowed out of her. She felt like… like… Tessa!

They heard the sound of a door opening and both stood. 'The forensic cavalry's here,' Tessa said. 'Let's head off to Chatsworth, they'll have it all set up by now. We'll add our bit about where she lives, then we'll get on a computer. Or get somebody a bit more computer literate to get on one, and get us some info on Nicola

Armstrong. I want to have contacted someone by tonight to let them know she's dead.'

The room loaned to them by the Duke was warm and noisy. A crime board had been set up, with a picture of Nicola Armstrong on it, and computers were on.

Tessa walked to the front and stood by the whiteboard. 'Listen up, everybody,' she called, and the clatter died down instantly. 'Hannah and I have been to the victim's home, and had a brief look around while we were waiting for forensics to arrive. We now need information. Who was she? Does she have family? She had a child. Where is he? He's called Danny, so it's presumably Daniel Armstrong...' she hesitated. 'Bloody hell, Daniel Armstrong.' She dropped her head in thought, and Ray Charlton helped her out.

'Boss, Daniel Armstrong's the young lad snatched about ten years ago. His mother always thought her ex-husband, the lad's father, had taken him, but whatever happened we never found either of them.'

6

Tessa pushed the file into her bag, and stood as Martin walked into her office. She felt grateful that most of her team were still at Chatsworth, including Hannah; she had taken advantage of the Daniel Armstrong paperwork being at Chesterfield, and had driven back to headquarters alone.

'Are we still okay?' Martin asked, unsure whether he should smile or not. He felt nervous, something he hadn't experienced for a long time. Looking forward to an event made it so much worse when it was cancelled, and he desperately didn't want Tessa to say I'm sorry, but...

'I'm good, if you are,' she said, and finally his own smile arrived to match hers.

'Then let's go before something happens to change that,' he said, and held the door open for her.

They agreed to go in separate cars, and meet up at the Cricketers Arms. Tessa arrived first and waited for Martin to lock his car before getting out of her own. She slung her bag on her shoulder, not wanting to leave it in the car; the file was too precious, and as such represented her bedtime reading.

They decided to go with the carvery, and ten minutes later settled down with a hefty meal and a lemonade each.

'You don't drink?' she asked.

'Not when I'm driving, but to be honest I've done too many autopsies on drunk drivers. Nothing on this earth could persuade me to have any alcohol and get behind the wheel of a car. You the same?'

She nodded. 'I like the odd glass of wine at home, and will probably have one later when I read the file in my bag, but I don't drink when I'm driving.'

'You take work home?'

'Don't we all? Something odd has cropped up with regard to our Chatsworth lady. It seems she's the mother of Daniel Armstrong, a five-year-old little boy who went missing nearly ten years ago. It was presumed at the time that his dad had taken him, and they'd just disappeared, but in view of her murder I have to consider the possibility of a link between the two cases. I've pulled the main file on Daniel to go through it tonight.'

'I vaguely remember that. It was the mother who insisted her ex had taken Daniel, wasn't it? Presumably that was never proved.'

'Nothing was ever found. If his father did take him, he hid him very successfully. Maybe Nicola's death will flush him out and we can close a cold case.'

Tessa pushed her plate to one side. 'I can't eat any more. Why do I always feel the need to load up my plate when I have a carvery?'

Martin laughed and pointed to his own plate. 'Look at mine. There's no way I can eat all that. I'll struggle manfully on, but I feel as though I'm fighting a losing battle.'

. . .

With the meal finished, they walked outside to return to their cars, still talking, still happy to be in each other's company, much to Tessa's surprise. She hadn't expected anything from the evening, but it was proving to be extremely pleasant, and when Martin asked her if he could see her again, her smile gave him the answer.

'You like curry?' she asked.

'I do.'

'Then if you'd like to, I'll cook us a curry at my place. Tomorrow okay?'

'I'll bring wine and a bottle of lemonade,' he said with a grin.

She climbed into her car and lowered her window. 'I'll text you my address,' she said and he leaned down and kissed her gently on the cheek.

'Thank you for tonight,' Tessa said. 'I really enjoyed it.'

'Me too. I'll look forward to tomorrow.'

The more Tessa trawled through Daniel Armstrong's file, the more the memories of the case came flooding back. She had only been a WPC, involved on the periphery of the case, joining in searches and occasionally accompanying the then DI, Peter Jenkinson. She quite clearly remembered going to DCI Jenkinson's funeral so there would be no help coming from that quarter.

There was very little to read through. Adam Armstrong had disappeared at the same time as his son, and it didn't take a genius to work out that they had gone together. Nicola Armstrong had been distraught, and had never given up on her child, but to that day he hadn't been seen.

Tessa closed the file with a sigh. She leaned against the back of the sofa and closed her eyes, only to have to immediately sit up to answer her phone.

'Hannah?'

ANITA WALLER

'Yes, boss. Nicola Armstrong has a sister and a brother. Simon Vicars and Debra Carter.'

'I know. I was just deciding what to do about it. Their names are in the old file from when Daniel went missing. But it's after ten, so I think we can give them one last night of peace before we tell them. We'll go early tomorrow morning, about half eight, to see Debra Carter. Can you make sure the address we have for her is up to date, please, Hannah? She used to live in Buxton, let's hope she's moved.'

'We'll go on a sledge,' Hannah laughed. 'I'll check the electoral roll, boss. You have a good night then?'

'I've spent it reading this file.'

'Oh yes, of course you have. Has the lovely doctor been reading it as well.'

'That's for me to know, and you to find out,' was Tessa's sure-fire response.

Hannah disconnected with a laugh, and brought up the electoral roll. Tessa had got her wish; Debra Carter had moved, and much closer to her sister. She lived in Eyam.

'Good morning, Kat. How's the world with you?' Tessa's voice sounded crackly.

'I'm good. About to take Martha to her nan's. You want something?'

'Only to give you a bit of a head's up that you'll probably see my car when you go out. I'll be next door to you. We're going to see a Mrs Debra Carter.'

'Debbie? Is everything okay? She's lovely, I hope nothing's wrong.'

'You've presumably heard of the body found at Chatsworth? It's Mrs Carter's sister. We're off to break the news.'

'Oh no, she'll be devastated, I'm sure. I've never met her sister. Does she live locally?'

'Baslow. There's a slight complication… Look, I'll not talk about it over the phone, I'll come down to the office later, possibly this afternoon unless anything breaks in the case. Have we got biscuits?'

'We do. And you haven't met our new receptionist Luke yet. It'll be good to introduce you to him.'

'I'll ring if I can't make it. About two okay?'

'It is. It seems ages since we've caught up with each other, it will be good to see you. Our offices have changed a bit.'

'I'll bring Hannah as well. She was moaning the other day we hadn't seen you all since before Christmas. This damn snow's stopping us getting anywhere.'

'Don't be late,' Kat laughed. 'It's chocolate biscuits.'

Tessa and Hannah walked up the snow-covered path and rang the house's bell. The laughter they had heard immediately stopped, and a few seconds later the door was tentatively opened by a young girl of about ten or eleven.

'Hi, is your mummy in?' Tessa asked, fixing a smile on her face.

'She's changing Charlie.'

They heard a crash followed by 'bloody hell', and then a voice called from somewhere in the house. 'Who is it, Bridie?'

'Two women!' her daughter shouted.

For a second, Tessa felt out of her depth. The job of death notification was difficult enough, without it having to be conducted by shouting it out on a doorstep.

'Bridie, we're police officers.' She held out her warrant card as proof of it but the little girl simply stared at her, her blue eyes widening by the second.

'Mum, it's the police!' she shouted, and waited for instructions.

They heard footsteps and a woman appeared with a baby tucked onto her hip.

'I'm sorry.' She sounded flustered. 'You came at the wrong moment. I would advise not going into the kitchen, I've just changed Charlie's nappy. Can I help you?'

'Debra Carter?' Tess asked.

'Debbie, yes. What's wrong?'

'Can we come in for a moment, Mrs Carter?'

Debbie held open the door, and the two officers stamped snow from their boots and followed her through to the lounge. There was a baby gym on the carpet and Debbie placed her son in the middle of it, where he bashed the various hanging toys with some brutality.

'Okay,' she said. 'Is this about Danny?'

'No, I'm sorry, it's about your sister.'

Debbie waited, unspeaking.

'Your sister is Nicola Armstrong?'

'She is.'

'Then I'm sorry to have to tell you your sister is dead.'

'Really?' Debbie looked around the room, her face expressionless.

Tessa and Hannah glanced at each other. 'Is there anybody we can contact to be with you?' Hannah asked, 'and we're very sorry for your loss.'

'I'm not,' Debbie Carter responded. 'We haven't spoken in years, had very little contact. How did she die?'

'You may have heard on the news about a body being found at Chatsworth? In the grounds? It was your sister. We will be going public with her name once we've had contact with your brother.'

'Simon will be here in about ten minutes. He's an electrician, and he's putting us some extra sockets in. Don't expect weeping and wailing from him either. Can I get you both a cup of tea while we wait for him?'

They thanked her, and watched as Bridie sank to the floor to play with her baby brother.

A few minutes later, Debbie returned carrying a tray of four drinks. 'Bridie, can you put on your coat and get your bag, please? You'll be going in about five minutes.'

The little girl stood and left the room, then came back with a blue bag proclaiming itself to be a book bag, and a bright red coat.

'Bridie,' her mum said, a note of warning in her voice. 'No mention of these ladies when you get to school, okay, love?'

'Okay, Mum.' Bridie leaned forward and kissed her mum, then walked out the door. 'I'll wait at the gate,' she called, and they heard the front door open and close.

'A friend collects her every morning to save me having to get Charlie ready,' Debbie explained. 'She takes half a dozen or so kids, it's quite a sight to see them, especially all trudging through this deep snow. School initiative, called a walking bus. The kids love it.'

She stood and watched through the front window until she saw her daughter safely collected, then returned to the two police officers. 'Simon's just parking the van. Then you can fill us in on the details, and we can forget about her for the rest of our lives.'

The front door opened with a clatter and curses as Simon Vicars stamped his feet to get rid of the snow. 'Bloody weather,' he called out. 'Is the kettle on?'

'In the lounge, already made,' his sister responded, and she looked up with a smile as her brother came through the door.

'Simon, these two ladies are police officers. I'm sorry, I still have baby brain and I can't remember your names,' she said, turning to Tessa.

'DI Tessa Marsden and DS Hannah Granger.' Tessa held out her warrant card once again, followed by a similar action from Hannah.

Simon frowned as he took in the possible implications of two police officers in his sister's home, then he sat down and picked up his drink.

'Is everything okay?' he asked.

'Nicola's dead.' The words coming from Debbie's mouth sounded brutal, almost cruel. 'It's her body they've found at Chatsworth. Karma, that's what it is.'

7

L uke saw the two women as they approached the office door, and he pressed the buzzer to release the lock. He stood as they came in, and he heard Doris's door open.

'Tessa, Hannah, it's good to see you. Let me introduce you to Luke, our new receptionist-stroke-investigator. Luke, this is DI Tessa Marsden, and this is DS Hannah Granger.'

Tessa shook Luke's hand. 'Good to meet you, Luke. In here call us Tessa and Hannah, but outside of this office please use our titles.'

Doris laughed. 'You don't need to worry about that, he calls me Mrs Lester, and he's not graduated to Mouse yet, still calls her Beth. It'll be a while before he graduates to your Christian names, trust me. Am I right, Luke?'

'Could be,' Luke said. 'I'll make some coffee, shall I?'

'We'll go in Kat's office; it can just about accommodate the six of us.'

Luke smiled. 'You want me in there?'

'Luke, you're a member of our staff, and you want to learn the job from the bottom up, don't you?' Doris said. 'Well, this is the bottom up.'

'Huh, don't believe anything she says, Luke,' Tessa said. 'This is top down.'

'Are we here to socialise, or to talk about... something?' Kat looked at Hannah and Tessa.

'Both,' Tessa said. 'We're here partly to drink your coffee and eat your biscuits, but because you know Debbie Carter I'd like to fill you in on what's happening. Six heads are better than two. I imagine Doris has drilled this into you a hundred times, Luke, but I have to reiterate – what is said in this office stays in this office.'

Luke glanced across at Doris. 'Do you really think I would dare go against Mrs Lester and repeat anything of what's said here? Don't worry, DI Marsden, I'm not risking losing this job for a bit of tittle-tattling.'

Tess smiled. 'I like this lad. You want to be a policeman, Luke?'

'Not on your life. I'm okay here with my ladies.'

They sat down with much clattering of chairs, and Tessa took out a folder. 'Here's what we have so far, and it's not much. It's early days. As you've probably heard on the news, a body of a woman was found in Chatsworth grounds, and it was obvious it was murder. She had been strangled with a rope, washing line to be more accurate. We found her handbag which had been thrown into a clearing behind where she was left, propped up against a tree. It snowed heavily, making everything doubly difficult.

'Robbery wasn't the motive. There was an expensive iPhone in the bag, about a hundred pounds in cash, various cards including one credit, one debit. She also had another phone in the back pocket of her jeans, but it only had one number in it. No name in the contacts, just XXX.'

'A lover then? *Cherchez l'homme*, Tessa, *cherchez l'homme*,' Kat said.

'It could be anybody, couldn't it, if she's substituting exes for a name.'

'What if it's kisses?'

Tessa stared at Kat. 'Little miss clever clogs strikes again. That really didn't occur to me. It's with the tech boys at the moment. If they can't tie it down to anybody, then I'm going to ring the number and see what happens. Anyway, we found out she's called Nicola Armstrong, lived in a lovely big house in Baslow, and she is the sister of your next-door neighbour, Kat, Debbie Carter. There's no love lost between them; I think they were sisters in name only. While I was at the house telling Debbie, the brother arrived. Simon Vicars. He wasn't quite as openly hostile as Debbie, but I got the impression he didn't see much of Nicola either. I'm not sure why there's all this animosity, not yet, but I will find out.'

'They weren't upset?' Doris looked troubled. 'That's dreadful. Siblings are usually very close, aren't they. Nicola must have done something to really upset them, to cause such a massive rift.'

'They weren't upset, no.' Hannah threw her opinion into the mix. 'But they were surprised. Simon more so than Debbie. He moved across to her and put his arm around her shoulder, but she shrugged him off. She was sort of saying she didn't need comforting; she simply didn't care.'

'Luke,' Tessa said, 'any thoughts?'

'Not really. You've obviously to do a lot more digging into the family background. I have trouble understanding how siblings fall out to this extent. I have two younger sisters, and I wouldn't let anything happen to them, wouldn't allow anybody to even look at them a bit odd. That's what you do for sisters.'

'Oh, we'll be digging. It starts when we get back this afternoon, now that we've notified next of kin. We've got a roomful of people working on it at Chatsworth already, digging into backgrounds, looking for any trace of the husband and child.'

'Husband and child?' Kat stared at Tessa. 'Whose husband and child?'

'Nicola Armstrong had a little boy, Daniel. He disappeared ten years ago, and she always said her husband had taken him. Exhusband. Does the name Daniel Armstrong ring any bells?'

'It certainly does.' Doris spoke slowly, as if gathering in her memories. 'It made big news at the time. The two of them simply disappeared, both on the same day, which kind of leads you to one conclusion, that the husband took his child. So they've never been traced? It's a cold case?'

Tessa shook her head. 'I've obviously not had chance to look closely at it yet, only had a quick skim through the file, but we don't know if the two things are connected. Nicola's murder could be down to something entirely different. Don't forget we have this phone with only one number in it. Once we find out who that number is, that will open up endless possibilities.'

Tessa reached across and took another chocolate biscuit. She stared at it in disgust. 'This is my third. What am I doing?'

'Don't swallow it,' Doris advised. 'It's the only way to stop the calories counting.'

With a sigh, Tessa bit into it. She needed the extra fat to keep her warm in this cold weather.

'Debbie Carter's nice, isn't she?' Kat drew them back into the conversation. 'When we moved in, she came around to ours with a bottle of wine and a box of scones. Bridie was only little then, but she's had Charlie since. We talk baby talk together now.'

'I briefly met Bridie; she was off to school on the walking bus. Genius idea. But Debbie came across as quite aggressive. She obviously had nothing to do with her sister, and I got the impression she wanted to blame me for not finding her nephew ten years ago. Have you met the brother, Kat?'

'Yes, he did some electrical work for us. Complete rewire

actually. Nice man, quiet, just got on with it, did the job perfectly and went. Debbie recommended him when she brought the wine. You saw him this morning?'

'Yes, he's working at Debbie's today. He said very little, but I've got this feeling...'

They waited.

'I think he's been seeing Nicola without letting Debbie know it. As you said, he is quiet, and I'm guessing he wouldn't want Debbie finding out. It would mean trouble for him; she would see it as disloyalty. I don't know why she didn't get on with Nicola, but it goes back a long way. Probably to Daniel's disappearance. I'm not saying she's in any way involved with Nicola's murder, I'm just saying she's coming across as unfeeling, uncaring and quite aggressive. Which all seems the opposite to how Kat has known her.'

'You taking on the cold case as well?' Mouse spoke for the first time.

'Not without my DCI's say so. Solving this won't be easy. Nobody is going to walk into the police station and say I've come to confess, are they. And we have a specialised unit for cold cases, they can tackle it if somebody wants one last push on it. But don't forget no bodies were ever found. During the month before they disappeared, Adam Armstrong systematically took out five thousand pounds in small amounts from their account, two or three hundred at a time, and he's never used the account again. She had no idea the money was being removed, he apparently dealt with the finances. They could be dead. Or they could have effectively started a new life. Surely that ten-year-old unsolved case can't impact on this one...'

'With your luck? Yes. I'd say it could,' Kat laughed. 'But feel free to drop in here anytime. We can provide four pairs of ears now. Another coffee?'

Tessa shook her head and stood. 'No thanks, Kat. We'd best get back, see if anything's turned up at Chatsworth. I'm assuming there's some info on the mobile phone, but if not I'm going to ring the number. We don't like to do that, ring blind, because it alerts the person on the other end, but sometimes we have no choice. These burner phones are a bloody nuisance. The mobile phone companies don't do the police any favours... well, apart from being able to triangulate calls and such, anyway.' She finished her grumbling with a laugh.

Luke stacked the cups onto the tray, clearing Kat's desk for her. He clicked the lid back on the biscuit box, thinking he'd maybe have to raid the petty cash once more and restock. His ladies could certainly knock back the chocolate digestives. He'd been much too nervous to eat anything, but he knew he would feel so much better next time – maybe he'd manage one or two biscuits then.

The three Connection ladies walked into reception with Tessa and Hannah and amidst good wishes, they left.

Everyone else drifted back to their own offices as Luke disappeared into the small kitchen to wash the cups. He wiped down the tray and stacked it by the side of the microwave. He had learnt to balance it carefully; the kitchen was too tiny to be anything but precision tidy. He'd just put his hands into the soapy water when the reception phone rang.

He grabbed a tea towel and quickly dried his hands before picking up the receiver.

'Connection, Eyam,' he said into the phone.

'Oh, hello.' The voice was tentative.

'Hi there. Can I help you?' Luke smiled. He'd read somewhere that if you smiled when on a phone call, it showed in your voice to the person on the other end of the line. As a newcomer to reception work, he needed all the tips and hints he could muster.

'I'd like to make an appointment, please.'

'Certainly. Let me just pull the appointments screen up on the computer and we'll see when we can fit you in.'

'It needs to be soon. If it isn't soon, I might change my mind.'

The appointment screen flashed up and he scanned for the following day. Both Doris and Mouse had three appointments each, Kat only one, at church, and it was an early one. He also checked the physical diary, aware that Kat sometimes put things in it when she picked up random bookings such as Martha's injections. Nothing had been added, so he lifted the receiver once more.

'I can book you in with Mrs Rowe at ten o'clock, if that is any good to you,' he said.

'Thank you. That will be perfect. I'll have to bring the baby with me, but I'm sure he'll be sleeping after the walk down into the village. It's with Kat, at ten?' the woman confirmed.

'It is. You know Mrs Rowe?'

'I do, we're neighbours.'

Although he knew the answer, he had to ask the question. 'Can I have your name, please.'

'Yes, it's Mrs Carter, Debbie Carter.'

8

Tessa checked her emails as soon as they reclaimed their desks at Chatsworth. The report on the phone found on Nicola Armstrong revealed nothing other than the one random number. The phone hadn't been registered to her, a throwaway once it had served its purpose. If Luke was right about the three Xs, she guessed it wouldn't have been thrown away.

The number she had called possibly only minutes before Nicola died wasn't attributable to anybody, so Marsden took out the phone from the evidence bag. She waved across at Ray Charlton who gave her a thumbs up to show he was ready, took a deep breath and rang the number.

There were five rings before it was answered. 'Nic, for fuck's sake, it's over. I can't take any more. That was just one time too many.'

Tessa had to think fast. From somewhere deep inside herself she produced a tearful voice, keeping it quiet. 'Why?' She prayed this man wouldn't be able to tell it wasn't Nicola.

'Why?' His voice rose an octave. 'Why? Try the broken wrist, sweetheart. You can't bash somebody with a baseball bat and not expect something serious to happen. I had to tell Paula I'd fallen in the snow. So that's it, Nic. No more. It's over. I'm dumping this phone now, I suggest you do the same with that one, and get out of my life.' His tone was becoming angrier.

Tessa tried again. 'But...'

'But nothing. All that talk about wanting to become the next Mrs Ireland... listen, sweetheart, I don't even want to see you again, never mind marry you. Paula might be a boring old fart, but she's never put me in hospital.'

Tessa was writing furiously. She had names. Time to let him know who she was.

'Mr Ireland,' she said. 'Thank you for being so helpful. My name is DI Tessa Marsden, and I'd like to come and have a chat with you.' Ray walked across and pushed a piece of paper towards her. Baslow. 'Now I know you live in Baslow, so can you give me your full address, please.'

There was silence and then the man spoke again. 'What? Police? Where's Nicola? This is her phone...'

'We are aware of that, Mr Ireland. Now, your address, please.'

'No...'

Tessa sighed. 'Mr Ireland, it will take us approximately thirty seconds to find it, you may as well tell me what it is.'

He sounded a broken man as he told her where he lived. She suspected he was trying to come up with something to tell the boring old fart, but guessed he might need a bit of luck on that one.

'Thank you, Mr Ireland, you've been very helpful. So far. Please do nothing with that phone, you don't want a charge of obstructing the course of justice hanging over you, do you. We'll be there in about fifteen minutes.'

She hung up, and grinned at Hannah. 'Yes,' Tessa said and punched the air. 'Did I sound like a broken-hearted lover?'

'Not exactly, boss, but down a phone line you would. We going now?'

'We are. Then we'll head off home, unless he falls prostrate at our feet and confesses to murder, but I hardly think that's going to happen when he clearly doesn't know she's dead.'

Neil Ireland opened the door to them, his face immobile. Nothing showed, no anger, no upset, just piercing blue eyes that settled first on Hannah, then on Tessa. He was a tall striking-looking man with short steel-grey hair that lightened to a white grey around his ears. His skin was tanned, and Tessa guessed he'd been somewhere warm for Christmas. With Nicola? With Paula? His left arm sported a cast, presumably doing its work healing the broken wrist.

They held out their warrant cards and he nodded without speaking. He held the door open and they entered the hallway. Wooden floors with brightly coloured rugs welcomed visitors to this home, despite the current frostiness of the male resident.

'First room on the left,' he said.

The lounge was beautiful. It was exquisitely decorated in grey and pale mustard, with two huge sofas also in grey. The fire was burning brightly, and they waited patiently for him to ask them to sit. He didn't, so Tessa moved towards a chair, sat, and took some papers out of her bag.

'Hannah, can you take notes, please?' she said, and for the first time Neil Ireland began to look uncomfortable, rather than pissed off.

Hannah sat at the other end of the same sofa her boss had commandeered, and took out her notebook and pen.

She waited patiently for something to happen, but when it did it made her jump. The lounge door swung open, and a striking blonde woman came in, carrying a tray with drinks. She was around five feet nine, and carried her height gracefully.

'I hope you drink tea,' she said, and Hannah thought they wouldn't dare deny it.

'This is my wife Paula,' Neil said, and Paula inclined her head. She placed the tray on the coffee table then sat at one end of the other sofa. Neil took his place at the far end. There was an ice-cold space between them.

Tessa leaned forward and grasped one of the cups. She added milk, passed it to Hannah before doing the same with her own drink, and then turned to speak to her host. 'Thank you, Mrs Ireland. This is very welcome. It's so cold out there.'

'My husband says you need to have a few words with him. I trust it's okay if I'm here as well.' The frostiness had passed from husband to wife. The husband seemed to be deflating in front of their eyes.

'That's fine, Mrs Ireland,' Tessa said, and watched as Neil Ireland dropped his head. 'We have found a body at Chatsworth. Before we go any further, Mr Ireland, may I have the phone on which I contacted you earlier?'

He reached into his jeans pocket and eased out the mobile. Paula stared at it, but said nothing.

Tessa leaned across and took it out of his hands. 'Thank you. We'll have our tech boys recover everything that's ever been on it. Did you buy it new?'

Neil nodded; misery was written all over his face. The bravado when he had first opened his front door had gone.

'We now know the body is of a woman who lived in Baslow, Nicola Armstrong.'

Tessa heard Paula gasp, but kept her eyes on the man in front of her slowly imploding.

'No...' he moaned.

'Neil? What's wrong?' Paula turned to her husband.

Tessa interrupted, not wanting this domineering woman

interfering with anything her husband might be about to say. 'Can you tell me where you were between the hours of 10pm and midnight on Monday, please?'

'He was here,' Paula said. 'It was Monday when he fell in the snow, and we didn't get back from the hospital until about nine. He went to bed almost as soon as we got in. He took some painkillers and when I went up about half past ten, I checked on him and he was fast asleep.'

Neil lifted his head, ignored his wife and looked at Tessa. 'She's dead? She rang me about ten that night but I didn't answer. I didn't want to speak to her, or ever see her again. This isn't the first time she's hurt me, but this is the most serious. I realised it couldn't go on, but I was in no state to speak to her Monday night. The pain was too bad. By the time you rang this afternoon, I was ready to tell her it was over. Only it wasn't her…'

'Do you have any idea why she would be in Chatsworth?'

'She died on the estate? I know she liked to walk around the grounds, but not in the middle of the night in a horrendous snowstorm.'

Paula Ireland stood. Her face was pale, and her eyes remained fixed on Neil. 'You've had an affair with her? Nicola Armstrong?'

'You knew her, Mrs Ireland?' Tessa asked. She hated to see marriages fall apart so easily… and this one was. She suspected there hadn't been much love left anyway, and the ghost of the late Nicola Armstrong was hammering the final nail in.

'Of course I knew her. We spent bloody weeks tramping the moors looking for the kid when he went missing. Everybody knew that husband of hers had legged it, and taken the kid with him. But we had to look as though we were helping.'

Hannah was scribbling furiously; she needed to get everything down so they could pick over everything later. She made a note that Paula had gone very white, and that note caused her to look up and check her out.

She lifted her head just in time to see Paula storm out of the room.

'Let her go,' Tessa murmured.

'Mr Ireland, can we return to your relationship with Nicola Armstrong, please. How long had the affair been going on?' Tessa waited for him to gather his thoughts.

'About thirteen months. We met a few days before Christmas last year. I shared a table in the pub with her, because it was packed with people having a Christmas party. It was very noisy and we started to talk but could hardly hear each other. We left that pub, drove to the next one and went in there. It was Christmas party free, and we had a really enjoyable evening. We exchanged phone numbers, and I rang her the next day.'

'You bought simple phones to keep contact away from your main phones, I assume. When you spoke to me earlier, you insinuated it was Nicola's fault your wrist was broken. Is that true?'

It was clear he didn't want to speak, and eventually Tessa had to prompt him. 'Can you answer please, Mr Ireland?'

'Yes, damn it, it was Nicola's fault, She smashed a baseball bat down on to my arm, but I'd started to move it and my wrist took the full force of it. It's the third time she's attacked me, and I decided enough was enough. That's why I didn't respond to her call on Monday night.'

'What other damage has she caused to you?'

'The first time she scratched me. I know that sounds like nothing, but they were deep channels down my back. Her nails ripped through my shirt and then through my skin. I had to go see my doctor because they became infected, and I pretended to him that I had fallen against a fence and it was barbed wire that had caused the injuries. I kept it away from Paula, but that's not difficult. We have separate rooms now.'

'And the other time?'

'She didn't actually cause any damage; she held a knife to my throat because I had to attend a function at work and Paula was going with me. Nicola was livid, said it was time I stopped being spineless and divorced Paula, then she could be Mrs Ireland. She scared me, and I managed to get away from her and headed home. She rang me the next day, full of apologies, in floods of tears, promising she would never hurt me again. I met up with her Monday morning and again she started going on about me leaving Paula. I said no, I wasn't ready for that level of commitment and she grabbed the baseball bat she keeps behind the front door and brought it down with an almighty thump on to my arm. She was screaming after me as I headed down the path to drive home. The pain in my wrist was unbearable; fortunately my car is an automatic and I managed to get home without much bother, but I had to lie to Paula and tell her I'd fallen in the snow. My wrist was an odd shape, so she drove me to the hospital. She's quite right, it was about nine when we got home. How did Nicola die?'

His question came across too abruptly, and he looked at Tessa. 'I'm sorry, DI Marsden, I don't seem able to grieve. Do I sound as heartless as I feel?'

'At this stage, Mr Ireland, I can't give out details of how she died, but I can tell you it was murder.'

'And she was found in Chatsworth?'

'She was, and we believe she was killed shortly after she made that phone call to you. She died sometime between 22:03 and midnight. Was it a habit of hers to go out walking late at night?'

Ireland shook his head. 'Not as far as I'm aware. However, I never stayed overnight with her, so maybe she did go out. I can't really help with that.'

Tessa stood, and Hannah took her cue from her boss, slipping her notebook back inside her bag. 'Thank you, Mr Ireland. That's all we need for now, but we may need to speak to you again, possibly at the station for a more formal interview. Whichever way it's done, we will be needing a statement.'

Neil Ireland gave a lop-sided grin, which didn't reach his eyes. 'That's fine, but believe me, your interrogation, even if it's under torture, will be nothing like as horrific as what's heading my way in the next few minutes. Can't I go with you and seek asylum?'

'Sorry, sir,' Tessa smiled. 'If you change address, please keep us informed,' and she handed him her card.

His sigh came all the way up from his feet. 'Thank you for not judging me.'

'I think you'll have enough judgement coming down on your head as soon as we leave. Good luck with it,' Tessa said, and she and Hannah left the warmth of the house and trudged back to their car.

9

Debbie Carter shivered as she pressed the bell and waited for the door to open. She felt nervous, as if she was doing something wrong. But how could it be wrong to want to find her nephew and his father? Hopefully they would be alive and Danny a handsome fifteen-year-old, but if they were dead at least she could reconcile herself to that. Living in this cruel limbo had been hard for too long, too many memories.

Luke glanced up from the pile of post he was sorting, and clicked on the release button. He stepped around the reception desk and welcomed her with a smile. 'Kat is waiting for you, Ms Carter.'

He knocked on Kat's door, murmured 'Ms Carter' and showed her through, helping her to manoeuvre the pushchair through the narrow doorway.

'Thank you, Luke,' Kat said. He closed the door and returned to his post sorting – almost equal amounts for his three ladies. He knocked on Doris's door and handed her the envelopes, and she handed him a sheaf of papers.

'Look through these, Luke. See what you think. There's no

rush, but we need eventually to think about you being licensed. This will be the start of it.'

He stared at the papers, hardly daring to breathe. See what he thought? He already knew what he thought without looking through them. His three ladies were on a pedestal, and he wanted to be up there with them.

'Will I be 007?' he asked, flashing Doris his devil smile.

'Not an earthly, that's my number. You could be 002 and a half, I'm sure 008 and 009 will agree to that.'

He blew her a kiss and returned to his desk. Doris had printed the papers for him, and he meticulously put them into sections, found an empty file folder and proudly wrote LUKE'S STUFF along the top of it.

He checked his small bank of three lights under the top shelf of his desk, saw that none of the women needed him for anything, and settled down to what he felt was the most serious work he would ever do. 002 and a half meant business.

Debbie finished filling in the client form and passed it across to Kat, who skimmed through it, and put it in her top drawer. Kat pointed to the recorder, received permission to use it and switched it on.

'Okay, Debbie,' she said gently, 'talk to me. I'm so sorry for the loss of Nicola, it must have hit you very hard.'

'Not as hard as losing her son. Nicola was a nasty piece of work at times, and I struggled to keep any sort of relationship going with her. But I loved Danny. And that's why I'm here.'

Kat settled back in her chair, and looked at her neighbour with interest. 'The police will find who did it.'

'I'm not really bothered whether they do or not; she's gone, we'll bury her and that will be the end of it as far as Nicola is concerned. Since Daniel and Adam disappeared, I've seen her maybe half a dozen times, that's all. I always buy her a gift for

Christmas, and that's when I see her, but occasionally she hasn't been in when I've called with that so even half a dozen times might be stretching it. She certainly wasn't there when I called this Christmas. I left the gift and the card in the shed and pushed a note through her door.' Debbie took out her phone. 'This is the text I got back.'

Thank you. Will drop bag of gifts off for all of you tomorrow.

'No kisses, no anything. She left a bag in my blue bin, and it contained gifts for me and the kids, and a joint gift for Simon and his partner Greg. And that was it, really. I messaged her to say I'd got the bag.'

'Why?'

'Why what?'

'You must have been close at one point. So why the distance now? You're sisters, and I imagine quite close in age.'

'There's two years between us,' Debbie confirmed. 'But according to my mum, we never got on from the minute Nicola first saw me. Simon was three years older than her, and it seems that he spent his childhood stopping her killing me. We laugh about it now, but she was pretty violent, and not only towards me.'

'So how can we help you? We can't get involved in anything that would compromise the police investigation, you do know that?'

'Okay. I'm here representing Simon as well as me. We will go halves on your bill, but we need some answers. Neither of us has ever believed Daniel and Adam are dead. Our hope is that once Adam sees his wife is gone and no longer a threat to either of them, he will return, with Danny. But hope isn't going to make that happen. He could just as easily say thank God for that, and never contact either me or Simon again. The thing is, Kat, we need either closure or a happy ending.'

The sleeping baby in the pushchair snuffled. Debbie reached

out to the handle, to gently push the pram backwards and forwards.

Kat was silent for a moment. Despite having been neighbours for around six years, she hadn't known of Debbie's connection to the little boy who had disappeared ten years earlier.

Kat eventually spoke. 'Okay, I'll speak with Beth and Doris before I firmly commit. We have to make absolutely sure we're not stepping on police toes; I'll get back to you by tomorrow at the latest.'

Debbie reached down and removed a large carrier bag from the tray underneath the pushchair. 'This is everything I've collected since he went missing. Copies of both birth certificates, newspaper reports, photos… everything I could possibly get my hands on at the beginning. I always thought Danny was taken by his dad, but I also thought Adam took him to keep him safe.'

'Safe?'

'My sister had psychopathic tendencies, Kat. How Adam put up with her I don't know. He was always injured in some way, and then one day Danny turned up with a cast on his arm. Two days later, Danny and Adam disappeared. That's why I know they're out there somewhere. I can't, hand on heart, say Nicola would have killed them, because that wasn't what she was about. She just enjoyed inflicting pain. Adam could have walked away, but he was an amazing dad and he wouldn't have left Danny with her to become the punchbag.'

'Have you said all of this to DI Marsden?'

'No,' Debbie said, with an emphatic shake of her head to stress the word. 'The police gave up too quickly, and I always thought it was because everybody assumed he was with his daddy, and therefore that was okay. He was safe. But the real truth is that they're investigating Nicola's murder, and that is their priority. They won't be looking into a ten-year-old disappearance, will they?'

'They might if they suspect Adam. Or even Daniel. He'll be fifteen now, won't he.'

Debbie Carter looked horrified. 'What? No...'

'Debbie, I'm just playing devil's advocate here, but don't assume the police won't dredge it up, because they just might. You need to be aware of that, so you can handle the inevitable questions that will follow. Is Rob okay with what you're doing?'

'Rob? Why would it bother him what I do? He left three days after Charlie was born. He's living with somebody in New Mills now. You hadn't noticed?'

'I'm so sorry, Debbie, no I hadn't noticed he wasn't about. Winter months send everybody scurrying indoors and we don't know anything that's happened. I hope you know that if ever you have a problem, we'll help.'

Debbie gave a slight laugh. 'My problem would be if he ever tried to come back. I've been so much happier since he went, so his new love is welcome to him. He sends money each month for the kids, takes them out for a couple of hours every two weeks, and that's enough. Simon constantly checks on me; it seems to bother him that I'm on my own, but it definitely doesn't bother me. And I'm in no rush to replace Rob either. I like being me, not me and him.'

Kat began to put all the papers back in the bag, and as if on cue there was a small cry from inside the pram.

'I'll get Charlie home,' Debbie said. 'He's probably hungry. You'll let me know if you can take the case?'

'I will. I'm going to call a meeting with the others, show them this pile of paperwork, and we'll take it from there. I'll have to notify DI Marsden, tell her what we're doing, because treading on her toes isn't a good idea.'

'I understand. I'll look forward to hearing from you.'

Debbie manoeuvred backwards out of the doorway, and swung the pram around in the reception area. Luke held the door open for her, and she stopped to thank him. 'It's Luke, isn't it? Luke Taylor?'

'It is. Have we met before?'

'No, I know your mum. She's very proud of you, and pointed you out one day. We always have a chat when I go through her checkout in the Co-op. Lovely lady, very helpful and friendly. So you're working here... that'll be good for you. Connection has an excellent reputation. See you again, I hope,' Debbie said, and he closed the door gently as she left.

When he reached his desk, a red light indicating Kat needed him was glowing. He knocked on her door and opened it slightly.

'You need me?'

'Yes, come in, Luke.'

He sat across from her and waited. A large carrier bag was in the middle of her desk and he eyed it with some concern. It looked like a lot of filing.

'I need some advice,' Kat said.

Luke waited. Advice from him?

Kat patted the bag. 'Can this lot be scanned or whatever it's called, and sent to our computers? It just seems like such a lot of photocopying if it can't.'

He nodded. 'It can. I'll scan each piece, put everything into a file and send all three of you the file.'

Kat stood up. 'You see, I knew we'd employed you for a reason! Don't do it yet, I have to talk to Nan and Mouse first, to confirm we're taking the case, but one thing's for sure; I want you fully involved with it, and keeping this file up to date, so you might want to open a document or something on your own computer for this file to land there. Am I making sense?'

'Nearly,' he said with a laugh.

C CTV showed nothing helpful. No cars had gone through Chatsworth on that wintry night, although the camera on the entrance gates showed Nicola Armstrong entering the grounds, alone and staggering slightly, at around ten minutes to ten. On such a bitterly cold night she was well-wrapped up, a scarf around her neck, her hood up to cover her head, gloves and long boots. If they hadn't had the actual clothing in their evidence bags, they would not have been able to tell it was her.

The briefing was lively, but nothing new had come to light other than the interview with Neil Ireland. Tessa took them through everything, including the violent relationship Neil and Nicola had shared, which led to the phone call she made to her lover being ignored.

'Could that phone call have been a cry for help? Was she scared? Did she think someone was following her? Let's see if we can pinpoint exactly where that call was made from, let's try for some sort of location on it. And we need to know where she was going. Why did she take her bag? If she was going out for a last walk of the evening, why would she drag her bag along? Her phone was in her back pocket. Or was she going to meet somebody? She was smartly dressed underneath all the outer winter clothing. And I want details ASAP of calls into and out from her home, on the landline. Do we think this murder could be connected to the disappearance of her son and husband? According to her sister, they're still married. Is he still alive? Are we going to have to open a ten-year-old cold case to solve one from a couple of days ago?'

Tessa sank down into her seat with a thud, and everyone began to return to their own designated desks. Hannah moved across to her and pulled up a chair.

'Well done, boss,' she said quietly. 'You think there could be anything back at the Armstrong house that we've missed? Should we go and have another look?'

'I think we should. Just the two of us. We'll take our time and go through everything. But not today. It's getting dark, so we'll go tomorrow morning. I'll see you here for about half past eight, then we'll leave the troops to pound the computers. We'll head off to the house. There's something we're missing, somewhere. Let's go find what the hell it is.'

Doris, Mouse, Kat and Luke sat around Kat's desk, the carrier bag still in the middle of it.

'This,' Kat said, lightly touching the bag, 'is ten years of gathering paperwork. There are photographs, letters and all sorts of stuff in it, and Debbie wants us to take the case. She wants Danny, her nephew, in her life, so she wants us to find him. I think she's quite prepared for either outcome, either closure if we discover he's dead, or a meeting if we find him alive. I've talked to Luke and he can document...' she hesitated. 'Well, he can do something with them that will end up in a file we can all look at on our computers.'

. . .

Luke tried so hard not to smile, but he saw Mouse's roll of her eyes, and was lost. The smile became a guffaw, and he felt he had to apologise. 'I'll scan them into a file, and send it to each hard drive,' he explained. 'That's what Kat's trying to say.'

Doris patted his hand. 'Don't worry, Luke, we understood. So shall we listen to the recording now?'

A disgruntled Kat reached for the recorder. She thought she was getting on top of this computer stuff. She pressed play, and they sat around with notepads, each of them making the occasional comment on the paper for discussion later.

They reached the end, and Kat stood to replenish drinks. She handed the coffees around, and then sat quietly, thinking.

'Luke?'

He glanced down at the page in front of him. 'Why does she buy her sister a Christmas present if she doesn't have anything to do with her? It seems strange. And from what she says, it could be a two-year gap between seeing each other, and yet they exchange Christmas gifts? I don't get it.' He glanced around the table. 'That's just first thoughts from listening to that. Sorry.'

Mouse smiled at him. She was getting to like him more and more every day. 'Look.' She pushed her own notebook across to him. It said *Christmas presents? Why?*

He high-fived her.

'I agree with Luke,' Mouse said. 'There's something not ringing true. I could understand it if there had been Christmas presents for children involved, but with the disappearance of Danny, that left Debbie the only one to have children. How old is Debbie's daughter?'

'Bridie? About ten or eleven.'

'Which means she was born when Danny went missing.

Maybe the explanation is simple. Maybe Nicola felt she had to continue the exchange of gifts because of the children, so Debbie felt she had to send something to Nicola. I'm sure we all send a Christmas gift or card to someone we really don't care about.' Mouse paused. 'So do we take it on? Are we comfortable with it? We'll have to bring Tessa and Hannah in on this decision, and take bloody good care not to impact on their investigation. And, Kat Rowe, no bodies. You know Tessa has the face on with us if we give her corpses.'

Doris smiled. 'Corpses aren't good for business. I propose we do take it on, that Luke scans this lot into a file, and we spend tomorrow going through it and familiarising ourselves with everything. Then we'll send Mouse into the undergrowth of the Internet to see what we can track down. Luke, how far do you want to be involved with this? You can man the office for us, or you can go out into the field and accompany us. I'm conscious that you're very new and I don't want you to feel overwhelmed.'

'I need to accompany you. You promised full training on the advert,' he said with a huge smile. 'That's what I want.'

'Okay. Let's have a vote, girls. Take it on or leave it alone. Luke, you can't vote in this.'

He willed them to say take it on. To his deep satisfaction, they did.

Kat spoke to Debbie, explained the costs involved, and said they would be returning the carrier bag full of documents as soon as they had been scanned into the computer. She had written the word "scanned" on to her notepad before making the call. It wouldn't help if clients thought she was a numpty when it came to technology.

To Kat's surprise, Debbie burst into tears. 'You've made me a very happy person,' she blubbered. 'Find Danny and Adam for me, please, Kat.'

'I promise we'll try. You need to understand he's been missing for ten years, and picking up any sort of trail won't be easy, but we'll give it everything we've got.'

'Thank you so much, Kat.'

Kat replaced the receiver and frowned. Unease still sat heavily on her, but she had no idea why.

Kat walked across to the church and leaned against the back pew, surveying the interior. She loved the place, found peace and solace there, and also did a lot of thinking – usually on the third pew from the front.

She headed down the aisle towards it, dropped a kneeler to the floor, and dipped her head in prayer. All sounds disappeared and she remained kneeling for five minutes, before she felt a gentle hand on her shoulder.

'Thank you, Kat, for looking after him,' the woman said, turned and almost ran down the aisle, as if embarrassed at disturbing someone immersed so deeply in prayer. Just for a moment Kat's brain went into freefall, and she eased herself back onto the seat.

'Craig's mum!' Kat said aloud. 'Sally Adams.' Craig Adams had been the first person to be murdered by Leon, and when Kat discovered just how evil her husband had been she'd promised Sally she would take care of her son's grave. Sally lived some distance away and as a non-driver, couldn't get easily to Eyam churchyard where Craig had been laid to rest next to his father.

Kat sat for a short time, her thoughts drifting back to two years earlier when her world had begun to implode. On discovering what Leon had done, and had been doing for a long time, she had got through the whole horrific period with the help of Mouse and Doris, and her parents.

That was the moment she knew that they had to give everything to try to find Daniel Armstrong. He was still a minor; they had no idea what his life was like. He may be in a good place, and if so, they could tell him about his aunt and give him the choice of whether to return to meet her or not; but similarly, he could be in a bad place, without choices.

Kat said a silent thank you to her god, and left the sanctuary of the church to return to the office.

'I'm going home,' Kat announced. 'I need to feel Martha's arms around me. She stayed at Mum's last night, and I need her now. Okay?'

'Okay,' Doris said with a laugh. 'Kat Rowe, get lost. And bring her here tomorrow, we all miss her.'

'I haven't even seen her yet,' Luke said. 'Can she switch on a computer?'

'Depends whose genes she got more of,' Kat said with a smile. 'If it's mine, then the answer is probably no. You going to teach her?'

'In time,' he said gravely.

'Joel? It's me.'

'Mouse, I know. It said so on my phone screen.'

'Smart arse.'

He laughed. 'You want something, beautiful lady?'

'Yes, you. But that's what I'm ringing about. I can't come to Manchester tomorrow. We've taken on a biggish new case that I need to be here for. So I'll have to forego those long tanned legs, that stunningly beautiful chest, the amazing kisses, and...'

'Whoa! Are you in the office with anybody?'

'Only Nan.'

'What?'

'Stop panicking,' Mouse laughed. 'It's just me. You want to make your way over to Eyam, big boy? Maybe at the weekend?'

'Let me see if I can rearrange something that's booked in for Saturday, before I make a firm commitment. So the answer is yes, I do want to make my way over to Eyam, but I can't say I can do it for definite yet. That okay?'

'It'll do. I'm missing you.'

'I know. I'll work something out. Gotta go, I'm late for a conference call. Love you, Mouse.'

He disconnected and she stared at her phone. Love you. Had he really just said that? Love you. That sounded so good, she felt she could maybe get used to hearing it.

She put down the phone, swivelled her chair to stare out the window, and whispered, 'Love you too, Joel.'

Harry Hardy walked into the kitchens of Chatsworth and helped himself to a bacon sandwich, the bacon topped with tomatoes that soaked rapidly into the huge breadcake.

He headed over to the table in the corner and glanced up at the clock. Nearly nine and he was bang on time. He could take his half-hour break, then go and meet up with the chap from the horticultural company who wanted to see around the greenhouses. He apparently could supply Chatsworth with all their gardening needs... Harry grinned to himself. The idiot couldn't possibly have any idea of the scale of requirements for the huge area that made up the Chatsworth estate. Still, it was part of his job to meet up with all salespeople, so meet up he would.

He'd had an interesting hour chatting to the assorted police personnel working in the large room down the corridor from the kitchens. He'd given his statement, signed it, then talked for a while about the stages they were at.

There had been some admiration for the fact that he had been at Chatsworth all his working life, and would be there until the Duke made him retire.

'I simply can't imagine working anywhere else,' he admitted, when PC Fiona Ainsworth finished with his statement. 'I'm happy with my work, it's mainly all outdoors, and nobody bothers me. I know the job, know what has to be done, and my employers are amazing.'

'Do you see much of the Duke?' Fiona asked.

'Every day at some point. He keeps a close eye on the running of the place. I think he's quite taken by the change this murder has brought into Chatsworth, but don't tell him I said that,' Harry said with a laugh. 'Have you taken young Davy's statement?'

'We have, it didn't take long. He didn't find her, so it was more making sure he didn't touch the body at all, that sort of thing.'

He nodded. 'I was a bit worried he would be affected by it. He couldn't even look at that poor lass, so I just kept talking to him to keep his mind off it. It was a relief when your DI Marsden turned up, I can tell you. I could get him back here to warm up, then the Duke sent both of us home.'

Fiona laughed. 'And did you go home?'

'No. I'm here to do a job. I made sure Davy went though.'

Fiona shook his hand. 'Thank you for being here so promptly, Mr Hardy. I hope I haven't kept you from anything important.'

'My breakfast, and my name is Harry.'

He picked up his jacket and walked out of the room. The smell of the bacon drew him towards the kitchens, and he remained in the warmth until the sales representative arrived.

'Iain Sherwood,' the dark-haired handsome man said to Harry, and held out his card.

Harry thought he looked a little young to be tasked with selling products to Chatsworth, but he looked at the card, read the information on it, and held out an arm to guide him around to the gardens.

'You've a couple of days to spare then,' Harry said. 'I take it you've never been here before.'

'No I haven't,' Iain said, looking around him. 'Impressive, isn't it? According to my information, it's twelve thousand acres in the Chatsworth estate alone, and thousands more spread out across the whole of Derbyshire. Is that right?'

'Aye,' was all Harry could say.

They moved into the kitchen garden and both of them walked around the vegetable beds, the raised beds, the fruit trees. Iain spoke into his phone rather than taking physical notes, and Harry finally began to realise that maybe the young feller knew a bit. Still, it was going to be a long day for both of them. They had a lot of ground to cover.

'Your greenhouses are situated somewhere else?' Iain asked.

'They are. Do you want a drink first? It's bitterly cold out here.' Harry hesitated for a moment, and then decided not to say anything about soft southerners not being able to take the northern climate.

'That would be good,' was the response, and Harry watched as Iain switched off his phone and dropped it into his inside pocket.

It was gardening staff that sat around the table this time, and they were all soon in animated conversation with Iain. He showed them leaflets of different products, chatted to them about their wish lists for improving the crops, keeping predators at bay, and other such horticultural advice. Harry enjoyed the time spent drinking tea, but eventually he stood, told the others they were heading over towards the greenhouses, and he and Iain moved back outside to continue the tour.

As they walked down the hill heading towards the greenhouse area, Harry felt inordinately proud of what was in front of them. The sun was shining with very weak and watery rays, but it created a sparkling effect, like twinkling stars, on the windows of the greenhouses.

They went in the first one, quickly closing the door behind

them to preserve the heat, and were assailed by a tomato fragrance. Once again the phone was brought into play, and Iain dictated his observations into it. He took his time, and Harry walked alongside him, impressed despite his earlier reservations.

The second greenhouse was filled with plants that had been started under glass, prior to them being transplanted in warmer months into the vegetable gardens. This was the largest of the glasshouses, with walkways down either side, and a large central growing area. They walked down the first side, with Iain continuing to list the plants into his recorder. As they turned around at the top to walk down the other side, Iain stopped, but Harry didn't. The collision caused Iain to take a step and he almost fell.

'Fuckin' 'ell,' he said, all pretence of having a posh accent vanquished. He dropped to his knees, and Harry, still behind him, stooped to pull him back up.

'Sorry, Iain,' he said, then froze. Iain's legs and arms formed a bridge over something lying on the ground. Something unmoving.

'Shit!' Iain scrambled to his feet, and Harry pushed by him before dropping to the ground himself.

'It's Olivia,' he said, placing a finger on her neck. Her skin was icy cold, and he knew he didn't need an absent pulse to tell him life was extinct.

Iain vomited. Harry took out his radio.

'Frank,' he said. 'I think I need some help.'

Frank chuckled. 'Harry,' he said, 'the last time you said that to me, you'd found a dead body.'

'Yes, Frank. Get some of those police round to Greenhouse B, will you. Best bring them yourself. And don't let any of the kitchen staff come down for anything. Nothing, you hear me? Where's young Davy?'

Frank hesitated. 'He's checking on the deer, he could be

anywhere. He's not far from finishing his shift, he started at six today. Wanted an early finish for a dental appointment. I'll get hold of him and send him home.'

'I don't want him here. He's too young. And bring a bottle of water, will you? I think Iain needs a drink of something.'

Iain Sherwood's face, despite his winter suntan, was chalk white. 'You know her?' he whispered.

'I do.' Harry's tone was grim. 'Her name is Olivia, and she's part of the Duchess's staff. Lovely girl. Just had her twenty-first birthday.'

'And she's…'

'Dead. She is. I hope you've no more appointments today, Iain, because the police will be interviewing everybody.'

'No… I only had here.' He looked up as the door slid open, and several people came through. None were in uniform, but Iain Sherwood was in no doubt that they were police. They immediately took charge, and he apologised for the pile of vomit in the corner.

Harry had a quiet word with Frank, then Harry and Iain left the greenhouse and climbed the incline up to the main house, with instructions to go nowhere, speak to nobody, and sit tight until somebody could talk to them.

They opened the door, and the atmosphere was sombre. Nobody spoke, and all five people present turned towards them. Harry held out a chair for Iain, fetched a small glass and took out his hip flask from his pocket. He poured a generous measure of whisky and handed it to the young man, whose hands were visibly trembling.

'Drink this,' he said, and Iain did so, giving a small cough as the whisky hit the back of his throat.

Harry turned to face the other five sitting around the small table. 'You've been told to wait here?'

They nodded, and one, a buxom woman on the cleaning staff, spoke to him. 'We've been told not to chat about anything and not to speculate.'

'Quite right,' he said. 'But we don't have to sit in silence. Anybody fancy a brew?'

The buxom lady stood. 'I'll do it.'

'Thank you, erm…'

'Judy, Judy Jones.'

Harry smacked his forehead. 'That's it! I'm brilliant with faces, but names I can't remember! Sorry, Judy.'

She smiled. 'No worries. Sit down. Everybody want tea?'

They nodded once again and Harry joined them around the table. He looked into their faces, and knew they were waiting expectantly for him to divulge some information, any information. He lowered his eyes and they knew they would have to wait.

Iain said nothing. All he wanted to do was sell some fertiliser, some tomato growth product, to this magnificent stately home. Instead he had quite literally fallen over a dead body. And now he could do nothing; he was tied to this place until the police said he could go. He took out his phone to ring his company, and then realised he couldn't even do that. The others in the room would hear every word.

They remained silent, waiting for Judy to carry the tray of drinks across to them.

Judy tried to smile as she placed the tray on the table, but it was a very weak one, and disappeared almost instantly. They each took a mug, and sat with hands wrapped around it, seeking comfort from something about which they had no knowledge, just guesswork.

Finally Judy broke. 'Is it like the other one?'

Harry sighed. 'I don't know. And I'm not allowed to say anything, so please don't ask.'

'Other one?' This time the question was short, sharp, staccato, and fired at Judy. Iain's head was raised and his eyes were fixed on her.

'A death. A few days ago. In the grounds.' Judy felt she was being pushed into talking about something that she shouldn't be talking about, and she didn't know how to handle it. 'Harry knows more than we do. He found her.'

Once again they fell silent.

Iain looked deep in thought. Suddenly he stood. 'Where are the toilets?'

Harry pointed. 'Through the door over there.'

Iain disappeared, and the others looked towards Harry. 'What can you tell us, now he's gone?'

'Nothing. They asked me to say nothing.'

Iain returned, slipping his phone back into his pocket, and Harry knew he had been in contact with someone; maybe his family, maybe his employer. Either way, he knew very little and could cause no damage.

They sipped their drinks, waiting for something to happen, anything. When Frank came through the door, they stood as one.

'Has Harry said anything?' he asked, and he received a mass shaking of heads.

'Then I can give you limited information. The dead woman is Olivia Fletcher.'

There was a gasp, an explosion of shock from everyone sat around the table.

'Has Her Grace been informed?' Harry asked.

'Yes. They're both away, don't forget, until the week after next, but this will probably bring them back.'

'And is it connected to the other death?' Again it was Harry speaking.

'Nobody has actually said it is, but if it isn't, who the hell thinks it's okay to keep dumping bodies at Chatsworth? And how the fuck are they doing it under our noses?' Frank sounded angry. 'I'm sorry for the swearing, ladies, but she was just a sweet twenty-one-year-old kid, and some bastard has snuffed the life out of her.'

Forensics spent a long time in Greenhouse B and when Tessa finally left the glass building, she felt she knew nothing further. The girl's name was Olivia Fletcher, and she was on the staff of the Duchess, and that was basically it. It seemed she lived with her parents, but as yet the address hadn't been handed to Tessa.

She felt tired; the chest infection she had been battling for a couple of days was wearing her down. The cough was keeping her awake at night, and it was starting to look as though a visit to a doctor was called for. She had no idea when that would be possible.

Hannah and the rest of the team were waiting for her in the control room. A second murder board had been set up, although as yet nothing had appeared on it. Tessa walked into the room and went straight to a radiator, leaning against it to try to warm herself. The temperature was dropping dramatically as the afternoon wore on.

'Boss?' Hannah said. 'You want anything?' She was aware that Tessa was under the weather.

'I'll take a couple of pills,' Tessa said. 'They'll help a bit.'

'What do we know?' Ray Charlton moved to the board and picked up a marker pen.

'Not a lot,' Tessa said, and smiled gratefully at Hannah as she handed her two white tablets and a glass of water. 'The deceased is Olivia Fletcher, aged twenty-one, believed to live in Bakewell. We need an address as soon as possible; we have to inform her parents. It's looking as though it's strangulation again, but no time of death yet. Martin Robinson will let us know as soon as he does. He thinks it was early this morning, but that's not confirmed. Can someone find out what time she was due to start work today please. And do it without alerting the staff to what has happened to her. Frank Norman is probably the best one to ask. He knows he's to say nothing yet.'

'How was she strangled?' Ray's pen was poised ready to write on the board.

'Ligature, and it looks to be the same as the earlier death.'

'So we're looking at a possible serial killer?' Fiona Ainsworth asked what everyone was thinking.

'I hope not, Fiona,' Tessa said. 'At the moment it's a double murder. Three turns it into a serial killer, so be very careful how you phrase things. And now we have a bit of a problem. When forensics have finished, I want some of you in the greenhouse, going over it meticulously. There's a walkway goes around the plant tables about a yard wide either side, so there's not much room to manoeuvre. Bear that in mind, and try not to kill any plants.' She coughed, struggling to breathe.

'Boss,' Hannah said. 'Go home. Get an early night. Nothing's going to happen before tomorrow morning, and I promise if it does, I'll call you.'

Tessa slumped onto a chair and sat for a moment before lifting her head to look at Hannah. 'You're right. I'm going to raid the first chemist shop I come across and get enough medication to cure a carthorse. But, Hannah, you ring me if anything happens. I mean it.'

'I will. Now go. As soon as we get the address, I'll take Ray and we'll go and do the notification. You're not fit to do it anyway. You can talk to her parents in a couple of days when you're feeling better.'

So Tessa went.

Hannah and Ray knocked tentatively at the house in Bakewell. The front garden was tidy, although at that time of year bare of colour. The net curtains moved slightly, and a woman called from the other side of the front door. 'Who is it?'

'Mrs Fletcher?'

'Yes.'

'Mrs Fletcher, it's the police. Can you open the door, please?'

The door opened slightly, and then stopped, halted by the door chain. Hannah held up her ID. 'DS Hannah Granger and this is DC Ray Charlton. Can we come in, please?'

The door closed, the chain was removed, and they were allowed over the threshold into the wide hallway.

'Can't be too careful,' Alison Fletcher said, unsmiling. 'What can I do for you?'

'Can we go in and sit down, please, Mrs Fletcher? Is your husband here?'

She hesitated. 'Tony, can you come here a minute?'

The door at the end of the hall opened, and a heavyset man in a wheelchair came through. He stopped when he saw them, and waited.

'It's the police,' his wife said.

'Oh. And what can we do for you?' His tone was bordering on belligerent.

Hannah was insistent. 'Can we go and sit down please?'

Alison moved to the left and opened a door leading into a large lounge. They all went in, the wheelchair gliding smoothly on the laminate flooring.

'Is this your daughter, Olivia?' Hannah asked, picking up a photo frame from the mantelpiece.

'It is. Is she in trouble? She's at work. She works at Chatsworth.' Alison was babbling. 'What's wrong with her?'

Tony Fletcher grabbed hold of his wife's hand. 'Come on, lovely. Calm down. She was fine when she went to work this morning. Don't go upsetting yourself.'

'Mrs Fletcher,' Hannah said gently. 'Come and sit down.' She sat on the sofa and patted the seat by her side.

Ray stood by the fireplace, hating what they were about to do.

Alison Fletcher was clearly unnerved. She sat by Hannah's side and listened to the detective tell her how she was very sorry, but her daughter was dead.

The wheelchair was almost silent in its movement and Tony pulled his wife against him. He held her tightly, almost as if he was trying to smother the moans coming from the depths of her.

'No, no, no, not Olivia. She wouldn't hurt a soul. Not our Olivia.'

Tony looked at Hannah. 'How?'

'I obviously can't go into details. There hasn't been time for that, she was found about two hours ago. We'll know more tomorrow morning when we receive forensic reports…'

'I said how,' he repeated.

Hannah took a deep breath. 'Olivia was unlawfully killed.'

A devastated Alison screamed, and she clung on tightly to her husband.

'Oh God, Tony, she was murdered.'

The man's belligerence had gone, now he looked grey and bewildered. 'But who would want to kill our Liv? She was the world's gentlest person.'

'We have no answers yet. Ray, can you make tea for everybody, please.'

Ray disappeared to the kitchen, leaving Hannah to talk to the distraught parents. He hated having to do this job, had always admired Hannah and the boss for taking it on every time it was required.

He switched on the kettle and reached up to the cupboard to take down some mugs. A box of tablets was to the left of the kettle on the work surface. They bore Tony Fletcher's name and Ray quickly took photographs on his mobile while he waited for the kettle to switch off.

There was a quiet sobbing coming from Alison when he returned, and he handed round the drinks. He was grateful for the hot tea, his own nerves frazzled by the experience, and he couldn't begin to imagine how the Fletchers must be feeling.

Hannah moved into the hall and quietly rang Tony's sister, who said she would be over within quarter of an hour, and they eventually said goodbye and left, telling them someone would be in touch as soon as they had any information.

As they got in their car, a little Smart car pulled up, and a woman hurried along the path.

'They'll be okay,' Ray mumbled to Hannah. 'That was horrible, wasn't it?'

'Always is. Usually I'm in your position, because the boss takes the lead. I feel drained, but she was in no fit state to do it. We'll go back in a couple of days and start with some questions, but we couldn't do it today. Come on, let's head to Chatsworth. See if anybody knows anything we don't.'

Ray took out his phone and handed it to Hannah. 'Go into the pictures. I took a photo of Tony Fletcher's medication, in case we needed to know what we were dealing with. None of it rang any bells, but we can look it up when we get back.'

Hannah moved her fingers and enlarged the picture. Ocrelizumab. Avonex. She clicked off the picture and handed the phone back to him.

'We don't need to Google anything,' she said with a deep sigh. 'My mum has these. It's multiple sclerosis. No wonder Mrs Fletcher seems to be in such a nervous state. It can't be easy for them, and now their daughter's been murdered.'

Tessa overdosed on everything and climbed the stairs wearily, hoping she would get a better sleep. The previous night had been horrendous, and had been spent mostly propped up into a sitting position by multiple pillows.

Her body felt worn out, tired enough to sleep the instant her head touched the pillow; her brain said differently. She went through everything so far, each of the murders, trying to find the link. She knew there was one, and recognised it may take some delving to track it down, but she trusted her team. They would find it.

One piece of commonality was Chatsworth. Whoever had killed the two girls clearly knew the estate, and knew how to move around it without fear of being discovered. Every member of staff would have to be interviewed, and questioned in depth, but so would previous staff members who had left the employ of the Duke and his wife. Maybe some had left under a cloud, or with bad feelings towards the Devonshires. She couldn't imagine it, the Duke had been wonderfully helpful towards their investigation, but he was top of the line and grudges can rise pretty high.

Tomorrow, she thought as her eyes finally closed, *tomorrow at the briefing I'll relay all these thoughts…*

. . .

Hannah spent half an hour on the phone with her mum. Talk of her illness with Ray had kick-started thoughts that they hadn't chatted in a while. Oh, they'd had quick phone catch-ups, but no lengthy proper talk for months.

She came off the phone, feeling much better about things. She'd told her mum, against all instructions, about the day she'd had, culminating in the notification visit with Ray.

Joan Sharpe had sensed instantly the distress that Hannah was trying to hide, and had talked her through it. When Hannah's tears came, her mum knew she would be okay.

Joan put down the phone and sighed. She had always held back from ringing her daughter because she didn't like to intrude on the life she led, but it seemed as though she had been wrong. She needed to speak with her much more regularly, she needed to let Hannah talk about everything and anything, secure in the knowledge it would go no further.

She would text her in the morning, send her love and then ring in the evening, just to let her know she was there. Always.

13

<hr />

Without knowing it, all three women opened the file sent to their hard drive within a minute of each other. Luke had already gone through it and made notes and observations, so he busied himself with the bits of post that had arrived, and updating the diary. He grinned when he saw that Kat was having a date afternoon with Carl Heaton and she'd put it into the physical diary, but done nothing with the online one. He entered it in and put a little red heart at the end of it.

He held a bottle of water to his lips and took a deep drink, then opened up his notepad. Computers were brilliant, but when you're sat around a table discussing the contents of a file of multiple documents, the only thing you needed was a notepad and a pen. He had no doubt there would be a myriad of things he had missed that would be picked up by his ladies, particularly Kat, but for now he wanted to be au fait with the stuff he had noticed.

His notation of the broken arm and the writing on the back of the photo of Daniel with a cast on the arm were uppermost in his mind. *What did she do to him?* was written in red ink on the back, and it seemed that Debbie Carter had probably taken the picture of her nephew. But that needed checking… Luke ran a highlighter across his words to remind him to bring it up.

There was also a photo of a man's back with huge welts across it, deep purple bruising that hadn't begun to yellow. There was nothing written on the back of that picture, but Luke guessed it would be Adam Armstrong, the husband who had had enough.

Luke had written up a mini profile of both Adam and Daniel Armstrong, using whatever information he could find in the papers, but it was copies of their birth certificates that gave him the most.

Adam Armstrong was born on 3 June 1978, making him forty, which in turn meant he was around thirty when he'd disappeared. His mother was Yvette and his father John Armstrong, and the address at the time of his birth was 3 Jasmine Dell, Hathersage. Luke highlighted Yvette and John, and their address.

Daniel Armstrong was born on 30 May 2003, and his address at the time of his birth was the same Nicola Armstrong had still lived at until her death a few days earlier, 27 Linwood Cottages in Baslow. Danny's birth certificate confirmed his mother and father as Nicola and Adam Armstrong. Danny, if he were still alive, would now be fifteen.

Luke flicked through the rest of the pages of notes, highlighting where he needed to make important points, then waited patiently for his ladies to summon him into the sanctuary of Kat's office.

Kat's new cupboard, with shelving from about halfway up and a large space at the bottom to house six extremely comfortable stacking chairs, had been an inspired idea by Stefan Patmore. Luke lifted out three of the chairs, and they sat around the beautiful oak desk Kat had chosen for her office. She threw them the coasters she kept in her top drawer for their mugs of coffee, and the meeting started.

Kat began. 'First of all, I'm sure you're all extremely grateful to me for putting this file together so quickly and so perfectly, without having to ask anybody for help...' She looked around at the faces in front of her, and collapsed into giggles. Martha, playing in her pram with a rag doll, beamed at her mummy.

Kat held up a hand. 'Okay, I give in. Luke, this was a magnificent effort. I hadn't realised quite how much stuff was in that carrier bag, and you've put it all in separate places...'

'Folders, Kat,' Luke said.

'Okay, clever clogs, folders, and even I can understand it. Can we give him a raise?'

'No,' said Doris.

Luke grinned. 'That's okay. Just give me a partnership.'

Martha's beaming smile moved from her mummy to Luke. She and Luke had mutually fallen in love when Kat arrived with her two hours earlier, and he waved at the little girl and blew her a kiss.

'So, who came up with what?' Mouse asked. 'And thank you, Kat, for all your hard work.'

Doris spoke first. 'If she didn't kill them, I think they're alive. As soon as Daniel became seriously hurt – and remember, we don't know if she hurt him prior to this breaking of his arm – it looks as though his dad took him. He took him to keep him safe. It's obvious Nicola Armstrong had serious anger issues, and for some people they never resolve them.'

Luke flicked through his comprehensive notes and drew a line through his own version.

'Luke?'

'I'd thought exactly the same thing,' he explained, 'and I've now crossed it out so that I can see if there's anything left at the end when you've all finished talking.'

'So tell us something in your notes.'

'I made sort of mini profiles of both of them, dates of birth, where they were born, that sort of thing. I didn't have time to delve any deeper last night because I had to go out and pick Mum up from her quilting group. I think there'll be something in there that's hidden at the moment, but won't be when we get a proper picture of Adam and Danny. Like you ladies, I think they're alive, but I also think Adam must have spent a lot of time planning the disappearance. It was very successful, and it's been silence from both of them for ten years.

'One other thing that occurred to me while I was dropping off to sleep was we maybe should try to track down a will Nicola Armstrong may have left. It seems she didn't divorce, so technically she's still married to Adam. Presumably he was co-owner of the house, so therefore it's now his. And that's where DI Marsden's case and ours do a crossover, because wouldn't that give him a motive for murder? Or even give Danny a motive for murder... If Adam has subsequently died, Danny would inherit.' Luke stopped. 'Tell me to shut up if I've overstepped the brief.'

Kat's eyes were wide. 'For goodness sake, give him the raise, Nan.'

'He's certainly taking over from you as our thinker,' Nan said. 'You thought of all of that as you were going to sleep?'

'Yes, it's why it's not in my notes. It might all be absolute rubbish, because they might not have been co-owners, but even if Adam didn't have a half-share in it, Danny presumably now inherits the lot if he turns up. If she owned it outright, Danny is her next of kin.'

Mouse was scribbling furiously, her mind jumping to the actions she would have to take to follow the leads being suggested by their young colleague. They needed facts, and not what-ifs.

'It's fascinating, isn't it?' Luke smiled at them all. 'This is my first real work with Connection and I'm more convinced than ever that I was right to apply for the job. The only thing that's a bit out of control is I can't stop thinking about it. This must be how authors feel when they're writing crime novels. The brain never stops.'

'And that's just as it should be, Luke,' Doris said. 'This may be your first case with us, but we've had lots and lots of cases ranging from following people who were doing things they shouldn't be doing, to being on interview panels for people applying for jobs, to assisting in solving murders. Kat even specialises in finding dead bodies. So welcome to our world. Just don't go on any jaunts with Kat, anything could happen.'

'You've said she finds bodies before. Are you serious? Kat?'

'I don't find them all,' Kat said with a laugh. 'But I found one a couple of months before Christmas, in Eyam churchyard. And Mouse and I found one in Hope last summer...'

Luke shook his head, almost in disbelief. 'And DI Marsden suggested I join the police! How boring would that be, compared to this.' He pulled his notebook towards him. 'Anyway, I also thought about the brother, Simon. He's sort of in the background, but he was also in the background when Adam and Danny went missing. Somebody needs to talk to him, I reckon. Just supposing he helped them...'

'You think that's a possibility?' Doris found herself fascinated by Luke's quick thought processes.

'I do. He wasn't just Nicola's brother, he was Adam's brother-in-law, and very often that relationship is a good one. Don't forget that Debbie said Simon spent his childhood stopping Nicola killing her, so he was well aware of the volatile nature lurking inside Nicola, and if he saw the injuries on Adam, I reckon he would help him.'

Kat picked up her cup and sipped at the coffee. 'Okay, let's make some plans. Mouse, I assume you'll share the Internet side with Nan, but how on earth you'll manage to find anything, I have no idea. The first thing Adam would have done is change their names. This investigation is going to make finding Ewan Barker's son look easy-peasy, isn't it. Shall I take the interview with Debbie and Simon? Luke can go along for the ride, and learn how far he can go, given that we're not police officers. How do you feel about that, Luke?'

Luke's face turned pink. 'Oh my god! Real work? Proper interviews? It sounds ace. Are we going now?'

Kat laughed. 'No. In case you hadn't noticed, I've got Martha with me. We'll go tomorrow. Martha's going to Meadowhall apparently, for a new outfit, so I won't have to worry about her. Between now and then, we need to come up with some points we need answers to, so that's this afternoon's work, along with whatever is required of you from Mouse and Nan. We'll put our heads together first thing tomorrow morning, then set off around ten to speak to Debbie. I'll warn her tonight that we'll be calling, make it sound official rather than a friendly neighbour chat. I'm not going to mention Simon, we need to interview him away from Debbie, because if he did help Adam, he won't admit it in front of his sister.'

'My nan says something that maybe I should remember,' Luke said with a grin. 'She says slowly, slowly, catchee monkey. I never really took much notice of it until now. Listening to your plans, Kat, I think I understand what she means. And when we get to Debbie's house, I'll keep quiet. I'll listen and learn.' He picked up his own cup and took a long drink. He calmed down and absorbed the rest of the comments as the three women worked through their own lists of thoughts. They mirrored his own in the main, and he felt good about that. He remembered another phrase his nan used, and he knew there were no negative nellies in his trio of ladies. It was all about getting on with it, using their own specialities to find answers. Definitely no negative nellies.

The meeting broke up, and Mouse and Doris returned to their

offices, having drawn up a plan for the avenues that needed exploring, possibly deeper into the Internet than they usually went. Both of them loved this side of the work, and Luke saw no flashing lights on his small console for the rest of the afternoon. He concentrated on potential questions for Debbie Carter, and then moved on to the paperwork Doris Lester had given him.

He went home that night feeling well pleased with how the day had gone. He had been included in the discussion far more than he could ever have imagined, and he was looking forward to the next day, to watching Kat Rowe interview someone in that oh so gentle way she had, that he suspected could be quite cutting when required.

14

Tessa woke to the sound of her alarm, feeling grateful that she had slept most of the night. She had woken just after four, repeated the medication she had taken eight hours earlier, and drifted back to sleep.

The gentle ringtone on her phone pealed out. 'Hannah? Everything okay?'

'I'm outside. I need to come in and make toast and coffee for us.'

'Oh. Right.'

Tessa went to let her DS in, and shivered as the arctic blast came in with Hannah. 'You've never made toast and coffee for us before.'

'First time for everything. And don't get used to it, it's because you're poorly. I'm taking you into work, you're not driving, and I'm only taking you in because I know you won't stay at home.' Hannah paused. 'How *are* you?'

Tessa's voice was raspy. 'I'm feeling better than I was yesterday. I've actually slept. Just one slice for me, I've got to get it past my tonsils.'

'No problem. Go and have your shower, you'll feel better after that.'

Half an hour later they were finishing off the toast, and talking about murder. 'We need to see Olivia's parents. Thank you for doing that awful job, Hannah, having to notify them.'

'No worries, boss. It had to be done. I don't think Ray appreciated going with me though. It's not one of the nicer parts of police work.'

Tessa stood. 'I'll have a word with him, thank him for doing it. Nice toast, by the way. Why wasn't it burnt?'

'I turned down the timer on the toaster. Maybe you won't need to grumble about your bread being burnt black from now on. Now get your coat. Time to rally the troops, and solve two murders.'

The room was noisy as the team arrived in dribs and drabs, ready for instructions on what they would be doing. Computers were glowing around the room, and Ray was adding items to the whiteboard.

'Morning, everybody,' Tessa tried to call. Nobody heard, nobody responded.

'Oy!' Hannah yelled. 'Listen up. The boss needs to speak and she can't talk properly, so shut up.'

The room fell silent, and everyone turned towards Tessa and Hannah.

Tessa feebly held up a hand, trying to rein in the laughter. 'I'm sorry. You'll have to listen carefully. I've got a squeak instead of a voice.' She walked over to the whiteboard and looked carefully at it.

'Okay, we need to know these people inside out. I want our IT guys on the computers, and I want to know everything there is to know about Debbie Carter, Rob Carter even though he's no longer on the scene and not been interviewed yet, Simon Vicars, his partner Greg Littlewood, Neil and Paula Ireland, Adam and Daniel Armstrong, although that may prove a little difficult, Harry Hardy and Frank Norman. That's just for starters. The second murder of Olivia Fletcher will throw up a different wave of suspects. Olivia's autopsy is scheduled for ten, maybe we'll know more after that.'

Tessa placed a hand on her chest and tried to take a deep breath. Talking had been a massive effort. The coughing bout drained her, and Ray Charlton handed her a glass of water.

'Go home after the autopsy, boss,' he said. 'You shouldn't be here. We know what we've to do. Another day in bed might make all the difference.'

'I can't, Ray. We have to stop this double murder becoming a serial killing spree.'

The autopsy revealed that Olivia had received a blow to the head severe enough to have caused unconsciousness. It was then relatively easy to put the ligature around her neck and asphyxiate her. The line used to strangle her matched that from around Nicola Armstrong's neck; it had been a longer piece originally, and the cut ends were a perfect fit. It briefly occurred to Tessa that she hoped it had only been cut into two parts.

Tessa headed to Martin's office and waited for him to join her. It was worth the wait. He took her in his arms and kissed her. 'You sound dreadful,' he said when they'd greeted one another.

'Thanks.' She smiled. 'I sound better than I feel. I've given the troops their orders, and I'm heading off home to bed. Hopefully by tomorrow the worst of it will be over. It's got to be. Two bodies in less than a week, that's scary. And apart from the location of their deaths, Chatsworth itself, we haven't come across a link to tie them together. They don't live in the same areas – one is Baslow, the other Bakewell – and they don't work together. Olivia was a member of staff, and currently we don't know what Nicola did. An Internet search had produced nothing on the woman. Interviews start in depth as soon as I've got a voice. I've enough medication to cure half the world of flu, and I'm taking it all this afternoon.'

Martin hugged her. 'I'll leave you to sleep. Only contact me if you need me, I won't ring you. You need me to run you home? Please tell me you're not driving.'

'No, Hannah brought me. I said I'd ring her when we'd finished here.'

'Then ring,' he said. 'Stop being a brave little soldier, and give in to it.'

Alison Fletcher also gave in to everything and took to her bed. Tony was changing in front of her eyes; his anger was building, and the frustration increasing because he didn't have enough strength or movement in his legs to get out of the damn wheelchair.

Damn was always the adjective that went in front of the word wheelchair whenever Tony spoke of it. He hated it, hated the limitations it created, and he always said the day he agreed to have one was the beginning of the end for him. Then, of course, he hadn't taken into account losing Olivia.

Alison had come to bed to wallow in her own grief, and because she couldn't stand the way Tony's grief was taking him. He couldn't stay still. The wheelchair was constantly on the move, the soft swish swish of its tyres ever present as it moved backwards and forwards in the downstairs rooms. She had kept their bedroom upstairs as her own, and they had created a bedroom for Tony on the ground floor with a wet room, but she knew it had emasculated him. He felt less of a man because he had to give into his weaknesses.

Trying to sleep, she lay for a while with her eyes closed, but eventually tears opened them. Olivia had looked so beautiful on the evening of her twenty-first birthday, and now there was nothing.

Alison knew that at some point they would be called upon to identify their daughter, and she wasn't convinced that she could be the one to do it. She needed to remember that beauty, the girl that would always be her best friend, her Olivia.

Alison edged herself wearily from the bed, and was halfway down the stairs when the doorbell pealed out its silly tune.

She opened it and saw Hannah. Silently Alison held the door back, and waved her through.

Hannah followed her through to the kitchen. Tony's wheelchair was pulled up to the table, and he was attempting to do the crossword in the newspaper. He looked up at Hannah.

'I can't do it,' he said simply. 'I can't do the bloody crossword I do every day of my life.'

She sat down opposite him. 'Of course you can't. Did Olivia used to help you?'

He nodded. 'Yes, she used to put any words in that had the required number of letters, she didn't even read some of the clues.' He paused for a moment. 'She was our life, our whole life.'

'Then fill the crossword in with Olivia words. Start with a four-letter word and put LOVE in it. Then go from there. Don't shut her out because she isn't here.'

Tony lifted his head to look at Hannah. 'Thank you.'

The kettle switched off and Alison made drinks for them.

'Just what I needed,' Hannah said. 'I wasn't going to come this morning, I intended leaving it until tomorrow when hopefully my boss will be well enough to talk to you, but I want to get the ball rolling, give her a bit of a break.'

'What can we help with?' Alison asked.

'I'd like to see Olivia's room, if that's okay with you.'

'It is. We had the forensic people here earlier. They dusted for fingerprints and such like, took our prints, although Tony hasn't been upstairs for the best part of two years now, so in theory there should only be mine and Olivia's in her room.'

Hannah nodded. 'So tell me about Olivia.'

The parents looked at each other, and both smiled.

Alison began. 'She was an absolute ray of sunshine. Never stopped smiling, adored her dad, and was my rock when it came to the bad days of Tony's illness.' Alison reached across and touched her husband's hand. 'He's doing okay at the moment, but in a week's time the pain may be overwhelming, or he'll only have partial sight, or his arms may be like useless lumps of lead. Those were the times when Olivia stepped up to the plate and we managed Tony between us.'

'It's MS?' Hannah said, her voice soft.

'It is. But we cope.'

'My mum has it,' Hannah said. 'We're getting to a point where instead of occasional use of the wheelchair when we take her out, it's becoming more of an indoor chair. She's accepted it in a fashion, she's trimmed it up with number plates and ribbons and bows, but it's kind of like a statement to the world. I'm in this chair, so let's make the best of it. She's even taught herself to crochet so that she could make a really bright blanket to cover her legs.' Hannah smiled. It had been a fun day taking her mum to pick lots of little balls of luminous wool.

'I need to learn to crochet?' Tony asked, and for the first time Hannah saw a tentative smile on his face.

'Why not? Looks good on a CV,' Hannah said, returning the smile.

They sipped their drinks, talking about Olivia, how she'd loved her job at Chatsworth, enjoyed cycling more than driving, and tended to use her bike for travelling to work every day.

'Did she take her bike yesterday morning?'

'She did. You'll know it's Olivia's bike because underneath the saddle, on the frame, she's tied a bright pink ribbon. Says it helps her go straight to it when she parks it in car parks.'

Hannah took out her notebook and added the description of the bike to her notes. 'I don't suppose you have a photo of Olivia with the bike, do you?'

'I do,' Alison said, and left the kitchen, leaving Hannah with Tony.

'It's knocked Alison for six,' Tony said quietly. 'I don't know what to do.'

'Want some advice? Talk. Talk about Olivia, about your memories, even about the future if you can begin to imagine one. Just don't stop talking. It will get you through it, I promise. And if you think of anything at all that might help, please ring me.' She pushed her card across to him. 'I'm kind of in charge at the moment, although hopefully DI Marsden will be back with us tomorrow. She currently has no voice and precious little energy so she's home and in bed.'

Alison returned with a picture. The bike was bright blue, and easy to spot with the addition of the luminous pink bow peeking out below the saddle. Hannah took out her phone, snapped the picture and forwarded it to Ray Charlton with a message.

Get everybody out on the estate and looking for this bike. Olivia Fletcher rode it to work yesterday. Please note pink bow under saddle.

15

Alison accompanied Hannah to Olivia's room, and had to frequently wipe the tears from her eyes. 'She kept it so tidy,' Alison said. 'She didn't like mess. Can I ask you something, DS Granger?'

'It's Hannah, and of course you can. I can't always give answers because it is an ongoing investigation, but if I can, I will.'

'Was she... was my Olivia raped?'

Hannah took a deep breath. 'I haven't seen the autopsy report. I can't give you a definite answer, but I can tell you that when Olivia was found, she was fully clothed, her coat was zipped up and she even had gloves on. I don't think she was assaulted sexually, but as yet we have found nothing to indicate why she was attacked. We haven't found her phone, or her purse. Didn't she take them? Are they still here?'

'No, but I can tell you where they should be. On the back of her saddle she has a small bag. She puts them in there so that she doesn't have to take a handbag. There'll be a nylon coat in there as well, one that she wears when she's helping on the cleaning side. It's got pockets, and she puts her purse and phone in them.'

They're cleaning chandeliers at the hall at the moment, and that was what she was doing. It was why she went in early. They were on the last two or three, and she wanted to get them finished.'

'She wouldn't have normally been starting at that time?'

'No, usually half past eight, but she left here before six yesterday.'

Hannah was writing rapidly in her notebook. Was it just bad luck that Olivia had been in the wrong place at the wrong time? Or did somebody target her, knowing she would be going in early, and there wouldn't be many people around?

She stood. 'Thank you for letting me have a look at Olivia's room, Alison. It gives me a general feel for her, and I can tell how much she was loved. If there's anything I can do at any time, Tony has my card.'

They went downstairs, and Hannah said her goodbyes, before getting back into her car and picking up her phone.

'Ray? You found that bike?'

'Not yet, Hannah, we've got everybody out looking.'

'There's a bag attached to the back of the saddle. Should be her purse and her phone in it. We need them, Ray.'

'Understood.' He disconnected.

Luke picked up the carrier bag of paperwork to be returned to Debbie Carter, and held the door open for Kat to go through.

The snow had almost gone, and Kat hoped the weak rays of sunshine filtering through the clouds would be enough to get rid of the last of it.

'Thank you, Luke,' she said, and clicked her car keys. She waited for him to fasten his seat belt, and fired up the engine.

'This is nice,' he said appreciatively. 'Bit bigger than mine.'

'This isn't the sort of car you start off with,' she grinned. 'You work towards this. And I need one this size because of the stuff that goes with Martha whenever we go out. You've not got that problem yet.'

'So if I have a baby, I get a car like this,' he mused. 'That's worth thinking about.'

'Then think about the sleepless nights, the constant feeding, being tied to the house because it's too much trouble to go out, and stick with your little Peugeot.'

Luke thought for a moment. 'I'll maybe buy it some new seat covers,' he said with a laugh. 'This is a really nice car though.'

They put the car on Kat's driveway and walked to Debbie's house.

She opened the door immediately.

Luke handed her the carrier bag and Kat spoke. 'Thank you for these, Debbie, we've copied everything, and are working our way through all of it. Mouse and Nan have their heads stuck in their computers as we speak.'

'Good. I have no idea if they'll be able to track Danny down, ten years is such a long time, but I'm keeping everything crossed that they can. Danny was the reason I had Bridie. He was such a lovely child, no trouble at all, and he turned me maternal,' Debbie said with a laugh. 'I desperately want to know he's okay, that he had a good life with Adam. It's what everybody thought, you know. Nobody believed we were looking for bodies, we all guessed Adam had taken him.'

Debbie led them through to the kitchen, a familiar room to Kat who had shared quite a few moments with Debbie over the past five years or so. Not close friends, but friends.

'Coffee?' she said, holding up the jug. They nodded, and Debbie poured out the drinks.

'Okay,' she said, finally sitting down with them. 'What can I help you with?'

'Tell us about Adam Armstrong,' Kat said.

. . .

A smile flashed briefly across Debbie's face. 'He was one of the nicest people you could ever meet. As you know, Nicola and I are – were – very close in age, less than two years between us. This meant that we were in the same school for quite some time in our teenage years. During that time the school had some big anniversary. I think it was a hundred or something. Anyway, they took all the pupils on coaches to Chester to celebrate, to the zoo.'

She paused briefly to enjoy the memories. 'I've always been a little nervous of anything like that, so I stuck with Nicola's group. Everybody was fine with it, except Nic of course. No street cred in having the kid sister hanging around, I suppose. Adam seemed to sense the problem, and he stayed with me for most of the day. We had a picnic lunch, and he sat on the grass with me, and when we had our photo taken, he was with me on that. Would you like to see it?'

'You still have it?'

'It's in a drawer, I don't have it on display or anything, but it was a memorable day, not least because I got a good hiding from Nicola afterwards.'

She moved into the lounge, returning with a dog-eared large photo. She handed it to Kat, who studied it.

'This is you and Adam on the grass? And that is Nicola?'

'How on earth did you know that?' Debbie was surprised.

'She's glaring at the two of you.'

Debbie laughed. 'Yeah, I suppose it does give her away. I wrote all the names on the back as soon as we got the photos. Her photo was different; she was with a group of girls from her class. I don't know if she still has it, but I'll always treasure mine.'

Kat studied the picture carefully. There were six boys and four girls in total. 'You didn't send this down to us with the other documents?'

'No. It's a picture from the pre-Adam and Nicola days. Adam didn't even like her at this stage, he told me I was so much nicer than my sister. Unfortunately for Adam, Nicola decided she wanted him, and she set out to get him. On their wedding day he jokingly said to me that he hoped he'd picked the right sister.' Debbie hesitated for a moment, lost in her memories. 'It was at their wedding that I met Rob. A bad wedding all round really.'

The baby monitor burst into life and Debbie stood. 'Excuse me a minute. I'll just go and get Charlie.'

She left the kitchen and Kat took out her phone. She snapped both sides of the photograph, counted the names and bodies on the picture. They tallied, and the written names were annotated as top row, middle row and grass. She put her phone away as Debbie returned carrying her little boy.

'Sorry about this, he doesn't sleep for very long in the morning. So, what else can I tell you?' She stared thoughtfully into the distance.

'At first they seemed happy enough, and during this time, right at the beginning, Adam's dad died. He received a pretty hefty inheritance, and they were starting to look round for a new home when my mum died. The house in Baslow was left to Nic, me and Simon, to be shared equally. Nic and Adam proposed they have it valued, and buy Simon and I out, so they could keep the house. We agreed. That's how I could afford to live at Eyam. Simon stayed where he was, and presumably still has his share. The family home then became jointly owned by Adam and Nicola.'

'And when did things change?'

'I saw Adam with a slash down his arm that was very angry looking, and I said it looked infected and he should see a doctor. He said he'd fallen on some broken glass. Anyway, he did see a doctor, and all was well in the end. But one day I asked Nic how his arm was, and she flared up, had a proper go at me and said he'd obviously told me how she'd slashed him with a knife.'

'That was the first time you became aware of her temper?'

'Not really. She'd always been quite violent towards me, and occasionally Simon. I honestly was shocked that she would have attacked Adam though. He was, is, such a nice bloke. I'm praying you find him, Kat. I would hate to think he was dead.'

'And Danny?'

'Her pregnancy seemed to quieten her down, and some of the love came back into the relationship. They set up the nursery, shopped together for everything they would need, and I think it was the best time in their marriage, because as soon as she had the baby, she changed back to the screaming harridan she was before she got pregnant. At first, Adam said it was her hormones, but pregnancy hormones don't last five years. He constantly made excuses for her nastiness, and then one day I put my arms around him when he was really upset. He yelled out in pain, and I made him take off his shirt. That photo in the paperwork is what I saw. In real life it looked much worse than on the picture. She'd gone for him with that blessed baseball bat she keeps in the hall behind the front door.'

'And the picture of the little boy with the cast on his arm?'

'Danny.' There was a long pause. 'My lovely Danny. He was just five and she knocked him down the stairs because he said he wanted to go out with his daddy. It was obviously the end, because two days later they disappeared. I… I encouraged it. I told him he couldn't stay with her, that Danny was at risk, that he was at risk. He simply nodded. He said nothing about any plans, and even now I don't know whether he left or whether…' There was a choking sound in the back of Debbie's throat. 'Or whether she killed them and hid their bodies somewhere. I always thought he would have contacted me at some point. He knew how I felt, and we used to joke about me being Team Adam, and not Team Nicola.'

The tension in the air was palpable, and all three of them sat back in their chairs and allowed their minds to settle.

. . .

'You really think they're dead?' Luke opened his mouth for the first time, unable to exit the story.

Debbie turned to him and smiled through her tears. 'No I don't, Luke. I've never thought they were dead. And I need them both to know that they can come home, finally. I need Connection to find them for me, and tell them they're safe.'

16

D oris and Mouse listened intently to the recording of the interview with Debbie Carter, while Luke and Kat made additional notes to the thoughts they had already garnered from the morning's work.

Luke had spent the journey back to the office apologising for speaking out, but Kat had said it was the right thing to do, and what he had said was exactly what was needed. It had clarified the whole conversation.

On their return, he had taken Kat's phone from her and printed off four copies of the photograph showing the school friends at Chester Zoo, along with the names from the reverse side.

Once the recording had ended, they each pulled a photo towards them and studied it.

After a while, Kat sat back in her seat. 'Thoughts?'

'Plenty,' Mouse said. 'It seems to me that there was something between Adam Armstrong and Debbie. Look at the way she is with him. And his hand is over the top of hers. But it's equally clear that Nicola isn't happy about it. Her eyes are on both of them, rather than turned towards the camera and laughing like

109

the rest of the group. I wonder what it was that made him choose Nicola. I know Nicola was the same age as him, they were in the same year, but Debbie was only two years younger. This is something we need to ask Debbie about.'

Doris picked up the list of names, and pursed her lips. 'I know this is just a thought, and it's off the top of my head, but if you needed to escape, as Adam and Danny did, how would you do it? You'd have to have somewhere to go, for a start, because you can't sleep on a beach somewhere with a five-year-old in tow, and I'm guessing there would have to be an instant name change for both of them. And with that comes documents like birth certificates, passports, a driving licence. Plans would have been made, and I suspect he would have turned to a friend. Possibly an old school friend.' She tapped on the names in front of her. 'Instead of this being *cherchez la femme*, it could be *cherchez l'ami*. I think Mouse and I need to take these names apart, follow them as deep as we can, and see if there's anything that makes us stop and think. Seriously stop and think.'

Mouse pulled the names towards her. 'Okay. Six boys and four girls. We can take out Debbie, Nicola and Adam. That leaves us with seven. Nan, will you take four of them, and I'll take the other three? I've some work to do for Manchester before I can tackle this.'

Doris looked down at the names. 'Okay. I'll go with the first four on the top row, the ones who are standing, then if you take the middle row with the two girls, and the last boy on the end of the top row. That means you get Zak Garside, Susie Long, and Wendy Thompson. Can you manage them?'

'I can. Thanks, Nan. We need to keep our bread and butter sweet, as well as our other clients.'

'Joel's bread and butter, is he?' Doris laughed. 'I'd got him down as being pure chocolate doughnuts. So that leaves me with Mark Brogan, Barry Earnshaw, Ethan King and Kenny Wilkinson. Agreed, everybody?'

Luke finished his note taking, and nodded. 'I've written everything down. I'll type it up and let you all have copies. Can I do anything to help on the search side, Mrs Lester?'

Doris shook her head. 'Not on deep searches, Luke. I'd hate to see you locked up.'

Luke grinned at her. 'Okay. I'll stick with Kat. But if you ever need to know the codes for the nuclear missiles, just ask me.' He gathered up the cups and went to refill them from the freshly brewed coffee.

'You believe him?' Mouse asked, pulling her laptop towards her.

'Every word,' Doris said.

'And I definitely do,' Kat joined in. 'He even managed to print that photo off my phone! How do you do that without breaking the printer?'

The doorbell went and Luke jumped. He'd been immersed in the course he was taking; his ladies were quiet, and he thought he could complete part two easily. He pressed the door release, and Hannah came through.

'Anybody in?'

'Me,' he smiled.

'I can see that, numpty. Any ladies in?'

'All of them at the moment. Which one would you like.'

'Kat. She busy?'

'Let me check. She might be asleep. I understand Martha wanted to play at two this morning.'

He knocked on Kat's door and opened it slightly. 'You asleep, Kat?' He laughed.

'I would be if I didn't have cheeky brats opening my office door. Problem?'

'No. DS Granger is here.'

'Hannah? Send her through.'

'I've only come for a coffee,' Hannah called.

'Then you're very welcome,' Kat called back to her, and waited for Hannah to close the door before saying anything further.

Luke went back to his computer, and his legal section about surveillance.

Kat leaned back in her chair. 'Something wrong?'

'Lots at the moment.' Hannah cradled the mug of coffee, staring thoughtfully into the outer regions of space. 'I needed time out. Sometimes Tessa does that, and now I know why.'

'Seems strange to see you without her.'

'I know. I'm doing her job for a couple of days, she's so poorly. Chest infection, I think. She's no voice, can't breathe, and she's got this cough that is just about finishing her off. As a result I had to do a death notification which has left me feeling… wiped out.'

'The second death at Chatsworth?'

'Yes. She was only twenty-one, Kat. Lovely girl. Harry Hardy, who found Nicola Armstrong's body, also found this one. He was showing a rep around the glasshouses and she was lying on the floor.'

'There's a connection, isn't there? It's linked to Nicola's death, and it's not just that the same man found them both.'

'You're right.' Hannah sighed. 'Same line used to strangle them. The cut ends of both pieces are a perfect match. But other than their deaths, I'm damned if I can see a link between the two women. They simply didn't know each other. Nicola lived at Baslow, Olivia at Bakewell. Olivia is a generation away from Nicola, she still lived at home with her mum and dad. Telling them was really hard, as I'm sure you realise. Her dad has MS and is in a wheelchair, so her mum has enough on her plate with that. It's been a shitty couple of days, so I thought I'd take half an hour out and come here for some lunch.'

'You want me to ask Luke to fetch you a sandwich?'

Hannah waved a hand. 'No, course not. I don't actually want food; I just want the concept of a lunch hour today. I'll settle for a ginger biscuit to dunk in my coffee though. That's proper comfort eating.'

Kat smiled at her. She looked drained. Normally it would be Tessa sitting there looking out of sorts, but Hannah appeared to have shouldered Tessa's worries for the duration of a chest infection.

The biscuits were produced, and both dunked in unison. 'Luke and I went to see Debbie Carter earlier. You know she's employed us to find her nephew? And his dad, of course, but I think really it's all about Danny. We're being careful not to tread on police toes.'

'Luke's doing okay?'

'Better than we could have hoped. He's totally embraced the job, he's bright, willing to tackle anything, and polite. He didn't say a word when we interviewed Debbie, and we were there for about an hour. Right at the end a question burst out of him, but he listened and learned for the most part.'

'And what did he ask?'

'If she thought they were dead.'

'Mmm. So she'd been ambiguous about it?'

'She certainly hadn't come down on any side, that's for sure,' Kat conceded. 'But Luke's timely question, right at the end of the interview, made her smile, and she said she didn't believe they were dead.'

'And you? Do you have feelings on it?' Hannah was curious; she was aware of the regard Doris and Mouse held for Kat, always saying she was the brains, the thinker in the group, and usually correct.

'I believe they're alive. The timeline says they are. It seems Nicola was an abuser, and not only of her husband and child. She was pretty nasty to Debbie in their younger years. Danny's broken arm happened after he "fell" down the stairs, and I think it was the push Adam needed, no pun intended. He'd been building up to it in various ways that included stockpiling money, so he went, and removed Danny from the danger that was his mother. If this didn't happen, I don't think there's any doubt that Nicola killed them. I'm sure she was capable of it. But sooner or later, bodies tend to be found, and they never have been, so it's another reason for believing they're still alive. Where they are is another matter altogether. But we're on it.'

'Really? Already?'

Kat tapped the side of her nose. 'Early days, Hannah, early days. But I promise if anything is thrown up that will help you with Nicola's murder, we'll pass it straight on to you, you know we will.'

The ginger biscuit box was looking depleted, so they had a second cup of coffee and continued dunking.

Luke was scrolling through what he had written when Hannah walked out of Kat's office. He stood immediately, and waited while she closed Kat's door before he headed towards the shop door to open it for her.

'I'm hearing good things about you,' Hannah said with a smile. 'Getting qualifications, studying at home as well as at work – you've landed on your feet here. I'm pleased for you, Luke. I've known these ladies for a couple of years now and like to think I know them well. They'll look after you, and if there's one piece of advice I could give you, it's don't ever underestimate their intelligence. At times it's scary.'

Luke laughed. 'Tell me about it. I see the certificates every day. And Mrs Lester and Mouse are both black belts in karate!'

'Have you seen the video of Doris taking down a man in this

office? Awesome. Ask them to show it to you,' Hannah said with a laugh, then waved as she walked away.

Hannah felt so much better for her time out. She switched on her car's engine, and sat for a moment, deciding what to do next. In the end she chose to head back to Chatsworth, do a roundup of any new information that had come in, and read once more all the statements they had completed.

She pulled down the visor; the low sun was shining directly into her eyes, and it felt comfortably warm in the car. The green fields had lost all their white covering, and she knew lambs would be appearing any time. She loved her county in the spring, not so much in the summer when it was overrun with tourists.

She realised she hadn't revisited the poor lover who had an angry wife to contend with, and mentally put him on her list of things to do. Neil Ireland, Paula Ireland, second interviews, Simon Vicars first interview, Debbie Carter temporarily on a back burner; must do items for the next day. It felt strange to be thinking and planning ahead. This was normally Tessa's remit, and Hannah wasn't convinced she was making the right moves, the right decisions. *Come back soon, boss*, she thought. *I'm struggling!*

17

Two nights of almost undisturbed sleep had given Tessa a new lease of life. Although her voice was still croaky, her head had lost its fuzziness, and she dressed in warm clothes. She didn't want to feel the alternate freezing and overheating she had experienced over the past couple of days, and knowing she would be out and about, she dressed accordingly.

Hannah had said she would be at Tessa's house by eight, and so Tessa went outside to wait for her arrival. A few seconds later Hannah's car pulled up in front of her.

'Good to have you back, boss. You're okay?'

'Better than I was. You solved this case yet?'

'Not quite, but I did have ginger biscuits at Connection yesterday. I only saw Kat and Luke, it seemed Doris and Mouse were beavering away on their computers. It's all about Danny and Adam Armstrong with them. They're trying to find them.'

'And they will. Think it will impact on our investigation?'

Hannah nodded, indicated and negotiated a tight right turn before speaking. 'I do, but it may be eventually rather than imme-diately. They've only just started, saw Debbie Carter yesterday morning. She's given them a whole load of paperwork to see if it will be of any help to them, but Kat stressed they would turn anything over to us if it concerned Nicola Armstrong. Their main area of interest is the father/son partnership.'

They reached the Chatsworth parking area designated for the police vehicles and both officers exited the car and stretched. It felt good to have some sun on their faces, even though it was likely to be fleeting; rain had been promised for later.

The room was busy, but not loud. Everybody was doing something, and it gladdened Tessa's heart that she never needed to push for action. They got on with it.

She walked to the front of the room and banged a marker pen on a desk. There was instant silence and some sporadic clapping.

'Thank you. As you can hear I still can't shout at you, so listen carefully. I need bringing up to speed with everything. Hannah's told me about the bike. Have we found it?'

Ray walked to the front and pointed to a map of Chatsworth. 'We're working systematically, boss. We have to do a sector at a time, it's such a huge bloody place. Definitely a haystack/needle situation. The sectors with Post-it notes covering them have been searched, and these remaining three,' he pointed with a biro, 'are being searched right now. We may have to dredge the river...'

'And information on both victims? Has anything come up that's made anybody think outside the box?'

She looked around to blank faces. 'Okay, keep going on that one. CCTV? Anything at all?'

'Olivia rode through the gates on her bike at 5.55. Then there's nothing anywhere. She didn't make it to the house. If she had she would have definitely been on camera. It's like a film set in there.'

'Thank you.' Tessa nodded to the owner of the voice that had just imparted the information. She didn't know him. It occurred to her they had a large workforce on this one... the Devonshires had influence, she guessed.

Tessa thanked everyone, said she was fighting fit and back on duty, then returned to her desk. Hannah followed her. 'You okay?' she whispered.

Tessa checked her watch. 'Medication time. I will be shortly. They work pretty quick. So, we need to speak with Neil Ireland again, get a formal statement of his philandering activities and, more importantly, the various injuries he received at the hands of Nicola Armstrong. I have an inkling...'

Hannah grinned. 'An inkling? An inkling led us to arresting Marnie Harrison. Let's trust your inklings.'

'I just think this woman's violence is at the root of it all. I think she was killed because she's attacked somebody, and unfortunately it may be somebody we know nothing about. Domestic violence against men is on the increase, but not talked about much because the men don't come forward. But it seems to me it's at the top middle and bottom of this. Where Olivia Fletcher fits in, I don't quite know...'

There was a shout from the other side of the room. 'Bike's been found, boss.'

Tessa stood. 'They retrieved it?'

'Getting it out now. It's in the river. Hang on...' He listened to what was being said on the other end of the phone and then punched the air. 'Good news, boss. Only the front end was submerged. They spotted the ribbon stuck out of the water. The contents of the bag are dry and were secured, before they attempted to move the bike. It's in an awkward place and they didn't want it going under completely with the stuff in the bag.'

'At last,' she breathed. 'Maybe a breakthrough. If it's any help to us, it'll be the first thing that has been.'

The largest evidence bag contained a pale blue button-up full-length nylon coat, used as a coverall when cleaning. The second contained a mobile phone, the third a small purse, and the fourth two sandwiches wrapped in tinfoil. The fifth one contained four pieces of a bar of Cadbury's milk chocolate.

'The last bit of her life,' Tessa said quietly. 'How sad is that. And such a lovely girl, so young.' She put on gloves, and removed the mobile phone. Going into calls, she saw the last one was to Olivia's mum the night before the day of her death. The one prior to that, some thirty minutes earlier, was to a number with the name Joker allocated to it, and it had lasted ten seconds only. Tessa stared at the strange number, then wrote it down on her notepad. She couldn't remember the number of the phones used by Nicola Armstrong and Neil Ireland; she needed to check that this number on Olivia's phone wasn't the same as either of those.

She moved into texts and croaked 'Bingo!'

Hannah moved around to stand behind her, and then punched the air.

'Hannah,' Tessa said. 'Shout and get them all to shut up.'

Hannah banged on the desk and shouted, 'Quiet, everybody. Listen to this!'

There was an instant hush and they swung their chairs to face Hannah and Tessa.

Tessa handed the phone to Hannah. 'You read it to them. They'll not hear me.'

'Okay,' she called, raising her voice a couple of notches. 'The night before she died, Olivia Fletcher made a phone call to a number with a name allocated to it, but that doesn't tell us who it is. The name is Joker. The call lasted ten seconds. She then texted the same number. This is that text. *Don't put the phone down on me, moron. Not joking now are u? You know I saw u, and now she's dead.* She got a reply. *What time you starting tomorrow? Meet me in glasshouse B. I'll explain. I didn't touch her.*'

The air was electric as they all listened carefully to the words. 'Then she sent a further text. *Starting early. 6. This had better be good or I go to police.*' Hannah looked up. 'There's one more text from Joker. *I'll be there.*'

'It seems,' Tessa croaked, 'that once we tie this number to its owner, we have our man or woman. I'm passing it to the tech guys to see if they can trace it before I have to do my impression of somebody they might know.'

She sat down and there was muted chatter. They all knew the chances of finding out who it belonged to were negligible, but at least they now had a reason behind Olivia's death. She had seen the perpetrator following the victim.

Her purse revealed very little. It contained a debit card, a credit card, a library card, and a couple of loyalty cards. It also contained a receipt for a small bottle of whisky, the receipt timed at 21.47 from a convenience store in Baslow. She would have been passing the gates of Chatsworth around the time Nicola was entering the estate. Had he or she been waiting inside the gates, aware of the camera trained on them?

Olivia had obviously seen him or her following Nicola, but hadn't made the connection till much later. It had cost her everything, that small bottle of whisky.

She took out the nylon workwear but it held nothing that could help them; it was clean, pressed and had nothing in any of the pockets. The sandwiches and chocolate were opened up and rewrapped before everything was replaced in their evidence bags. Tessa handed the phone over to the tech guy waiting for it, but it wasn't long before he brought it back to her, saying the number belonged to a throwaway not registered to anyone.

Once more Hannah silenced the room and Tessa used Olivia's phone to ring the number. *Welcome to the O2 messaging service. The number you are calling is unable to take your call.*

Tessa replaced the phone in its evidence bag and put all the items into one large bag to ensure they were kept together until somebody could give them an extra search.

Tessa was in bed by nine, warm, medicated and with soothing

music playing courtesy of her Echo Dot. She opened her kindle, and tried to concentrate on *Cujo*, but sensed maybe Stephen King wasn't going to cut it for her that night.

She felt the edge of the bed sink slightly and turned over with a smile. 'You've locked everything up?'

'All secure. Now go to sleep. And tell Alexa she can sleep too. Wake me if you want anything at all during the night.' Martin reached across and kissed her. 'Alexa, goodnight.'

'*Goodnight. Sweet dreams,*' was the response and the music died away, returning when Alexa had finished speaking. 'Alexa, stop.'

'Do I have to wait until I wake for this "wanting something during the night"?'

He looked at Tessa, his face creasing into a smile. 'You're a brazen hussy, DI Marsden. The medication's working then?'

He switched off the light, and helped her to get better.

18

Doris began. She put the file containing her notes on her laptop screen and started with Mark Brogan, reading the details out to Kat, Mouse and Luke.

'Mark Brogan was the youngest on that photograph, apart from Debbie. He wasn't sixteen when the picture was taken, the others were. There's no evidence he was particularly close to Adam, just in the same class, but he clearly spent this particular day in Adam's company.

'He is now married to Lisa, has two girls and is in charge of a recycling plant. He stayed in touch with Adam for a few years, because there's a picture of them at a football match together. They did a fundraiser at half time and they had a photo taken for the newspapers. The fundraiser was for Cancer Research, but I can't track down why. Usually it's because someone close has cancer, but nothing is standing out. That's the last time I can connect them.'

Doris reached across for her water, and took a sip. 'Any questions on Mark?'

'Not questions really, more an observation. Is he as nice as he sounds?' Kat asked.

'I think so. No financial problems as far as I can see, been married for nine years. They live in a semi-detached, with a massive back garden.' She clicked on a picture and swung her laptop around. 'This is their home. Nothing too ostentatious but very nice. However, I have flagged Mark onto the list that says further checking required on the strength that he's moved some distance from here. I think Adam would have had the common sense to get well away, and Mark Brogan was working for the recycling company in 2008 when Adam and Danny disappeared.'

Doris swung the laptop to face her and sighed. 'Our next young man, Barry Earnshaw, was very close to Adam right through school. They lived next-door-but-one to each other, grew up through all school levels together. Then in 2012 he died, came off his motorbike. However, this doesn't mean he didn't help Adam. Adam disappeared four years before Barry's death. Research shows me that Barry didn't have any sort of official partner, and although he lived in Monyash at the time of his death, in 2008 he was living in Cornwall, working as a surfing instructor during the summer. He lived in a campervan, but that in itself presented problems tracking his life. It was definitely a hippy lifestyle. Would Adam consider that to be the right environment for his son? I don't know, but I suspect not. For all these reasons, I've removed him from the possible list, because no matter that he was Adam's closest friend, he certainly isn't helping him now, and likewise can't help us either.'

'Nan, did you work on this at home?'

'Might have.'

'Did you?' Kat looked concerned. 'Didn't we say it was a big job, and to not take it home because it would be a sleep wrecker?'

'Did we?' Doris looked singularly untroubled by the questions.

'And have you got a headache this morning?' Mouse's tone was accusatory.

'I only had one gin and tonic, and half a box of Ferrero Rocher.'

Kat's mouth curved as if fending off a laugh. Luke guffawed. His laughter set everybody else off.

'Nan,' Mouse said, wiping tears from her eyes. 'How old are you next month?'

'Sixty.'

'No, you're seventy. Now will you start to accept your limitations, please? The ruling about not working on this at home was meant for all of us, not just you. It's intense, it can be upsetting digging into people's pasts, and you took it home! Which part of don't take it home didn't you understand?'

'Don't.'

'Don't what?'

'Don't. That's the part I didn't understand. You said which part didn't I understand. The part was don't. Stop being obtuse and difficult, Mouse.'

Mouse looked at Kat and Luke. 'Has this just swung around to me being in the wrong?'

Luke stood. 'Another coffee?'

They all pushed their mugs towards him, Kat still mopping up the tears of laughter. She really wished Mouse would learn she was never going to better her nan. When the blank innocent look was on Nan's face, it meant she had already won.

Biscuits accompanied the coffee, and Doris wisely sat without speaking for a few minutes. To calm everybody down, they chatted about Luke's predicament with regard to his two younger sisters both having birthdays in the same week, both enjoying different things and both wanting presents and not money. The birthdays were a week away and he still hadn't come up with ideas for them.

Kat's suggestion of a package of cinema tickets, popcorn and sweets for each of the girls, with their big brother taking them, ended up being the suggestion he thought was brilliant. Kat suspected it was because he could do the main part online, and nip across the road for two gift bags and some sweets.

With that important issue resolved, they turned back to Doris who was ready with her next name.

'Kenny Wilkinson. Now called Kenny Wilkinson-Starr. Lives in Bakewell with a chap called Alan Wilkinson-Starr, married two years ago. I worked extensively on Kenny, because they took the same GCSEs, and it occurred to me they would have been close because of that. Same classes, possibly study after school, but I can find nothing to link them at all after they left school. It's possible they moved in completely different circles, if Kenny was discovering his homosexuality. Anyway, I've taken him off the list temporarily. I've other things I can check with Kenny if necessary.'

Doris picked up her coffee and took a long drink. 'Thirsty work, this talking. Have you any questions so far?'

'Would we dare?' Mouse smiled. 'No, seriously, Nan, you've left the third on your list till the last. That's significant. You think Ethan King could have helped Adam?'

'Clever clogs. When I started to look into Ethan, I began with the photo. He's the one immediately behind Susie Long, but she is quite tiny and his focus is on Adam. And he's smiling, but not for the picture. He's smiling at the back of Adam. Is he pleased Adam is sitting with Debbie? I suspect he is. Maybe he doesn't like Nicola. Anyway, that's all supposition of course, but you can tell a lot from faces.

'So, I began with a young Ethan. I had a feeling… Anyway, he was born to parents who were seemingly quite well off. His father had a business... wait for it... a printing business. King-Press. Heard of it?'

Everyone around the table nodded. 'And are you all starting to get a feeling now?'

'I definitely am,' Kat said. 'How handy would that be if you needed documents to start a new life. Did Ethan go into the business?'

Doris nodded. 'Straight from school. By the time Adam disappeared, Ethan's father had retired, and Ethan was in full control of the business. Still is, of course. It's a huge set-up. They've expanded, have a massive warehouse for stationery goods, and they employ a hefty-sized workforce. It's an online business, although they do have a small on-site shop that caters to people like me who can't resist stationery. I imagine his father is very proud of him.'

'We need to go visit Ethan?' Kat asked. 'Are we open about why, or do we need some story just to get us in there? I'm always in favour of being as near to the truth as possible, because he'll have heard that Nicola Armstrong is dead. I think we go in telling him we've been employed to search for Adam and Danny, and we're looking to interview everybody on that photograph who remained friends with Adam after leaving school. He'll not think he's being singled out then, and maybe we'll pick up something.'

'I agree,' Mouse said. 'We were open with Michael Fairfax when we went to tell him his father was our client, and look what repercussions came from that.' She glanced at Doris, hoping she hadn't upset her by bringing Ewan Barker into the conversation, but her nan didn't even flinch.

Luke said nothing. He didn't know details of the case, but guessed there had been a personal element to it. It occurred to him that maybe he should know... just in case. He'd ask Kat, make sure he had the facts. Nobody was allowed to upset his ladies, ever.

'To go back to Ethan. He has an impressive portfolio of properties in Norfolk. It's a separate website that deals with this. I reckon Norfolk's far enough away from Derbyshire to be a bolthole. I will need more time to pursue this line, because we're talking around twenty-five properties, and I need to check out which are holiday lets and which have tenants. I'll let you know when this is complete, because I'm making Ethan King my priority now. You can start the application process for one of these properties online, but it states very clearly a formal interview will be required.'

Doris looked around the table. 'So that's the end of my report. Or it is up to a point, anyway. I'm really going in deep, find out everything I can about these properties Ethan King owns. Once we have all the facts at our fingertips, we'll go see him. Unless we find Adam first, of course. Mouse, you have anything interesting?'

'Not really, but I didn't take my work home with me,' she said, fixing her eyes on her nan. Doris smiled. 'I didn't spend much time on Zak Garside because he lives here, in Eyam, and is a carer for his mother. You know him, Kat?'

'I know Emily Garside. She was in an accident while riding her horse, caused all sorts of problems for her. She doesn't walk very well, but manages to get to church occasionally. I knew her son was her carer, but I didn't know his Christian name. Nice man, very polite. I've never seen him with a girlfriend, or even a boyfriend, so presumably his life is his mum.'

'I made a start with Susie Long, and it seems she lives in Canada. I've put her to one side because it's harder to track when they're in another country, but it's also ideal for hiding someone, so I'll do as comprehensive a check as I can. Wendy Thompson lives in Kent, and as such, merits a much closer inspection. I'll concentrate on her initially, and leave Canada alone for the moment.'

'I'm going to ring Debbie. There's a little niggle in the back of my mind, set off by that picture. I think there was something between Adam and Debbie, but he ended up with Nicola. Was it just the supposed pregnancy that drove them together? And now Rob, her husband, is out of the way, is that why she wants to find Adam so desperately? Everything seems to be falling into place for Debbie, and it's making me feel uneasy. I hope she's got a good alibi for Nicola's time of death.'

19

The convenience store in Baslow was tinier than Tessa expected. She bought some paracetamol, then showed her ID. 'Are you the owner?'

'I am. Can I help?'

'I hope so. I have a receipt from a couple of nights ago, when a young girl came in to buy a small bottle of whisky.'

'Yes, I remember her. I tried to persuade her to buy a bigger bottle because it was only a couple of pounds dearer, but she explained she was buying it for her dad, and his hands couldn't hold the bigger bottle. She said he'd just dropped one of the smaller ones which was why she was there to buy one at that time of night. It helped him sleep, she said. Lovely girl.'

'Was there anyone else around?'

'Not with her. She came in alone. I remember saying to her she was only just in time. I close at ten. There'd been somebody hanging around and I was really ready for closing. I felt uncomfortable.'

'This other person. Man or woman?'

There was hesitation. 'I'm not sure. My first impression was it was a man, but very slim so it could just as easily have been a woman. They had on a black baseball cap, pulled low, so I couldn't really tell. I'm sorry, I'm not being very helpful, am I?'

'Did you see this person go through the Chatsworth gates?'

'No. After the young girl spoke to the person, she drove off and I didn't see the person in the dark clothes again. I did see a woman go in through the gates, but she was a bit worse for wear, definitely wobbly. That young lass tried to steady her while she was talking to the other person, the one dressed in black. Is this about the body they found?'

'It is. Thank you for your help. And can I suggest you close a little earlier until this investigation is finished. Stay safe.'

Hannah had waited outside while Tessa went in. Hannah stepped forward and opened the car door for Tessa. 'You okay? She understood your croak?'

'She did. It seems Olivia saw the suspect here. She actually spoke to him or her, and she also saw Nicola Armstrong, definitely unsteady on her feet. Olivia tried to help her, but she went through the gates and Olivia drove off.'

'And now she's dead, and all because she was doing something really nice for her dad. It's a shitty world at times.' Hannah felt anger overwhelm her for a second. 'Let's go get this prick, shall we?'

'Hi, Debbie, it's Kat. I've a couple of questions that have cropped up since we were with you. You got five minutes?'

'Oh, hi. I have. I've just put Charlie in his bedroom, and now I can sit down with a big mug of hot chocolate and read. What do you need to know?'

'The first thing is on the day that Adam and Danny went, where was Nicola? I'm assuming the police asked the question when they first started looking for them, but we don't have access to police files.'

'She was at the hairdressers. She had an appointment, she said, for half past nine but it was a little delayed. Then she went to do some shopping, and got home around noon. By that time Danny and Adam had vanished. Nobody saw them go, there was only one suitcase missing so they didn't take much, and they went in Adam's car. He left everything else.'

'Thank you. Did he leave a note?'

'Nothing. Took Danny, a few clothes, and we haven't seen or heard from them since.'

'Thank you. And one more thing. It was clear from the picture you showed me that Adam had a thing for you. Why did he end up marrying Nicola?'

There was a moment of silence. 'She told him she was pregnant. She set out to trap him, to get him from me, and she succeeded. He was devastated. They married quickly, no big wedding, just a simple registry office one, and then two weeks later she told him she was miscarrying. Neither of us believed for a minute that she had been pregnant, we think she had a period, and said she'd lost the baby. He stayed with her and then she did become pregnant for real with Danny, and things improved between them. I'd met Rob of course and we'd become an item. It was one big mess. I wanted Adam, Adam wanted me, and we ended up with different people.'

'Thank you, Debbie. I need to speak to Simon. Get his memories of that time. I'll give him a ring and organise it.'

'You have his number?'

'I do. In my phone, and clearly marked "electrician". You don't lose important numbers,' Kat said with a laugh.

Simon was surprised to hear from Kat. He had assumed that Debbie would be her point of contact, but clearly that wasn't the case. He agreed to see her at four, and put down the phone with a frown. He almost felt out of the whole situation; he hadn't spoken to anybody on the police side since the snowy morning they had notified them of Nicola's death, and Debbie had been the one to hire Connection to try to find Danny. He was on the periphery of it all, and yet Kat wanted to speak to him.

His phone pealed out again, a strange number, a possible new job. He cleared his throat and answered it with his posh voice in play.

'Mr Vicars? DI Marsden. We'd like to come around and have a chat with you, possibly tomorrow morning? Say half past eight?'

'Erm, yes, that will be fine. I need to be leaving home by ten, I have a job in Chesterfield. Will that be enough time for you?'

'Thank you, Mr Vicars, I'll make sure we're finished by then.'

He disconnected and sat down heavily. Suddenly he didn't feel quite so much on the periphery.

'Hi, Simon. Good to see you again.' Kat smiled at the tall good-looking man in front of her. It had been over five years since she had last seen him, and he hadn't changed at all.

'Kat. Please come in.' He stepped back and waited for her to pass by him before shutting the door. 'Straight on, it's warmer in the kitchen.'

The kitchen was toasty warm, and the air was redolent with something delicious cooking in the oven.

'That smells good,' she said.

'A simple stew. I'm not one for fancy food, never have been.'

He pulled out a chair from under the table, and Kat sat down. 'First of all, Simon, I'm so sorry for your loss. Death can be extra hard on people when it's a sibling.'

'Thank you. I'm not sure I've accepted it yet. Debbie has taken it so much better than me, but Debbie had written Nicola out of her life anyway, I fear.'

'And you hadn't?'

He hesitated. 'This conversation is between us?'

'It's between you and Connection. It won't go back to Debbie.'

He nodded. 'Thank you. I saw Nicola fairly frequently. I'm not saying we were best friends or anything like that, but she was an unhappy woman. I tried to be there for her. I could see both sides, Kat, with her and Adam. Oh, I saw his bruises and cuts – we were friends, and he made this house his port in a storm, but I knew it was something inside Nicola that she couldn't control. As a child I suffered at her hands, as did Debbie, but nobody seemed able to do anything about it.'

'So Debbie doesn't know you were in regular contact.'

'No. It's better it stays that way. It's irrelevant anyway now, isn't it.'

Kat could see the sadness in his face. 'Can we talk about Adam leaving?'

'Or otherwise?'

The room went silent. 'You think it's possible there's an otherwise?' Kat said.

'Kat, I've tried to explain how violent Nicola was. I honestly don't know what she was capable of. I can't believe she would kill Danny, not her child, but she came pretty close with Adam more than once. If Adam left through his own volition, I would have expected to hear from him at some point over the last ten years. I haven't. We were very close, more like brothers than brothers-in-law.'

'Debbie thinks he's still alive.'

'Debbie loved him. She'll never accept he's dead unless we find a body. She lives for the day when he'll walk through her door.'

'What did you think when he disappeared?'

There was no hesitation. 'I thought my sister had committed murder. She'd pushed Danny down the stairs two days earlier, and only another couple before that when she'd beaten Adam with the baseball bat. He didn't just let her do that, by the way, she knocked him out first. When he came to, he was in dreadful pain, but refused to send for the police. He and Danny turned up here, and I tried to help, but I knew he would take time. She arrived to take them home, and off they went. It was weird. It was almost as if he was embarrassed to admit he was being knocked about by a woman.'

'Have you thought about what she could have done with the bodies if she had murdered them? They've never turned up, so what on earth could she have done with them?'

He laughed. 'You've seen her house? No? Then I must take you. The dining room is a library; a beautiful room. It's filled with crime books. Real crime and fiction. It's all she ever read. She'd certainly know what to do with dead bodies. My guess would be they would be chucked in the sea. She'd make it look as though Adam had killed Danny, then committed suicide. It would be fifty–fifty whether they would resurface before the fish ate them, but either way she would be safe from prosecution. Some clever barrister would sort it out for her.'

Kat stared at him. 'You really believe it, don't you?'

'I'm sorry, Kat, I've lived with this nightmare, these awful thoughts for so long. I've never spoken to Debbie about them because she'd think I was mad, but I'm not. Nicola was.'

'I'm going to do my best to find this man for you, Simon. You need closure if he's dead, and if he isn't you need to be reunited. We're following leads that the police didn't know about when he first disappeared, so we're hopeful of a result. Have you given your statement to DI Marsden yet?'

'No, she's coming in the morning. But what do I know? She won't be here about Adam and Danny; she'll be here about Nicola's death. I'm not surprised Nicola died violently, it's how she lived her life, but I wouldn't have wished it for her, no matter what she's done.'

Kat stood. 'I have to go; my mum is bringing my daughter

back in half an hour. I'll keep in touch, Simon, let you know how we're progressing. Did you know any of your sister's classmates in her last year of school?'

'Not really. She only had eyes for Adam, and by the time she was in her last year, I was out earning a living in the real world. I remember she had a girlfriend called Wendy, but one day Wendy let on she fancied Adam, and that friendship disappeared. I can't recall any other friends she may have had.'

'Okay, no problem,' Kat said, and left him sitting at the table while she walked back to her car. In her eyes, he seemed a broken man. A man who missed his sister, despite her being a psychopath with a penchant for hurting men... badly.

20

K at's visit had woken latent brain cells in Simon, and he realised that at any future trial it would come out in court that he had seen Nicola a lot more frequently than Debbie knew about. He had no doubt in his mind that his current relationship with Debbie would disintegrate once she heard that little snippet of information.

As a result, when Tessa and Hannah called, the statement he signed was very brief. The family was dysfunctional, he had very little contact with his sister, and he really knew nothing of her life.

Hannah turned the ignition. 'That was pretty straightforward. A man of few words.'

'You believed him?' Tessa's voice was still croaky, but had flashes of normality.

'Think so. What did you pick up on that I didn't?'

Tessa didn't answer immediately. 'Something was off. Simon Vicars seemed to be a really nice bloke. A bit of a peacekeeper. Even a peacemaker. Know what I mean? I found it hard to equate that side of him with the side that didn't see anything, or very little, of Nicola.'

Hannah laughed. 'He doesn't want Debbie knowing he's been seeing Nicola, does he. As you say, he's a peacekeeper. You think we need to keep an eye on him?'

'No, I don't. If I had a brother I'd want one just like Simon. He's protecting Debbie, and he clearly kept an eye on Nicola. Wonder if he knew about Nicola's affair with Neil Ireland...'

'Should we ask him?'

Tessa shook her head. 'Not yet. Maybe not ever. He'll find out when it goes to trial anyway.'

'Wish I had a brother like him. In fact, I wish I had any sort of brother.'

'Yeah, me too. I think being an only child is overrated,' Tessa responded. 'Mum couldn't have any more after she had me, and I think she always regretted that. You want kids, Hannah?'

Hannah's tone was guarded. 'I like other people's kids, adore my nieces, but at the end of each day I can sit down with a glass of wine, tuck my feet underneath me and not think about another soul that I need to look after. That suits me.'

'Mmm...'

'You?'

'I don't know.' Tessa stared out of the passenger window. 'No, I simply don't know.'

Doris looked up from her cogitations as the door opened slightly. She closed the lid on her laptop, and watched as Luke's head appeared around the door.

'You need anything, Mrs Lester? I wanted to let you know I'll be missing for ten minutes. We need biscuits and milk supplies, so I'm popping over the road.'

'Thank you, Luke. And thank you for the minutes of the meeting from yesterday. We never did that. We just had meetings and everybody extracted what they needed out of it. This is much more efficient.'

'I like doing it. It helps me think. I've printed one for Kat, made her a cardboard file for them. I know she likes to read things properly.'

'You spoil that girl,' Doris said sternly.

Luke laughed. 'Some people don't like technology. Kat – and my younger sister – are part of that group. Imogen still plays with an Etch-A-Sketch, for heaven's sake. It's no trouble for me to accommodate Kat with that. So, you want anything from the shop while I'm going?'

'Let's have some cupcakes. Is there enough in petty cash?'

'I think so. You making any progress?' He nodded towards the closed laptop.

'Maybe.'

'007, don't go getting into any trouble,' he said with a grin. 'Stick to the grey side, not the dark side. And you didn't work from home?'

'Don't start again, young man. I only did half an hour... now go shopping, and we'll all have a break when you get back. Discuss what we've found out, if anything.'

'I'll take the minutes,' he said, and closed the door.

Luke warned both Kat and Mouse of an imminent meeting, and fifteen minutes later they each had a coffee and a cupcake. Kat had spent the morning putting finishing touches to a difficult sermon she needed to deliver the following Sunday, so she listened to what the other two had to say, having nothing of her own to contribute.

Doris began. 'The first thing I need to say is that Ethan King needs to up his security on his personal home set-up. That's where I began to look for his properties, half expecting them to be part of KingPress, but they're not. They're definitely on his home system, which is pretty sophisticated, I must admit, but I got in.'

'Easily?' Mouse asked.

Doris shrugged. 'So-so. Once I was in, it was simple to navigate. He actually has twenty-six properties, although only twenty-five are listed on the website. Of those, twenty are holiday lets. You can click on any of these for the details and ways to book. The other five are permanent lets. Four are tenanted, one is available as a long-term let. They're scattered around one small area.'

'And the twenty-sixth?' Kat asked.

'Exactly. The twenty-sixth. At the moment I can't find it. It's listed, but without a location attached to it, and it says it's tenanted. It seems Ethan King complies with the law regarding his taxes, but has to hide something with this one. Let's hope the thing he's hiding is Adam Armstrong.'

'We need to go and talk to him?' Mouse asked, a frown etched into her brow.

'No.' Doris was quick to answer. 'That's the last thing we need to do. One thing said out of place and Adam will disappear, if he is the one in the mystery house or flat.'

'So what do you propose?' Kat was intrigued.

'Give me time. As long as we don't alert Adam and Ethan to any activity, we're okay. I can go deeper to find this, but I have to be careful where I'm going. It may take a couple of days, but *if* we get what we want, and I'm still stressing the if bit, we'll put surveillance on the house, see who comes and goes. If we're on the right track with this, and the tingles in my fingers tell me we are, we may have to talk to Tessa. No, we will have to talk to Tessa. I imagine when Adam and Daniel went missing, the police removed items from the house that had their DNA on them. If we can get something of Adam's, we can pass it on for testing. His physical appearance could have changed dramatically, but he can't change his DNA. We can't approach anyone before we have proof and the police have been called in, because he will run. I'm sure of it. He's kept Danny safe for all these years, he's not going to put him in harm's way again.'

'Get any sleep last night, Nan?' Mouse asked quietly.

Doris grinned at her granddaughter. 'I put something on to run for half an hour, then closed it down. I read, watched the news and went to bed. Now stop nagging. Oh, and I had the other half of that box of Ferrero Rochers. I've run out now,' she added, lowering her glasses and staring over the top of them at Kat and Mouse.

'Now you're a partner they no longer form part of your consultant fee.' Kat tried to keep her face straight as she answered Doris.

For possibly the first time in her life, Doris didn't have a response.

It was a busy day for everyone in the cases connected to Nicola Armstrong. Olivia Fletcher's Mini had been seen on CCTV travelling both ways between Bakewell and Baslow with the precious half bottle of whisky on the return journey. The statement by the shop owner at the convenience store had been signed, and results were coming back from extended tests on the two bodies.

Neither woman had been sexually assaulted, although Tessa had guessed that. Undisturbed clothing was a pretty big clue. This case had never been about sex, it was all about Nicola Armstrong. What nobody could get a handle on was the reason for Nicola's death.

Her anger issues were well documented, but who would be so pissed off with her brutality that they would follow her steps towards Chatsworth, then kill her? Paula Ireland, the cheated wife? She hadn't even known her husband was seeing Nicola; that much had been clear when Tessa and Hannah had dropped the bombshell. She hadn't liked Nicola, that had been obvious, but that had been more about the enforced tramping over the hills of Derbyshire looking for two people that everyone knew would have left the area on the day they went missing.

Tessa pulled the printout of the autopsy results towards her. No perpetrator DNA apparent on either body, same rope, line, used for the ligature, with cut ends that matched with precision, and the rope could have been bought at any hardware store in the county, so generic was it. Both women had been hit over the head primarily, although this wasn't what had killed them. The rope had done that. The blow to Nicola's head hadn't been as severe as the one to Olivia's, but with the amount of alcohol inside Nicola, the effect would have been the same.

Tessa pushed back her hair, and felt the fringe flop back on to her forehead. She reached into her bag and took out the paracetamol, popped two out and swallowed them with the dregs of the now-cold tea. Although feeling much better in stretches of four hours, her body told her to take medication to get her through the next four. And she desperately hoped the tablets would eventually give her a voice that people could hear and understand.

'Hannah!'

'Boss?'

'Let's go to the Armstrong house. I know it's been gone over by forensics, but we haven't been back. Let's go and see how Nicola lived, see if there's anything at all that's been missed. We might get more of a feel for her, and her lifestyle.'

Hannah was putting on her jacket while Tessa was speaking. 'Come on, I'm driving.'

It briefly occurred to Tessa that they could have walked; Nicola did on that last night of her life.

They parked the car outside the house and walked up the path. There were brave signs of spring in the daffodil leaves pushing through the soil, and little blue plants that Tessa thought were rather pretty, despite her having no idea what they were.

Entering the house this time was different. Last time the heating had been on, thanks to Nicola having left it on before venturing out for that last walk that she fully expected to return from, frozen and needing warmth. Now it felt bitterly cold.

'Where do we start?' Hannah murmured, almost to herself. She ventured into the kitchen and Tessa entered the lounge.

Fifteen minutes had passed before they met up in the dining room. They looked at the books.

'Wow.' Tessa's poorly voice managed to deliver the one word that spoke volumes.

'Look at these,' Hannah said, awe evident in her voice. 'She has complete series of crime authors – all the Sue Graftons, the Patricia Cornwells, the Ian Rankin novels, the Henning Mankells, dozens of J D Robbs – this woman was a serious crime reader. And that side of the room is taken up with real crime. She would have been, in her own way, an expert criminologist. So... did her husband and Daniel leave her voluntarily, or was it something more sinister that everybody discounted? Tessa, we need to look at this differently, don't we?'

'We certainly do. Ring for SOCOs to come back. I want comprehensive photos of every shelf, every book in this room. Particularly the true crime ones. Let's see how her heroes disposed of the dead bodies they were left with.'

21

Doris pulled the map of Norfolk towards her and picked up the thick black marker pen. Sometimes, she reflected, you just needed pen and paper.

The list of properties was also printed on to paper; she wanted to be able to rule them in or out, again with the thick black marker pen. She had the printout on her left, the map on her right, and her brain somewhere in between. She had twenty-five addresses that she wanted to dot onto the map, and she didn't really know why. The twenty-sixth address was proving elusive, and she wanted to see if any areas had more homes owned by Ethan King than any others did.

You're struggling, old woman, she said to herself. The first address took a couple of minutes to locate on the large-scale map, and she put a dot on the exact spot. By the time she had located ten of the properties, it was clear that all of them were in one specific area, and all within five hundred metres of the sea. She continued until each home had been dotted, and then sat back and stared at the massed black marks. A very small area contained all the homes.

She sat for quite some time wondering what she had gained

from the exercise, and decided it was nothing. Picking up a red pen, she put a circle around the dots that represented the long-term rental properties. A pencil followed the red pen, and she connected the same properties, the line forming an almost-perfect pentangle amidst a sea of plain black dots.

Doris's top right-hand drawer revealed a pack of Blu-Tack, and she attached the large map to the wall. She studied it intently, wondering what had been in Ethan King's mind when he had designated these five properties to be the long-term lets, and not holiday lets. Surely it wasn't just a protective ring of trusted people around a man who had been threatened by his wife. It seemed a bit extreme, to say the least.

Or was the protection for Danny? As the adult, Adam had been the focus for her, but standing looking at the map of the coastal region of Norfolk, she knew it was truly about Danny, not Adam.

Doris pressed her buzzer for Luke, and he knocked and opened her door.

'Look at this,' she said, and waved her hand towards the map.

He stood for a moment; his eyes took in Cromer. 'These are the homes he owns? He either has a bit of a thing about Cromer, or he's set up an escape route for his best mate.'

Doris stared at the map. Could it be as simple as that? 'Let's get our brainstormer troops in. Are they both here?'

'Yes, Kat went out but she's back. I think she went for morning prayer. I'll get them.'

None of them sat down. They stood around, clutching on to the cups of coffee they'd brought with them, and simply looked.

'Luke, tell the others what you said, first of all.'

'I guessed – no proof at all, obviously – that Ethan King has set up an escape route for Adam and Danny. And I bet that when we find Adam, his house will have so much CCTV on it, it will be like a documentary being filmed for television. He will be able to see anyone approaching the house, any cars going past... do we know what he did for a living before he went missing?'

'No, we don't. I'll ring Debbie and find out.' Kat stepped closer. 'Did you think the pentangle was significant, Nan?' She laughed.

Doris smiled at her. 'He could have set up a magic thing, where he's protected from all evil by salt and garlic. No, it was actually to see where the centre of that five-house set was. Even then it seemed like a protection system.'

'Luke, can you give Debbie a ring and find out what job Adam did, and who he worked for, please.' Kat spoke almost absently, still engrossed in the map.

He disappeared, feeling inordinately pleased that Kat had asked him. He returned two minutes later with the news that Adam had worked for a company called Secure, and he worked from home, but travelled all over the country setting up security systems. When the police contacted Secure, trying to track him down, they said he'd not checked in for work since the day he disappeared.

'Then the only person he can see is me,' Doris said. 'If ever we track him down he'll disappear as fast as an express train, unless it's me standing at his door, a little old lady carrying a dog lead, looking for her dog who's slipped his lead. I can cry on demand, you know.'

'So our only problem is finding where his house is. Let's jump straight to the middle of that pentangle and start there.' Kat gave a short bark of laughter. 'Easy.'

'Or we could apply to rent this untenanted property,' Doris said. 'I could be the little old granny whose grandson lives with her, and we'd like to move to the coast. It's a Cromer Estate Agency who manages the properties, so we could approach them. We'll put that on the back burner though. I've got something

ANITA WALLER

running… if things go well, we'll have this last address, if not I'll buy a dog lead. Out of petty cash now I'm a partner.'

Mouse was still staring at the map. 'This is quite a little empire he has. I'm impressed.'

'He inherited twelve of them from his grandfather. He's bought at least one a year since then. Most of them are holiday lets, he just seems to keep this group of five as proper homes for people. You know, this is still all assumption that he is helping Adam, we've no proof at all. In the end, we may just be putting this theory to rest, and have to start over again. We may even have to consider that Adam and Danny are dead.'

The final home wasn't in the centre of the pentangle; garlic and salt didn't come into it. It was a house between two other tenanted properties. The tenant was James Owen.

Kat, Mouse and Luke trooped back into Doris's office, keen to see what her delvings into the grey shadows of the Internet had thrown up.

She had used a luminous green marker for the final house, and she pointed it out on the map. Then she handed out detailed printouts of the road. Using the same luminous green, she had highlighted the house, and back and front gardens. The alleyway down the side of the house was highlighted in luminous orange. A second, wider path running all the length of the houses, was highlighted in luminous blue.

'Nan, we could frame this and have it as modern art.' Kat held it against a wall, and Doris threw a paperclip at her.

'Any more sarcasm, young lady, and you'll be on the naughty step. So, if this is Adam Armstrong, the pathway running along the back of all the houses, at the end of their gardens, is his escape route. That's the blue on your maps. There's a lot of

Victorian houses in this country that have a path at the end of their gardens, not sure why but I guess there was a good reason when they were made. And I bet these tenants either side are there for a reason – to protect him. They're both very long term, one's been there eleven years, the other one nine. The first one was already in situ, the second one's tenancy started after Adam disappeared. It seems Ethan King can make things happen.'

Doris paused and stared at the map. 'Or am I being stupid? This is all supposition. What frightened this man so much that he hid away for ten years? And he must know by now that his wife is dead. It's been all over the news and I'm damn sure Ethan King will have been in constant touch.'

'Maybe he doesn't want anything to do with that old life. If he has a good one now, he'll not want to go back to the bad memories. And Danny probably won't remember much about it, so there's nothing to take him back.' Mouse too was staring at the map, as if it would give her enlightenment.

'But there is something to take him back,' Kat joined in. 'The house in Baslow now legally belongs to him. Unless he murdered her, of course, and then it doesn't. But why now? If he's the murderer, why has it taken so long for him to do it? He's quite successfully disappeared so doesn't need to come back into the limelight by killing Nicola. He's not on my radar for having done it. What do you think?'

'I don't understand it at all.' Doris frowned, continuing to look at the multi-coloured map as if seeking inspiration. 'We need confirmation that James Owen is Adam Armstrong before we pass this to Tessa, because if he turns out to be just a bloke called James Owen and nothing to do with the investigation, we'll look complete plonkers. We can always blame Luke, of course.'

Luke grinned. 'Hey, keep me out of it. This is fascinating, watching the way you three work. You just bounce the ball around between you. No wonder our police ladies call in here to sort out their heads. Are we going to check him out then? I'll volunteer to ride shotgun with Mrs Lester.'

'You think she needs protecting?' Mouse laughed and swung Doris's laptop around to face Luke. She opened the file containing a video from their CCTV. 'Come here, Luke, it's time you saw this. The man is an arsehole called Ewan Barker, who Nan had a couple of dates with, and then we found out what sort of a scumbag he really was. You need to see this so that you know just who your Mrs Lester is, and why you need never think about protecting her.'

Mouse held out the chair for Luke to sit down, and clicked for the file to open. 'Enjoy the movie,' she said.

Luke's mouth fell open as he watched the events unfolding on the screen, and when it finished with Barker prostrate on the floor clutching his groin, Luke clicked for a replay. Finally he sat back. 'If I go with you, Mrs Lester, will you promise to look after me and protect me?'

'Certainly, Luke,' Doris said with a smile. 'I don't act like that every day though. Only twice a week.'

Luke stood. 'I promise never to upset you. And you still train?'

'Of course. And never forget that Mouse is even more advanced than I am, so between us we can take on the world, and Kat will make everything better.'

Kat was still staring at the map, but her smile widened. And then her brain woke up.

'Hang on a minute,' she said, and left Doris's office, returning a few seconds later with her mobile phone.

She scrolled, then dialled. 'Simon?' They went through the formalities of saying they were fine. 'Simon,' Kat finally got around to the point of the call, 'did Adam support a football team?'

There was a short bark of laughter. 'We both went to every home match for a number of years. Manchester's not so far from here when you're a fan.'

'Which one?' she said, knowing she was right. 'Which team? Blue or red?'

'Red all the way, Kat. We lived for Man U, when they were probably the greatest team ever.'

Kat thanked him and disconnected. She turned to the others. 'That name had been bugging me. James Owen. And suddenly it clicked. Michael Owen, one of the biggest stars at Man U.'

'A bit tenuous,' Mouse said.

'Not when you know his name is Michael James Owen, it isn't. I'll wager next month's child benefit that Adam Armstrong took his new name from his beloved Man U.'

22

Tessa stared at the crime scene pictures of the library in Nicola Armstrong's house. Hundreds and hundreds of books, and with different murder methods in each one. Was it possible that she had disposed of Adam and Daniel? Had the anger had moments of uncontrollability?

Tessa thought back to other victims whose bodies had never been found – Suzy Lamplugh, Claudia Lawrence, Keith Bennett and many more, but the difference was that those victims were certain to have died. She couldn't say that about Adam and Danny Armstrong. Had Nicola come across something in one of these books that she had filed into her memory banks for a "just in case" moment?

Or was the answer much simpler – Nicola enjoyed reading crime novels. Nothing sinister, just a woman who found her escape in a book.

Tessa pushed the pictures to one side, and stared around the room. All the staff had been interviewed, alibis verified, and they seemed to be no closer to identifying this murderer.

Tessa picked up a pen and pulled a piece of paper towards her. Time to organise thoughts, see what hadn't been answered and what had. She drew a line down the middle of the page, and sat and stared at it.

Hannah walked across and stared at it too. 'No thoughts at all then?'

'None whatsoever. What are we missing?'

Hannah pulled up a chair. 'Okay, time to recharge brain cells numbed by medication. Make one side a list of people who really didn't like her, for whatever reason. You see, in the middle of the night it occurred to me that she didn't have anybody. We've found no friends, let alone close friends; is this because she's a very unlikeable person, or is it because she realised her anger issues were getting out of control and she was better being on her own?'

Tessa began to write. Accidentally picking up a red pen made the list stand out.

Adam Armstrong
Daniel Armstrong?
Neil Ireland
Paula Ireland
Debbie Carter
Simon Vicars?
Greg Littlewood
Rob Carter

The two women sat for a while just looking at the names. 'So that was her life?' Hannah said. 'If I made a list of people who didn't like me, it would be a lot longer than that, and I'm still alive! Are we seriously considering any of these could have murdered her? Adam is well out of it, as is Daniel. They've no reason to complicate their lives by coming to Baslow to kill her. That doesn't make sense. Yes, Adam would inherit the house, but not if he killed her to get it. There's no motive, no indication of where he is, unless...'

'Unless our friends at Connection have come up trumps again. Let's go and ask them. And I want to talk to Neil and Paula Ireland again. I want them both signing statements about where they were that night. We'll get Fiona on to checking if that wrist injury really is sufficiently serious to stop him strangling somebody.'

Hannah crossed the room to speak to PC Fiona Ainsworth, and then joined Tessa outside.

'Come on, let's go see what biscuits they've got. It's time to talk.' Tessa pulled her coat tightly around her, and they walked to the car park.

Luke was engrossed in his course, and didn't see the two police officers approach the door. It came as a shock when the buzzer sounded. He released the lock and stepped forward to greet them. 'Welcome, ladies. Do my ladies know you're coming?'

'Not unless they're psychic,' Tessa admitted with a grin.

'I wouldn't put anything past Mrs Lester. I'll let them know you're here, and find out which room they want you in.'

He knocked first on Doris's door, and she looked up, surprised. 'DI Marsden and Hannah are here,' he said, and smiled as she closed the lid down onto her laptop.

'Warn Mouse, will you?' she whispered.

He nodded, and knocked on Kat's door. 'Police in attendance, Kat,' he said, and she confirmed that they would use her office.

Mouse had already closed down her laptop, the voices having been loud enough for her to hear.

Tessa was quiet, and it was plain to see that the illness had taken its toll. She coughed intermittently, and it proved to be Hannah who led them into talking about Adam and Daniel Armstrong.

'Things are quite strange,' Hannah said. 'Nicola had no friends, or even acquaintances. Maybe that was through choice, we'll never really know, because she was aware of her temper. She was having an affair, but on the man's part it was over because she'd attacked him once too often. When she died she believed she was still in that relationship. That last phone call she made that night was to him, but he was in too much pain with a broken wrist to answer her. She hit him with a baseball bat earlier in the day, and he'd only just got back from hospital when she rang. We now wonder, of course, if she was ringing to tell him she was being followed, and she needed help. I suppose he'll always have to live with that thought.'

'And the second murder? You've found a connection?' Kat asked.

'Yes. It seems that Olivia saw whoever was following Nicola, and once the body was found, she texted him or her to say she was going to the police. He persuaded Olivia to talk to him first, and he killed her.' Hannah paused. 'The biggest problem of all is we can find no reason for anyone to kill Nicola. We have no reason to suspect the missing husband and child, it would make no sense for them to arrive back on the scene.'

'Have you found them?' Tessa asked quietly.

'Maybe.' Doris was equally quiet. 'We don't know for certain, because we've only found the missing bit of the jigsaw today, but one thing is for sure; if you send the police in, blue lights flashing, Adam will go. Let us confirm it is him, and then we can work out how to approach him without him using the escape route that has been in place for the last ten years.'

'You know his new identity?' Hannah's voice was strident, almost a demand.

Tessa picked up a biscuit. 'Hannah, leave it to Connection. They'll tell us as soon as something is confirmed. We're really struggling on this one, because everybody has an alibi. There was no DNA at either scene, we've interviewed all the staff except the Duke and Duchess, and we've found nothing. We don't even know why Nicola would be in Chatsworth grounds at that time of night. It must have been bitterly cold because the snow started soon after she died. We know she was drunk, but she was walking away from her home, not towards it. Come on, ladies, suggestions.'

'Interview the Duke and Duchess,' Mouse said with a laugh. 'I don't know what to say, Tessa. You're no further forward than you were at the beginning, except you've got a chest infection.'

'And we promise you,' Doris said, 'that if our thoughts do lead us to Adam Armstrong, we won't approach him, we'll tell you where he is. However, we are being paid to find him, so we will also be telling our clients. Now, if it does prove to be him, it will be visual confirmation only. I think he will be out of his home within ten minutes if anybody causes him any concern, because I think he has expected to be found ever since he left. He's protecting his child, and he'll take Danny, or whatever his name is now, and run once again.'

'Fair enough.' Tessa sipped thoughtfully at her coffee. 'Even if we interview him, I still think it makes no sense that he had anything to do with her death. He'd escaped the tyranny of living with her, and he'd managed to keep Danny as well. He's had ten years to build a new life, and I'm assuming it's some distance from Baslow... no, I can't make my brain think it's him.'

'So where do you go from here?'

'Mouse, if only I knew.' Tessa sighed. 'There are people on the periphery who we haven't spoken to yet, such as Rob Carter, Debbie's husband, and Greg Littlewood, Simon's partner, but that will be just a formality, I'm sure. Greg, according to Simon, has been in Holland since Christmas with his job, not due home until next week. I can't see that fitting in with murdering somebody in Chatsworth. And Rob Carter is living with somebody else and has very little to do with Debbie apart from sending her money regularly. What strikes me the most is that it was a strange dysfunctional family. Nobody really liked anybody else, and even now Debbie and Simon seem to only see each other if he's doing some work for her. Why can't people just be normal and stop killing each other,' she grumbled.

'We'd be out of a job.' Hannah grinned at her disgruntled boss. 'Are we going to call at the Irelands' home today?'

'We might as well while we're out.' Tessa put down her now-empty cup. 'Thank you for the chat, ladies and Luke, and the coffee and biscuits. We get scones up at Chatsworth. They've been remarkably accommodating.'

'Ah, but you don't get the sparkling repartee up there, do you.' Kat smiled as the two police officers stood. 'We'll be in touch very shortly, with a yay or nay on Adam Armstrong. Believe me, nothing's definite about this. We're like you, everything seems to be ifs and buts with this case. Have you ever considered they could be dead?'

Tessa halted, halfway through putting on her coat. 'That's a definite yes. I know you haven't been in Nicola Armstrong's house, but her dining room doubles as a library. It's full to bursting with crime novels, both fiction and true crime. It's an amazing collection of books, but it rather makes me think that Nicola was a potential expert criminologist, and would know exactly how to dispose of corpses, with very little effort. She had the full set of Patricia Cornwell's Scarpetta series, and I imagine from that one set alone, she could kill half of Derbyshire and get rid of the bodies.'

Luke escorted them to the door, then watched as they walked to their car before locking the door. He enjoyed having them drop in, enjoyed watching them trying not to give too much away. That day had been different in that he sensed if they'd had anything to say they would have done so. The whole case had stagnated up at Chatsworth; fortunately it hadn't in Eyam, and he was looking forward to heading off to Norfolk for his first crack at surveillance.

He gathered up the cups and took them into the kitchen. Washing and drying was his time to let his mind wander, and it wandered to the cinema trip scheduled for Saturday night. He'd be in a bit of a pickle if Mrs Lester decided Saturday was the day to visit Norfolk – he could just imagine what his sisters would say.

23

L uke breathed a sigh of relief that they were delaying their surveillance until Monday. They decided to be sensible, knowing the distance of the journey, and Luke booked two cheap hotel rooms for the Sunday night, so that they didn't have to leave Eyam at two on Monday morning. The plan was to leave around two on Sunday afternoon, check in to the hotel before having a meal, then get an early night for an early start Monday.

Friday proved to be quiet. Kat had decided to take the day off to spend it with Martha and Carl, Mouse came in for a couple of hours then announced she would be in her flat if anybody needed her, but it would only be if the office was on fire. Doris closeted herself in her office, ostensibly to double-check everything for Monday, but when Luke popped his head around her door to say he was going for some milk, she was reading a book.

'Any good?'

'Surprisingly so. I picked it up yesterday on that second-hand books shelf in the Co-op. It's an author I'd not read before, but will certainly read again, and actually buy it properly next time. Do you read, Luke?'

'Constantly. Can't beat a good murder. I'm nipping over to get us some milk. You need anything?'

'No, I don't think so. It's quiet in here today, isn't it? We'll give it until four, then we're closing. Mouse isn't ill, is she?'

He smiled. 'Nah... I saw Joel arrive. She's fine.'

Luke closed Doris's door and headed across the road, narrowly missing being mown down by a BMW being driven at speed. He used a word he would never dare use in front of his ladies... or his mum.

He grabbed a basket, checked out the bookshelf and chose a novel to pack in his travel bag on Sunday, got the milk and headed towards the checkout. He put the milk through first, getting the receipt he would later put in petty cash, then put the rest of the things through.

His mum laughed. 'You taking these to the cinema then?' She rang his goods through, but not before checking whether she would enjoy the book as well. 'See you later,' she said, as she handed him his change.

He checked more carefully before crossing the road, taking note that the traffic flow had increased over the last few days, a sure indication that warmer weather was approaching. It just didn't feel as though it was.

He put the milk in the fridge, his new book in his bag, and tapped on Doris's door before opening it. He placed the box of Ferrero Rocher in front of her and winked. 'You can't read without chocolate,' he said, and closed the door.

Mouse lay in Joel's arms, completely happy. His phone call that morning had been unforeseen – an unexpected chance for a day off, did she fancy meeting up? When she asked him where he was, he said Eyam.

He pulled her close and planted a kiss in her messed-up curls. 'You're beautiful,' he said. 'Did I tell you I love you?'

She stiffened, then forced herself to relax. 'You did,' was her quiet response. 'Last Thursday, on the phone. At 13:47.'

He leaned on one elbow and smiled down into her face. 'It had an impact then?'

'I told you I love you, as well.'

'When?'

'After you'd put the phone down.'

He sank back on to the pillow and laughed. 'You crease me up. Do you?'

'What?'

'Love me?'

'Yes.'

'Is that an emphatic yes, or a maybe yes?'

'It's pretty emphatic.'

'Wow.' He stared thoughtfully into space.

'You've gone quiet.' Mouse guessed she'd gone too far.

'I have,' Joel agreed. 'I'm trying to work out how to handle the next bit.'

'There's a next bit?' The surprise showed in her voice.

'Look,' he said, 'we've been seeing each other for over three months, and from our first date that wasn't a date it was a business meeting meal, I've wanted to be with you, to see you every day, but you're here and I'm there. You have responsibilities here, I know you do, whereas I... I only have a mum who lives in London and has a better social life than me. I hear from her once a month or so, love her to bits, but we don't need to be in each other's pockets. I do, however, need to be in your pocket.'

Mouse closed her eyes.

'Am I boring you? You going to sleep?'

She opened her eyes. 'No, you're scaring me. I don't know how to respond, or what to say.'

'Say yes.'

'To what? You know I can't get to Manchester any more than I do already. This is my business; I need to be here. And then there's Nan. And Kat. Kat saved my life. Not only with finding me very near death across the road, but she took me in, nurtured me, made me well inside and out. I love these two women, I can't get to you physically, you know I can't.'

'But, my lovely girl,' Joel said, turning Mouse's head to kiss her properly on the lips, 'I can move to Eyam.'

The shop door opened and Luke looked up in surprise. Mouse and Joel walked in, and went through to Doris's office.

'Nan, we have news.' The smile on Mouse's face said so much.

Doris went cold. She was about to lose her granddaughter to some two bit place the other side of the Pennines, and...

'Joel's moving in with me.'

Joel walked around Doris's desk, placed a kiss on her cheek, and said, 'Is that okay?'

Doris stood and hugged him, then walked around and did the same to Mouse. 'Just for a dreadful moment there, I thought you were going to say you were moving to Manchester. Congratulations. Take care of her, Joel. If you don't, there will be consequences,' she added with a smile.

Joel reached across her desk and stole a Ferrero Rocher. 'Love these.'

Doris looked at her granddaughter. 'He'll do.'

They closed at four and everybody went home. It was cold, and Doris looked forward to a night in, and the delicious smell of the stew she had put in the slow cooker that morning. No television, she promised herself, just the book from the Co-op charity bookshelf, maybe a glass of wine, and a few nibbles for supper should she feel so inclined. The new fleece blanket Kat had bought her for Christmas to match the décor in her snug was incredibly warm, and she loved it. Her thoughts were good all the way home, and she tried to clear her mind of anything to do with Adam Armstrong until Sunday afternoon.

She opened her door, and the warmth met her. It had been a sensible decision to set the heating to come on for three, when even mildly warm daytime temperatures began to drop. She hung up her coat in the tiny closet, and, following the smell of the stew into the kitchen, switched on the kettle. She took down the mug proclaiming her to be the best nan ever, and dropped a teabag into it.

The stew was going nicely in the slow cooker, but she decided to wait a while before eating. She took the cup of tea, headed upstairs and showered, putting on her pyjamas and dressing gown, ready for her planned chill-out evening in the glorious warmth of her cottage.

It was only as she reached the bottom of her stairs that she saw her post, still in the letterbox and not on the floor. She pulled it through, pushed it into her dressing gown pocket and went back into the kitchen, carrying her now-empty cup.

She set up her tray for her evening meal and left it on the kitchen side, ready for when she was ready.

Although the snug was warmed by the radiator, Doris decided she needed the comfort of the fire, so she placed a match to the newspaper twists, and watched with satisfaction as it caught immediately. It had taken some learning, but she could now light the two downstairs fires with ease.

The lights were flashing on her answerphone, and she walked across the room to press the button. The first one made her heart flutter a little. It was from Rosie, one of the village residents, who went on to explain that the vet had three kittens in his care, kittens that had been found dumped in the village. She knew Doris wanted one, and the vet was waiting for her call.

Doris dialled it immediately, already trying to work out in her head how she could handle having a kitten when she was going away overnight on Sunday. It was irrelevant. The vet explained they were three grey calicos, virtually identical, and available from the following Wednesday. Two boys and a girl were the choices, and Doris said she would love the little girl. He said he needed to check they were all fine, give them their injections and flea treatment, so if she could call around on Wednesday, the little girl was hers, subject to payment of their expenses.

'Put my name against her, please,' she said, smiling broadly, and put down the receiver. She then pressed the button to listen to other messages. There was only one.

Hi, Mrs Lester. It's Keeley, Keeley Roy, in Hope. I wanted to speak with you away from Connection, but... erm... I guess you're there. I'll maybe ring later – no, I'll write something down and pop it through your letterbox when I do the school run. I'm taking Henry straight up to Pam's for the weekend. Sorry for waffling, my mind's a bit... Thank you, Mrs Lester.

Immediately Doris's mind went back eighteen months or so to her first meeting with Keeley, and the subsequent case they had been involved with. So much good had come out of that time for Keeley, and they had all enjoyed her company. Now it seemed she needed help.

Letter. Doris touched the envelope in her pocket, and took it out. It simply said Mrs Lester on the front, so she decided to read it before contacting Keeley.

She slid out the piece of paper, a lined sheet that had clearly come from a reporter's notebook, and smoothed it on her knee.

Dear Mrs Lester

A few weeks ago I met somebody. We have had a few dates, and now I have let him meet Henry. I've also told Pam about him; I don't want anybody to think I am hiding anything. Pam and Henry, by the way, get on wonderfully well, it is lovely to see the relationship between them, a true nanny for him and he loves her.

I saw my new friend a couple of days ago, and we went for a walk with Henry, just around the village, and called at the pub to have our evening meal. He insisted on paying, as he has done every time (this was our third time), but when he came back from the bar after placing our order, he jokingly said something about me paying, considering everything that I have.

I have never said anything about my wealth. I don't flaunt it in any way, although I did have to get a new car when mine fell to bits. Other than that we moved next door (as you expected). He doesn't know we once lived in the smaller house attached to this one. He certainly doesn't know I own this one.

It has unsettled me. I thought of you, Kat and Mouse and your kindness towards me, but I don't want to make this into a big thing. I need to know who he is, and was it just a throwaway remark, or does he actually know what I'm worth, and he'd like some of it.

Can you help me, Mrs Lester, please? I'm worried.

24

Doris put the letter to one side, and closed her eyes for a moment. She knew this would be very easy to check, once she had the details of the man from Keeley, but she also realised that Keeley was being very naïve if she thought that her newfound wealth was a secret.

A definite source of that knowledge would be her neighbours on the tiny street where she had lived for a few years. Possibly another source would be speculative – the other mums at school, who would see the change in her, a young mum who no longer needed to work, who had acquired an extremely wealthy nan for Henry in Pam Bird. And after all that was taken into account, the man might be totally genuine, and it had been a throwaway remark based on little bits of her life he had gleaned from seeing her for a few weeks.

But Doris wanted to make it an official investigation. Working off the books wasn't the Connection way. She would have to make that very clear to Keeley – a contract, or you're on your own.

. . .

The stew was delicious, made all the more so by splashes of Henderson's Relish added to it. A Sheffield lass might leave Henderson's land, but the relish went with her, Doris mused, as she cleared her plate. She loaded everything into the dishwasher, switched it on and headed back to the snug. This was going to be a different evening to the one she had planned, but an idea was forming in her head, and it was time to put it into action.

'Luke. You busy?'

'I'm knocking Man U out of the FA cup.'

'Who are they playing?'

'Accrington Stanley.'

'Can they be taken off the pitch because of a sudden snowfall?'

'They can. You need me?'

'How would you feel about taking on a small case of your own? I'll supervise, obviously, and any searches you make will be surface ones.'

'I'll pop over now.'

Doris laughed. 'No, you're fine. I'm about to ring our client for any further details, but we can deal with it Tuesday. I can fill you in while we're sat in the car Monday.'

'But if you're ringing the client, shouldn't I be there right from the start, see how you handle it from the get-go?'

'Luke, it's Friday night. You're eighteen. Haven't you got anything better to do than go visit a doddering seventy-year-old?'

'Yes, but it's still snowing on Man U and Accrington Stanley. And I'm going out tomorrow night, don't forget, on a date with two beautiful young women. I live life to the full. And you're not doddering, I've seen the video.'

'They're your young sisters. That's not normally classed as a date. Okay, you're on, if you're sure you've nothing better to do.'

'I haven't. See you in fifteen.'

She shook her head as they disconnected. Luke had been an inspired choice.

. . .

He found the cottage easily, and smiled as he saw the plaque outside telling everyone and the postman that it was Little Mouse Cottage.

The warmth enveloped him as he walked through the door, and he sniffed as he caught the aroma of the stew.

'You've had something delicious.'

'Too right I have. Want some?'

He laughed. 'No thanks, I won't take the food out of a doddering old lady's mouth just because it smells so wonderful. I'm good.'

'I didn't ask if you were good, I said do you want some?'

'Yes, please.'

'I'll bring you a tray. Go in here.'

He sank into an armchair, and looked around him. He knew that if ever he reached the stage of wanting a home of his own, this would be the home he would want. From little things he had picked up around the office, he gathered that she hadn't lived here long, but it certainly looked as though she had.

The radio was playing softly in the background, the fire crackling, and the book she had been reading at the office was lying on the sofa, waiting for her to return to it.

Doris pushed the door open with her bum, and carried in the tray. He half rose to help her, but she said, 'Sit. And don't knock my Hendo's off.'

He did as commanded, then picked up the bottle. 'My mate uses gallons of this stuff.'

'He from Sheffield?'

'He is originally. I've had it at his house lots of times.' Luke shook the relish onto his stew, and began to eat. Pausing for breath he looked at a smiling Doris. 'This is superb.'

'You've not eaten at home, then?'

'No, Mum doesn't finish till eight on a Friday, so it's take-away night. I've told the girls not to worry about me, I'll get something when I get in. Now I don't need to! This is an ace job I've got.'

Doris stood. 'I'm going to get a glass of wine. Can I get you anything?'

'Just a water, please, Mrs Lester.'

'Okay. And when you've finished I'll read you a letter that was hand-delivered here earlier. Once I've filled you in on the background, we'll ring the client.'

Doris read out the letter, and told Luke to listen. Then she handed it to him to read for himself.

'Okay, I read it out to you because sometimes you can read something, but when it's verbalised, it takes on a slightly different... nuance. I'm not sure if this one will, because Keeley's quite an open young woman, but this case should be straightforward and we'll use it as training. Kat will get involved if any kind of distress comes from it, but I'm not expecting that. I'm hoping we can say he's fine, and get on with your life. She deserves some happiness. Mouse won't be involved at all; her remit is to focus on recruitment issues. So, before I ring Keeley, let me fill you in on everything.'

It took half an hour. It transpired that the case had resulted in Doris buying the cottage from a lady who had committed suicide, after she had murdered the wife of the man Keeley Roy had been in love with.

Luke listened to the whole story, trying desperately to remember everything. It also seemed it was how Kat had met Carl; Carl had been the forensic accountant from the Fraud

Squad who had managed to retrieve lots of money that had been embezzled along the way.

When Doris finished, Luke sank back into the armchair digesting everything.

'Thoughts?'

'Plenty,' he said. 'I know it's all irrelevant really, when it's linked to this letter, but how bloody convenient that Alice committed suicide. And how could someone that frail – you said she had advanced cancer – manage to overpower and stab a fit youngish woman? I don't buy it.'

'Tessa did. But Alice died on Tessa's watch. It affected her a lot, and of course Alice had left a confession. Everything worked out for the best, and Keeley inherited almost everything. I felt like you, that things didn't add up. But I had two traumatised girls to deal with – there was a lot of blood when they found the body – and I know it stayed in Kat's mind for a long time. I'm not convinced Tessa believed everything, it was all pretty much handed on a plate to her, but she had a confession, and it was allowed to be recorded as such. No trial, nothing. But that's all in the past.'

'So you're going to ring Keeley... then what?'

'We'll go and see her. Get the details, get her signature on a contract. I'll explain to her that we only do pro-bono jobs for people who don't have money, as we did the first time we met her. I'm unclear why she doesn't want it on our books. Maybe she thinks we would pass the information on, or something. She couldn't be more wrong about that. Anyway, let's ring her, see what transpires. I'll put it on loudspeaker.'

She dialled the number, and they waited for the connection. 'Hello,' came through very quietly.

'Keeley, it's Doris Lester. Are you okay to talk? I left it until I guessed Henry would be in bed.'

'Oh, hello, Pam,' came a much brighter, false voice. 'I'm sorry but Henry's already asleep. I'll let him ring you tomorrow morning. Is about ten okay?'

'Okay, Keeley, I'm assuming your friend is with you. I'll ring tomorrow at ten. Night.' Doris disconnected.

'He's obviously with her, so shall we nip down to Hope and see if we can see anything? Or do you have to get home?'

Luke laughed. 'Are you kidding? This is my first surveillance opportunity, and you ask if I want to go home? Shall we go in my car, in case anyone recognises yours?'

'Thinking like a professional, Luke.' She checked her watch. 'Okay, it's twenty past eight. Let's say we sit there until ten, then call it a day. I don't really expect to see anything, but I need to let you experience how boring surveillance is. You'll understand the back story better, if you grasp the location. It's literally two minutes away.'

He stood. 'Come on, Superwoman. Teach me how to people watch.'

'I'll get the camera. Try not to get overenthusiastic and break it. We spent a lot of money getting one that can take night-time shots without bringing the flash into play.'

'Wow! The night gets better and better.'

'If he's there, I'm guessing he will have arrived in a car, so you'll get the chance to use the camera. With the car registration, we can find out who he is. I'll make us a flask of coffee, it's a cold night, and we can't really sit with the car heater on.'

Luke laughed. 'We're going in my car. It has got a heater, but it's tepid at best. At worst it's simply not there. Take that fleecy thing, we can wrap it around our legs.'

She made the coffee, changed back into her outdoor clothes from the comfortable pyjamas and dressing gown, and five minutes later they turned off the main road and on to the tiny cul-de-sac that harboured six houses, all down one side of the road. The other side, bereft of any street lighting, led onto an uneven stretch of grassland, that, had there been children living on the road other than Henry, would have probably constituted their football pitch. Luke pulled as far on to the grass verge as he could, then switched off his engine.

'There's no heat at all coming from that heater vent,' Doris grumbled. She opened up the fleece blanket and they wrapped it around their legs.

'Let's hope we don't have to jump out and chase this feller anywhere.'

'What?' Doris looked across at her young assistant.

'We've no chance of getting untangled from this blanket, have we. And we'll probably have a cup of coffee each.'

'We're here purely to watch,' Doris stressed. 'I don't do chases on Friday nights.'

'Why not?'

'It's bad for your health. At least, it's bad for my health. I've had two glasses of wine.'

They settled down and looked around them. Cars were parked on driveways, but on Keeley's driveway there was an Audi with a *Child on Board* sign in the back window, and a smart-looking Saab parked by the side of it.

'The Saab's his,' Doris said. 'It's a man thing.'

'Certainly is,' Luke agreed, staring at the car with awe. 'Bet his heater works.'

'Now might be a good time to try out that camera. Point it and shoot, and we'll see what happens.'

25

The camera performed admirably. They had a clear picture of the number plate, there was no flash to warn anyone else that they were taking pictures, and just before ten, the door opened and a couple came out. Keeley didn't stay long; it was clear she was cold from the way she stood with her arms wrapped around her midriff. The man kissed her, then got in his car and drove away. Keeley walked back inside the house, and the light in the downstairs room went off.

Luke packed away the camera, removed the cover from his knees, passed his half to Doris who enjoyed the benefits of double insulation, and Luke drove them back to Little Mouse Cottage.

Doris went through to the kitchen and put some milk on to boil. They had decided on cocoa to warm them up, and while she made that, Luke downloaded the pictures to Doris's laptop.

He had taken six of the man, and hoped Doris would know him, but when she returned with the drinks, she glanced at the screen and shook her head.

'Nobody I know. Let's see what his car registration can tell us. You want to ring your mum?'

'I've texted her. Told her I have a date with you. She sent a smiley face back, so I think she approves.'

Doris pulled the laptop towards her, then worked some magic that she hid from Luke. He gave up trying to follow what she was doing, choosing to wait for the results instead. His cocoa was delicious, the room was warm, his eyes…

'Bingo,' Doris said, and Luke's eyes shot open. He hoped she hadn't noticed he was falling asleep.

'You've found him?'

'I have if it's his car. His name is Vincent Sanders, has an address in Hathersage. We can't do anything further tonight, but I'll speak to Keeley in the morning then pop down to have a chat with her.'

'You're taking me?'

'It's Saturday. Do you want to come?'

'Of course. As long as I'm home for four, so I can get ready for my cinema date with my two beautiful sisters, I'm free. Shall I pick you up?'

'That would make more sense than me picking you up. Be here for about nine, and we'll have a bacon sandwich before we set off on our travels to Hope. How does that sound?'

'Brilliant.' He put down his empty cup and stood. 'I'll head off home. Don't go on that laptop again tonight. Kat and Mouse will find out if you do, and things could become very unpleasant.' He grinned at Doris. 'But my money's on you coming out on top.'

She waved as he drove off down the hill, then locked everything up. The laptop was tempting, but she decided it might all be wasted effort. She didn't have confirmation that Vincent Sanders was the man under discussion, just that the car parked out front of Keeley's house belonged to someone with that name.

She made sure the fire was safe, folded her fleece blanket and placed it at the end of the sofa, then climbed the stairs to bed. It had been fun; Luke was good company, and pretty bright too. She simply didn't want to think about the conversation on Tuesday morning, when she had to come clean about the Keeley situation.

The pizza box was in the middle of the bed; glasses of wine were on the bedside tables. Tessa leaned her head against Martin's chest, and sighed.

'Something wrong?' he asked. 'I've not fed you enough pizza?'

She laughed. 'No, I'm full to overflowing. I'm feeling a little frustrated by the lack of anything in this blessed case, and it never leaves my mind. Why was she killed, Martin? Why was Nicola Armstrong killed? Opportunist, out for a run and took their chance? Or do you think she'd upset somebody. Paula Ireland? But I'd stand up in court and swear Paula knew nothing of her husband's infidelity that day Hannah and I turned up to interview him.'

'You need a list.'

'A list? Of what?'

'I know I'm only a lowly pathologist and you're a top-flight Wonder Woman of a detective, but it seems to me that if you make a list of everybody who has even the slightest of connections to Nicola, then work your way through it eliminating people, sooner or later you'll end up with a winner. Or a loser, whichever way you look at it.'

'Done that.' She sounded gloomy.

'And?'

'I eliminated everybody.'

He kissed her. 'Is this your way of telling me to shut up?'

'Not at all. I suspect you might be right, actually. It's likely that there's somebody who needs to be on the list who we don't know about yet, or who we consider insignificant. And if this lead that Kat and Mouse think they've got does pan out, it could bring

Adam Armstrong into the frame, and top of the list.' Tessa sat up and leaned forward, snagging a small piece of pizza. 'Maybe this little piece might clear my brain.'

'I don't think it's a medical way of clearing the brain, but go for it. You working all day tomorrow?'

'I am. Did you want to do something?'

'I thought I'd take my favourite person out to lunch. I know I'm on call, and you're actually working, but maybe the gods will smile down on us. Can you keep your lunch break free?'

'Take that as yes, but if anything crops up to spoil our party, I'll ring or text you. That okay?'

'It is.' He kissed her once again. 'You want any more wine?'

She shook her head, swallowing the last of the piece of pizza. 'No thanks. Really I want to sleep. After tonight I'm taking no more medication. I feel drowsy all the time, and I need to make a list which will require a clear head. But now I'm nodding off.'

He got out of bed, moved the pizza box and the wine glasses, and climbed back into bed. Tessa was already asleep.

Hannah had spent half an hour on the phone with her mum and was also feeling tired. She couldn't use the excuse of medication; the entire blame lay with sleepless nights because of the case.

She was tired, Tessa was tired, and she didn't doubt that most of the team members were tired.

A glance at the clock told her it was nearly ten, and a smile crossed her face. Friday night, traditionally given over to night-clubbing and debauchery, and she was wondering if it was too early to go to bed.

She checked the door and windows were locked, and climbed the stairs. Her teeth had a full ten seconds of being brushed and she headed for the bedroom. She picked up her journal and filled in her day's activities, completed her mood tracker which was starting to look like a long row of little green squares showing she was feeling down, and filled in her notes section.

Hannah flicked back through the previous week's notes and saw the names Adam and Daniel Armstrong highlighted in yellow. She couldn't for the life of her remember why they were highlighted, but somewhere inside of her she knew that when they found them, alive or dead, everything would be resolved.

They were the shadowy figures in the background, there but not quite there, and she knew she would feel gutted if they proved to be dead. Daniel had been a little boy of five when he disappeared, and it would be a disaster if he had been killed by his mother.

Reading the journal Hannah was meticulous about keeping, had woken her up, and she pulled her eReader towards her. Following on from the visit to the library in Nicola's house, Hannah had decided to revisit the Sue Grafton books, albeit in electronic form, and this time they would be in the correct order. She was halfway through *A is for Alibi*, and completely engrossed.

Five minutes later, the eReader hit her on the nose as her body gave in to the exhaustion.

She slept.

Kat wasn't asleep. Carl wasn't asleep. Martha wasn't asleep. Kat and Carl weren't asleep as a direct result of Martha not being asleep.

Martha wanted to play. Kat and Carl didn't want to play. Not with Peppa Pig anyway. Their play ideas were completely different to Martha's.

'Mamamamamam,' Martha said, and Kat groaned. 'Why is she so wide awake? I'm going to teach her to say Dadadadadadad instead. I'm sure it's you she wants and not me.'

'Sorry, sweetheart,' Carl said, trying to keep his face straight. 'It's you. She wants her mummy. You want Peppa or George?'

Kat shuddered. 'Neither, thanks. You think I'd be a bad mother if I stuck her in her cot with two pigs and left her to play?'

'Yes.'

'Will you tell social services?'

'Certainly not. They wouldn't want to play with her at this time either.'

'Fair enough.' Kat picked up the happy smiling baby and put her in the cot. The two pigs sat at the bottom end. Kat checked the baby monitor was working, dimmed the light until only the faintest of glimmers showed, and crept out to find out what had happened to Carl.

'Traitor,' she hissed, when she found him already in bed. She joined him, and he pulled her close. 'Night, God bless, my love,' he whispered in her ear. 'Peace at last.'

'Mamamamamam,' echoed through the baby monitor.

Mouse was looking forward to a reasonably early night. Joel was on his way back to Manchester after they had agreed to make the following Saturday moving day. Joel would spend the week packing everything up, organising a tenant for his flat, which he assured her was no problem because his friend craved it, and they would start their new big adventure. Together.

For the first time, Mouse hadn't felt upset at being parted from him. Her feelings had really escalated over Christmas, and she knew they were making the good decisions at last.

He hadn't wanted to go, but a Saturday breakfast meeting meant he didn't really have a choice.

'I'll not come over during the week,' he had said as she leaned into the car to kiss him. 'There's a fair amount of stuff to pack up, and I don't usually get home until about eight. That's definitely going to stop when I move in here. I want as much time as possible with my girl.'

She had felt a warm glow as she watched his taillights all the way through the village, and briefly her mum and dad flashed into her mind. Would they have liked Joel? Would they have welcomed him into the family?

Nan seemed to get on well with him; it was time for everybody to get to know him better, including herself.

Mouse climbed back up the stairs to the flat, tidied everything away and ran a bath. She soaked for an hour, then ran to answer the phone. She didn't need to see his name.

'You're safe,' she breathed. 'I hate it when you leave me to drive all that way.'

'Hey, stop worrying. I'm a safe driver. You ready for bed now?'

'I am. I've been killing time waiting for you to ring. I'm tired, but it's a lovely sort of tiredness. Happy tired.'

'Me too. Sleep tight, my love. I'll call you tomorrow. Love you.'

'Love you too.'

She snuggled into her pillow, pulled up the duvet until it encased her shoulders, but the smile on her face prevented sleep. She knew Nan hadn't been surprised at their announcement; Nan always knew what was going on in her granddaughter's head. Thoughts cascaded through her brain, and she eventually gave in and pulled a book from the bedside table.

The bookmark fell on to the floor, so she spent some time searching through the book for where she had left it. She read for two minutes, the bookmark fell back to the floor and the book closed, once more hiding the page she had just read.

Mouse slept.

26

Saturday was surprisingly sunny. Lambs had been seen on the hillsides, and that day marked the beginning of the annual influx of lamb spotters.

Doris and Luke had enjoyed their bacon sandwiches, and then the phone call had been made to Keeley, with Luke able to hear both sides of the conversation on loudspeaker. It seemed the name had been correct, so Doris agreed that they would go down to formalise things, and take any other details Keeley might have about him.

The journey was short but this time they went in Doris's car. The heater worked.

Keeley welcomed them both with a smile. 'It's really good to see you again. I'm sorry Henry isn't here; Pam collected him early, she's taking him out for the day.'

'I'm sure he'll prefer being with his nan to seeing the two of us. Can I introduce Luke? He's our new operative, still in training, and will be looking after your case. We have to make it formal, as I explained, but there will only be minimal charges. I will be overseeing Luke's work, although I'm sure he'll find everything you need to know.'

Keeley turned to smile at Luke. 'Thank you, Luke. I feel a bit silly asking you to check him out, but I'm really starting to enjoy being with him, and I have such a lot of money... come through to the kitchen and I'll make us a tea, then we can talk.'

Luke took out the contract, passed it across to Keeley and showed where she needed to sign it, then slipped it back into his bag.

He pressed record, and asked Keeley to tell him as much as she knew about Vincent Sanders.

'He seems fairly well off,' she said, 'which is why I think I might be being silly, but I have to protect my money, I'm really only the custodian of it for Henry. The money came from Henry's father. Vince has a pretty swish car, a Saab, which I know wouldn't have been cheap, and he seems to enjoy nice holidays. He has a house in Hathersage, up by the church where Little John's grave is, and he was talking about having some work done on his kitchen, so I'm presuming he owns it. He's forty-one, enjoys football, golf, the usual manly things, but he's quite a gentle person. Oh, I don't know, maybe it was just a throwaway remark. He's seen my car, my home, he must realise I can afford them. Perhaps I'm reading more into what he said than I should.'

Luke spoke calmly. 'Let's find out for you. I hope he is kosher, that everything checks out, and you can get on with the rest of your life. Keep your money securely in your own bank, and not in anyone else's.' He smiled at Keeley. 'Does he have family?'

'No parents, but I understand he has a brother living down south, somewhere just outside of London. He has friends, particularly at the golf club, which again speaks of him having his own money. I'm being daft, aren't I?'

'No you're not. If I need anything else from you, it will be me ringing. Thank you for trusting me with it, Miss Roy.'

'It's Keeley. And thank you. I don't feel as though I'm wasting your time now I know you're taking me seriously. And thank you, Mrs Lester, for making me wake up about it. I seriously thought I could just have a little chat with you, you would reassure me, and that would be it. But you're right, I do need you to look into it properly, and I'm delighted to be Luke's guinea pig. Do you need a retainer?'

Doris shook her head. 'No, we know you're good for it. It will just be a bill at the end of the investigation. And it shouldn't take long. We should have answers for you by Wednesday or Thursday. Luke and I have something on for Sunday, Monday and potentially Tuesday, but we'll get around to yours as a priority after that. Is that okay?'

'Of course. There's no rush, I don't think Vince is going anywhere. I just need to know he's with me for the wrong reasons.'

Doris laughed. 'Keeley, I think you'll find he's with you because you're a very attractive young woman. Does he get on well with Henry?'

'He does. I think that's really why I need to know Vince's who he says he is, no side to him, because Henry looks forward to him coming, and it would be awful if things were to go pear-shaped sometime in the future, and Henry got hurt.'

Doris stood, and Luke switched off the recorder and put it in his pocket. He held out his hand, and Keeley shook it. 'It was good to meet you, Keeley. I'll be in touch mid-week.'

'Smart arse,' Doris said, once they were back in the car.

Luke grinned at her. 'What do you mean, elderly lady?'

'Shaking her hand. Good to meet you. You went all polite and nice on me. Just warn me if you're going to behave like an adult and not a teenager. I need time to adjust.'

She drove back up the hill to her cottage, and Luke handed her the recorder. 'We really going to leave this until next week?'

'We are. Let's concentrate on Adam and Danny now. Go and enjoy your evening with Imogen and...?'

'Kerryn.'

'Pretty names. Yes, as I said, enjoy your evening. Be here for around two tomorrow, and we'll set off for Cromer.'

'Will do. We going in yours?'

'We are. I like to be warm, and clunk and bang free.'

He shook his head, as if in despair at her cruel words directed at his car. He waved and headed down the hill.

Tessa and Hannah checked in at Chatsworth, took a walk to Nicola's murder site, and decided to go see Paula and Neil Ireland. Statements were required.

The primary murder site had been cleared of all tape, and looked as if nothing had ever happened there.

'Why,' Tessa said. 'Why would anybody come here at that time of night, on one of the worst nights of the winter? What prompted her to do that? She didn't have a dog to walk. I can understand her wanting to burn some of that alcohol off, but in the grounds of Chatsworth? And why would the killer be here? He or she had to have followed Nicola, because nobody would be in the grounds at that time of night, simply on a whim. Did they lure Nicola to that specific spot? Or could Nicola have died anywhere, because the killer was determined she would die that night. If that was the case, Nicola turning into the blackness of Chatsworth would have been an absolute bonus.'

They walked up the slight incline into the heart of the small group of trees and looked around. 'I'm just trying to get a feel of what went off here that night, now it is back to being how it was.'

'And what are you feeling?' Hannah asked.

'Nothing. It's such an ordinary place. It's not near anything, it's just a small copse of trees. Nicola, what the hell were you doing? Meeting someone? Who would you want to meet so desperately that you came out on the coldest night of the year, only to walk straight into a trap.'

'Adam and Danny, that's who she would want to meet,' Hannah said. 'But that doesn't mean the communication drawing her here came from either of them. It could be someone using their knowledge of her circumstances who contacted her, pretending to be Adam.'

Tessa looked at Hannah. 'Clever clogs. Why haven't I seen that?'

'You've been out of it for at least three days, boss. Don't beat yourself up about it. We've got there now, but we still don't have any answers. In fact, I'm starting to think Kat probably knows more than we do, and they're not even investigating this aspect of the damn case.'

They took a last look around the copse, and stood for a moment in front of the tree trunk that had supported the dead body of Nicola Armstrong. Everything looked so normal, and Tessa shivered. 'I don't usually feel for victims, because it would affect my ability to find their killers if I did, but there's something different about this one. Her anger issues caused her life to spiral out of control, but sometimes there's nothing you can do to change things. How do you stop being angry, murderously angry? Maybe if she had sought some help for her problems, but we've come across nothing that suggests she did. As a result, she ends up dead, covered in nearly a foot of snow. I want her to know I care, and I kind of understand.'

Hannah nodded. This was something rare for Tessa to open up about feelings and thoughts so in depth, as these were. 'Then let's get the bastard who did it. Maybe by Monday night we'll know who Adam Armstrong is now, and where he lives. Even knowing that may not give us any answers, because I still can't get my head around him coming back here. He's been missing for ten years, and it was through choice. Protection of his son, protection of himself, they were his primary reasons for going.

Why on earth would he consider a return visit to Baslow? He wouldn't. But what could potentially tempt him back? Nicola's death.'

'And who would benefit from Adam coming back? Debbie Carter? Simon Vicars? Maybe even Neil Ireland if he couldn't think of any other way of getting out of such a controlling and abusive relationship.' Tessa felt she was almost on the edge of a breakthrough… something they had just discussed that had gone as fleetingly as it had arrived, and she couldn't pinpoint it.

Tessa touched the tree trunk for a moment. 'Tell us what we're missing, Nicola. Why did you come here?'

Neil Ireland stared out of his hotel room window and wondered how to put things right. Then he wondered if he wanted to put things right.

He couldn't help but consider that Nicola's death had been fortuitous; her attacks, sometimes verbal, sometimes physical, had increased, and he had known they were reaching the end. He had been scared of what she would do when that end came.

Neil hadn't foreseen what his life would become, how it would change instantly. Paula had packed his bags within two hours of DI Marsden's visit. Since then he had been stuck in a bloody Travelodge, unable to work because of his arm, and ever hopeful Paula would ring and say come home.

His decision to not notify the police he no longer lived at home had been arrived at because he believed Paula would take pity on him and make the call.

The strange number on his phone screen baffled him. Nobody had rung for four days, and he almost didn't answer. He knew it couldn't be Paula.

'Yes,' he growled.

'DI Marsden, Mr Ireland. Where the bloody hell are you, and why didn't you keep Chesterfield or me notified?'

'Sorry... I didn't think,' he mumbled.

'Well, think now. I want you at Chesterfield headquarters within half an hour. They are aware you're heading in, and they will be waiting to take your statement.'

'Can't I give it to you?' he gasped. She sounded furious.

'Yes of course you can, but you're not. If you change address in future, Mr Ireland, I'm the first person on your list to be notified. When I say keep me informed of your whereabouts, I mean keep me informed of your whereabouts. Is that clear? In fact, it couldn't be any clearer, could it? I suggest you get in that car of yours, and get yourself to Chesterfield, before I issue a warrant for your arrest.'

'I'm leaving now.' He was miserable. It appeared he was destined to be bullied by women.

'Mr Ireland. Where are you? You're still not listening. Keep me informed, I said.'

He told her his location while trying to steer his arm, complete with cast, into the sleeve of his coat.

'Thank you,' she said. 'You're down to twenty-five minutes. And don't speed.'

He threw his phone down onto the bed, and forced his arm into the jacket.

'Bloody women,' he growled and ran out of the room, fully aware he needed fuel before he could even think about going to Chesterfield.

Twenty-two minutes.

27

The radio played Frank Sinatra, Dean Martin, Perry Como, and one or two other smooth singers, people he hadn't listened to before, and Luke found it strangely pleasant.

'You always listen to this sort of music?' he asked Doris.

'On long journeys, yes. Calms me, stops me wanting to kill everybody else on the road. It's also my mission in life to educate the younger generation – that's you – in what good lyrics are all about.'

'It's kinda nice.'

'Kinda nice? Listen to it. It's more than kinda nice. And when they sing, all these crooners, you feel as though they mean every word. Today's songs are all about the choreography that goes with them, the video that's made. They're not about the music.'

The car travelling by the side of them in the overtaking lane put on its indicators and pulled in front of them, almost slicing off the front wing of their car. Doris swerved slightly and drew in her breath.

'Idiot,' she muttered.

'The music's not working then.' Luke smiled.

'Oh it is. I'll leave you to imagine what my words would have been if I hadn't been listening to Frank Sinatra. Anyway, you've not told me about last night. 'Was it good?'

'Surprisingly so. It was a Disney movie so the girls were happy. I figured I could stick my kindle on a dim light and read, but I actually started to watch it, and enjoyed it. They're good kids, so I didn't have to keep telling them to behave. Imogen's a proper joker, really quick with clever comments, and she had us laughing all night. They... no, we... consumed vast amounts of popcorn and chocolate, and didn't get home until half past ten. I think it was a success.'

'Sounds it. I would have enjoyed that. I love the Disney movies. *Beauty and the Beast* is my all-time favourite, but *Maleficent* is one I never miss.'

They chatted about other films they had enjoyed, and the miles disappeared under the wheels. They stopped for a toilet break and a coffee, and reached their hotel in Cromer just before six.

Doris organised their early morning calls and they went for a walk down into the town. It was pretty much deserted; out of season, only locals ventured out into the cold of the evening.

They had a meal in a local steak restaurant, then headed back to the hotel for an early night, but not without taking a slight diversion to find the cul-de-sac they would need the following day. The house was in darkness, the road quiet, and they located a parking spot around the corner which would give them a view of the house, without it being obvious they were there to survey the occupants.

They had a substantial breakfast, not knowing when they would get the chance to eat next.

'Fab night,' Luke said. 'I spent a bit of time with the camera, read through the manual, and took a couple of practice shots which I've now deleted. I feel a bit more confident with it now.

Then I read for all of five minutes before I zonked out, and didn't wake till the alarm call. Were you okay?'

'I was. I watched the news, read for about an hour, then fell asleep. I woke early though. A couple of emails pinged through around six and woke me. It seems I can go to Florida for £599, room only, including a car.'

'You want to?' Luke spread marmalade on his toast.

Doris shrugged. 'Might do, but I didn't want the option at six this morning. It is cold here, a bit of sunshine would suit me okay, I think.'

She pulled the little basket of jams towards her, and selected apricot. 'Sounds nice,' she murmured. 'You ever been to Florida?'

He shook his head. 'No, bit too expensive.'

'I have. Mouse and I went just after she came to live with me. We hired a car, did the theme parks, acted like tourists. It was amazing. But I'd like to go back on my own, forget there are theme parks, and just see Florida. Perhaps go in a more upmarket hotel than the one on International Drive that Mouse and I booked, so I can rest as well as travel. Maybe when I retire...'

He laughed. 'How can you retire? You've only just become a partner.'

'I know.' She smiled. 'But sometimes I have to accept that I am seventy. I am fit, I'll grant that, but I feel as though I should be winding down, taking things a bit easier. Is your nan like that?'

'Nope. She's like you. Although I don't think she could have handled that Ewan bloke in quite the same way you did. It seems seventy is the new thirty. So don't start talking about winding down, you'd be miserable. You were the first one to jump at doing this job, the other two just followed on from what you said.'

Doris laughed. She was really starting to get to know their protégé. 'It was more a case of wanting to follow through on something I'd done the bulk of the work for.' She held up her hand to indicate she wanted a second cup of coffee, and the waiter obliged. 'Mouse has enough on her plate at the moment anyway, with Joel's move to Eyam next weekend, and we try to keep Kat away from any long-distance trips because of Martha. And don't tell them, but I enjoy stuff like this.'

Luke finished his toast, and checked his watch. 'It's nearly eight. I'll go up to my room and bring everything down, while you're finishing your coffee. Then I can help you.'

'Luke, I have one very tiny suitcase. But you can bring it down while you're getting yours if you want.' She handed him her room key. 'There's my suitcase and my coat, that's all. I brought my bag down with me. I'll see you in reception in five minutes.'

Doris paid the bill using the Connection credit card, and carefully folded the receipt before placing it in her bag as Luke returned. 'I once went to pick up some business cards, paid for them with the company card, and lost the receipt. I got the look from Kat. Know what I mean? The look that Kat excels at that says how could you be so stupid. I'm more careful now.'

'The look works then. I've not experienced it yet. Don't want to either.'

They climbed into the car, and Doris turned on the ignition before doing anything else. 'It's time the weather was warming up,' she grumbled.

Luke placed the camera in the central storage compartment, then reached onto the back seat and pulled the fleece blanket on to his knee. 'You wrap this around your legs when we stop,' he said.

The parking place they had chosen the previous evening was clear, and Doris pulled up, and set the handbrake.

'Okay, Luke. We could be here for some time. We need to be

comfortable, so sort your seat out for the best angle, but don't fall asleep because you're too comfy.'

'As if,' he said. 'I'm proper giddy about this. What if someone comes and asks us what we're doing? Like a policeman.'

'I have my licence with me. If it's the police, I'll show that, explain we're on surveillance in a possible divorce case, and we'd be obliged if they'd bugger off and leave us to do our job without alerting the bloke who's committing adultery. That explains away the camera as well. They'll go, they'll know we're not here to be burglars. And I've arranged that if anything like that does happen, they can ring Kat and she'll confirm what we're doing. If it's a nosy neighbour, and not a policeman, we'll say we're here to pick up a car for you, a second-hand car, and the present owner is meeting us here to hand it over. Then we'll wait fifteen minutes and move, in case they come back to check.'

Luke looked at his mentor with admiration. 'Crikey. You'd thought this through?'

'I had,' she said with a grin. 'Last year we went on surveillance in the Ewan Barker case, and had to sit with the bonnet up for ages because Mouse decided our cover story was we were waiting for a rescue service to come and get us going again. A neighbour did ask us, and we told him the story which he believed, so I worked ours out, roped Kat in to confirm it, and we don't have to sit with the bonnet up, obscuring our view.'

Doris lowered her seat back slightly, and spread the blanket across her knees, guiding the other half over the gear stick. 'Here, tuck this around you. It will soon start to get cold.'

Luke followed instructions and lifted the camera onto his knee. He took it out of its case, quickly set the dials he now felt comfortable changing, and they settled in to wait.

They had an excellent view of the house, and Luke snapped three people as they left their homes on the cul-de-sac and went about their business. It was a quiet morning in a very quiet area. Despite Doris's careful planning, nobody approached them, and they laughingly decided neighbourhood watch didn't have many members in the cul-de-sac and surrounding streets.

Doris produced bottles of water and fibre bars from the depths of her handbag, and they munched away at them, more out of boredom than hunger. Kat checked in with them, saying everything was okay in Eyam, and Mouse had emptied her car, laid down the seats and shot off to IKEA, muttering things that sounded suspiciously like wardrobe and chest of drawers.

The sun came out and afforded them some warmth, but it disappeared late afternoon, and it really became quite cold.

Doris sighed. 'We'll stay here until six…'

Luke nudged her. 'Look.'

Coming out of the end of the alleyway that ran down the side of the house they were watching, was a man. A man in a red and white football shirt, and tugging a black wheelie bin behind him.

Luke took photographs.

The man walked back down the alleyway and returned a minute later with another black bin. He repeated the process, and a third bin joined the other two. The first bin he had brought out had a large Manchester United sticker on the front of it. The other two had simple house numbers.

Luke clicked photo after photo until the man disappeared and didn't reappear. Neither of them had spoken; in fact neither of them felt as though they had breathed.

'Thank the Lord for a council that collects bins in this area on a Tuesday,' Doris whispered.

Luke's hand was trembling. 'That was brill, Mrs Lester. Result! The pictures are close-ups and distance. Surely we can get an ID from these.'

'Let's hope so.' Doris removed the fleece from her knees and legs, and Luke threw it onto the back seat. 'Let's go before he comes out again and clocks us, or we get arrested. Fancy fish and chips? Out of newspaper?'

'I could be persuaded,' he said, feeling on such a high he wasn't convinced he could eat anything.

He carefully packed away the precious camera, and put it in the central compartment. All this, he thought, and fish and chips. Brilliant day.

28

Despite the lateness of their arrival home the previous night, Tuesday saw Luke and Doris in the office before Kat and Mouse. Doris downloaded the pictures and collated them all into one file, which she sent to the other three computers.

Mouse arrived carrying a travel cup full of coffee, and looking bleary-eyed. 'Good grief, you two are early. Couldn't you sleep?'

'We need to work through these photos, make our report to Debbie, and get Tessa here to show her. But Debbie has to come first.'

'You think it's him?'

'Pretty sure. He's older, his hair has a touch of grey, but he's still a good-looking man. If pushed, I'd say I'm ninety-five per cent sure. Debbie will be the ultimate yay or nay, of course, because she actually knew the man, whereas we only know the photographs. I've set up the file, take a look and see what you think,' Doris added.

'I'll have this coffee first,' Mouse said. 'I was still up at midnight putting a wardrobe together. I had a good look at what space I could free up for Joel's clothes, and it was clear the answer was none. I've picked up a wardrobe and a chest of drawers, and I haven't even started on the drawers yet. I get a degree in engineering when I've finished, I hope.'

'We need a quick meeting anyway, just to fill you in on our Friday night, Saturday morning, and all-day Monday activities. Luke and I have had a busy weekend. The other issue wasn't major, so I didn't trouble either of you with it, and Luke's handling it anyway.'

Luke smiled, and held up a thumb.

'The other issue?'

'I'll tell everything when Kat gets here. No point going over it all twice. You need help with the chest of drawers?'

'I'm currently considering handing Joel the box it comes in, and wishing him good luck with it. The wardrobe was bad enough, but I'm dreading this one.'

'Have you bought identical ones to those you bought when you moved in here?'

'Yes.' It was definitely a grumpy reply.

'And didn't you say all this when you put yours together?'

'Yes.'

'So it's not in my imagination that you said never again will I buy IKEA furniture?'

'No.'

Luke couldn't stand it any longer. 'Beth, when I've finished work today I'll put the chest of drawers together for you.'

She looked at him in shock. 'You're volunteering? Have you ever put furniture together before?'

'Mum's slowly replacing everything in our house with IKEA stuff. Guess who puts it all together.'

'Then you're on. Thank you so much. My god, where did we find him, Nan?'

'In the Co-op.'

. . .

Kat arrived ten minutes later and was immediately organising her seating arrangements for the meeting. She had been itching to ring Doris the previous night, but realised it would be a late return for them so abandoned the idea.

'Okay, let's crack on,' Doris said, once they were finally seated with drinks in front of them. Their laptops were open, and files clicked. They went through all the photos, then repeated the action.

Kat was the first to comment.

'It's him. He may have aged by ten years, but the basic head shape doesn't change, the nose doesn't change, even the overall shape of the man hasn't really changed. I'd place a bet on this being Adam Armstrong.'

Doris nodded. 'I think so too. Let me fill you in on the day, so that you're aware of how hard we worked to get these pictures.'

Luke looked at her and raised his eyebrows. Hard work?

'We got up at seven and packed our suitcases, then headed down for the biggest breakfast we could manage, because we knew it could be some time before we saw a proper meal again.'

Luke played an imaginary violin. Doris reined in the laughter.

'We finished breakfast, and then drove down to the site we had chosen the night before, while we were out having our steak meal.'

'So far,' Mouse said, 'you've had a steak meal and a massive breakfast. Is that right?'

'Sort of. We stopped on the way down for tea and a piece of apple pie at a services. Anyway, we parked up, decided on our story if either the police or a nosy neighbour turned up, and then made ourselves comfortable. Kat, the blanket you bought me for Christmas is wonderful. We were really quite warm under that. I'd taken some biscuit things to nibble on, so we were fine.'

'Oh good.'

'Mouse, was that a touch of sarcasm?'

'No, Nan, of course not.'

'Right. Back to our story. After our steak meal the previous night, I went straight to sleep, but Luke, bless his heart, stayed up and read the instruction manual for our swish new camera, so he was fully familiar with everything it could do.'

'Oh, bless his heart…'

'Was that a second touch of sarcasm, Mouse?'

'No, Nan. It is starting to sound as if you two had a lovely holiday.'

Doris ignored the comment. 'So… we sat there, Luke poised to use the camera. For practice, he took photos of people who live on the cul-de-sac leaving for work, but nothing happened at the house we wanted to show signs of life. Nobody challenged us, and we were in a perfect place for seeing it.

'It got to around five, and I'd just said we'll give it until six, when there was movement. Luke put on his photographer head, and took the first picture that's on your file. You get a really clear picture of the Manchester United shirt on that one and the next one, which is a close up of the same shot. I actually think that second picture is the best one we have of the face in a full forward-facing shot. That is the one that tells me it is Adam Armstrong.

'There are, as you have seen, twenty-four pictures of him and his actions over about three minutes; the last three pictures are the practice shots Luke took in the early morning. I don't know who they are, those people, but the first one came out of the house next door to Adam. Adam brought out the wheelie bins of his neighbours, as you can see by the numbers on the bins. The Man U stickered bin is his own, I'm presuming, as it was the first one he brought out.'

She sat back in her chair. 'Well?'

'Fantastic. Absolutely fantastic. And all this from lucky guess-work. We had no proof that he was anywhere near there, not even proof that he was alive. In fact, without that throwaway remark from Debbie about the old school photo, we would never in a million years have been able to come up with this.' Kat scrolled through the pictures again.

'So, now we have a dilemma.' Mouse was thinking things through in her usual careful way. 'We have a client who has asked us to find Adam Armstrong. We believe we have done that, although we could really use some proof other than a photograph. Our priority is to create our report, and invite her in to look at the photographs. We can either email her the file or print them off for her. But then we come to the other part.' She paused. 'It's easier fitting wardrobes together than juggling this overload of information. Right, the next step is Tessa. Adam Armstrong is a person of interest in the Nicola Armstrong murder. And if he killed Nicola, then he also killed Olivia, because, according to Tessa, she was killed because she saw who killed Nicola.'

Kat interrupted. 'But that's where it stops making sense that he's a person of interest. Olivia was killed because she knew the person who killed Nicola. She knew that person enough to have their phone number in her phone, even if it was just as a nickname. I'm not buying into this at all. And I'm sure Tessa will have realised all of that. She does need to know he's alive anyway, so she's not always in the is-he-dead/is-he-alive mode all the time. We'll have to make it very clear to Debbie that she can't contact him until the police have ruled him out of their investigation – or in it.'

Mouse looked at her nan and Luke. 'Cracking job, you two. If you give me all your expenses, I'll do a final bill for Debbie, and we'll get her in to look at these pictures for her confirmation of his identity. We'll make two copies, one for her and one for Simon.'

Doris went in her folder and produced a list of the expenses, and all the relevant receipts.

Mouse glanced down them.

'Seems you forgot to mention the fish and chips and the drinks for two. Oh, and the apple pie and tea on the return journey.'

'We didn't get around to telling you that when I was relating the story, because you were being sarcastic towards us, and you wanted to talk about other things anyway. You can't have surveillance done on a shoestring you know. And besides, Debbie Carter will be footing the bill for all of this. I think we earned this.' Doris patted the sheet of paper. 'I told you it was hard work.'

Kat and Mouse looked at each other, and could hold the laughter in no longer. 'You and Luke are perfect,' Kat said. 'You make such a good team. You even eat the same sort of food, for heaven's sake. Well done, Luke, on these pictures. Taken from inside a vehicle, and having to rely on the camera to get the close shots... you did really well. And thank you for looking after our nan, and keeping her in check.

'On our part, this case is closed, once we get confirmation from Debbie that this is her brother-in-law. It's all we've been asked to do, to find him. I think we have to withhold the address until Tessa has done her worst with it, and we're going to have to say this to Debbie. That means she will run the risk of losing him again if he decides he still wants nothing to do with this part of the world, because once the police have paid him a visit, he may up sticks anyway.'

'And so we're clear,' Mouse followed on, 'I can find no trace of a will from Nicola, but there may be one that the police know about. However, on the deeds the house is jointly owned by Adam and Nicola Armstrong. At some point he will have to deal with that.'

'Okay, who's going to ring Debbie and tell her we have news?' Doris asked.

'Shall I do it? She knows me best,' Kat responded, still trying to stifle the laughter.

'Yes, good idea, but make it tomorrow. Let's give Tessa a ring and ask her to call in today.' Doris sounded troubled, the frivolity slipping away fast. 'I feel uneasy that we have this knowledge, and it's our duty to inform her. It's important we maintain this relationship we have with Tessa and Hannah, and withholding stuff, even if it's for a day, isn't the right thing to do. Do you all agree?'

Kat and Mouse nodded in agreement, and Doris turned to Luke. 'Luke?'

'Erm, yes...'

'Luke, you've earned the right to this vote. You've done well this weekend, really well, and the way you conduct yourself is a credit to you. Or your mum. I suspect the latter,' Doris finished with a laugh.

Luke blushed.

'Okay, let's see if Tessa is free to call in this afternoon, and then we've got other things to tell you. In future, Luke and I will be known as the two-case kids, because we are perfectly capable of handling two cases at any one time.' She high-fived Luke, and he grinned.

'Sure are, Mrs Lester, sure are.'

29

'A second case? Sounds intriguing. Where did we get this from?' Mouse closed down her laptop and pushed it to one side. 'Is it second cup of coffee time?'

Luke stood. 'I'll do them.' He took the three mugs and Mouse's large travel mug into the kitchen and rinsed them. He could hear the muted tones of the others, and heard Doris say she wouldn't discuss anything without Luke being there, it was his baby.

He carried the mugs back through to Kat's office, and poured out the freshly brewed coffee. His ladies didn't seem able to function properly without copious amounts of caffeine. He handed them out, and looked at Kat. She nodded. He took out the ginger biscuit box and placed it centrally so they could all reach it.

'So? Stop prevaricating, you two. What have we missed?' Kat dunked her ginger biscuit while she waited for an answer.

Doris thought for a moment. 'It started Friday evening, after I'd gone home from here. I checked my answerphone and I had a call about…' her memory kicked in, 'a kitten!'

'We have a case involving a kitten?'

'No, silly. That was my first message, and I just realised I hadn't given you my news. Tomorrow I go to collect my new lodger, a tiny kitten. It's a little girl, so I might be a bit distracted for a few days, trying to come up with a suitable name for her. I've been putting the word out for a while, letting people know I wanted one, and the vet had three taken to him that had been abandoned. Two males and a female. I rang him, and he's going to flea and worm her, give her any injections she needs, and I can collect her tomorrow.'

'Fab.' Kat's eyes lit up. 'I love cats, as you know. You'll need a carrier to go and get her, so if you want me to bring mine in tomorrow, I can.'

'I've bought everything else, didn't think for a minute about actually transporting her home. Thank you, Kat. Okay, Mouse, you can close your mouth now.'

Mouse shook her head. 'Nan, you never cease to amaze me. So, that was your first voicemail.'

'Oh yes. The second one was from Keeley.'

'Keeley Roy?' Kat looked concerned.

'The one and only. She didn't really say much on the message, because I don't think she knew what to say. In the end she said she would write it down and pop the note through my letterbox. This is it.'

Doris dipped once more into her folder and produced Keeley's letter. She waited until Kat and Mouse had read it, and then explained she had rung Luke to see if he would like to take on the case under her supervision.

'I suspect Keeley is a little scared of having feelings for this chap, and wants it all to be perfect. As perfect as it was with Henry's daddy. Anyway, as a result of asking Luke, he stopped Man U being knocked out of the FA cup by Accrington Stanley and headed over to mine. But now comes the scary bit. We decided to go down to Keeley's as it's only two minutes away, and see if the chap was there. We went in Luke's car.' She paused dramatically, and with considerable acting skills, wiped her fevered brow with one hand.

'Oy!' Luke said.

'It was an experience. It doesn't have a heater. It clunks.'

'It does have a heater,' he said with no small degree of indignation. 'It just doesn't work. And the clunks are only when it goes around corners.'

'Anyway,' Doris continued, ignoring her co-conspirator, 'we took my new blanket and a flask of coffee, and Luke took the camera without really knowing how it worked, but we managed. We sat there for an hour, that's all, and we did see a car, a Saab of impressive proportions, parked on Keeley's drive, behind her car. She's driving a very smart Audi now, by the way. We photographed the Saab, and I accidentally found myself on the DVLA thing later, and managed to get his name.'

'Really,' Mouse laughed.

'Anyway, before I did that, the man went home. Keeley came out with him, kissed him and he went. We didn't follow him; I wasn't sure if Luke's car was up to it.'

'Oy!' Luke repeated.

'Nan,' Mouse laughed, 'stop digging that hole.'

'Sorry, Luke, it's a lovely car. The next day, on Saturday morning, Luke and I went to see Keeley. I'd filled Luke in on the whole situation, told him everything that had happened, so he was au fait with it all. He was a star. Looked very smart, incredibly polite and reassuring, and the upshot of it was that instead of the informal chat she wanted, I signed her to a contract. I've asked Luke to take it on, and I'll supervise everything, but it's a little case that will take hardly any research, and I'm pretty sure will have a good end result for Keeley. She's so afraid of doing anything wrong with this money. She doesn't see it as being hers, it's more about Henry. It's his inheritance. He'll be a very wealthy young man when he inherits this lot, I can tell you.'

'Does he have a name, this chap?' Kat asked.

'Yes, it's Vincent Sanders. He apparently lives in Hathersage, near that church where Little John's grave is. You know, the one with the long name.'

'St Michael and All Angels? Very nice. It's a lovely area to live in.' Kat looked at Luke. 'Bear that in mind. He'd have to have money to live there.'

Luke nodded. 'Thank you, I will. I'm making a start after we've finished here.'

'So is that it, can we ring Tessa now? And congratulations, you two. A productive weekend all round. All I did was panic I had no room for Joel's clothes, watch television, and try to plan my bedroom so that I could accommodate extra furniture. Nothing clever at all.' Mouse sounded a little disgruntled.

'We'll sort it all tonight,' Luke assured her. Those drawers won't take long, and we can get it exactly how you want it. Stop beating yourself up just because you're a mere woman.' He ducked as the pen that had been lying next to Kat came flying across the room.

'Get out,' she yelled as he escaped, laughing. 'And remember who the black belts are in this office.'

Tessa agreed to come over within the hour, and Luke began work on the investigation into Vincent Sanders.

He'd already spoken at length with Doris about the case, before Kat and Mouse had arrived at the office. He delved into all the sites that could give him information, and made notes on random pieces of paper that would eventually form a cohesive report that they could take to Keeley Roy, hopefully giving her peace of mind.

It seemed that Vincent Sanders was okay. He had three points on his driving licence for speeding, but Luke reckoned that minor infringement didn't mean he was after Keeley's money. And who wouldn't have three speeding points with a Saab? He could find nothing else. As Kat had said, his house was in a lovely area, and it was jointly owned by…

'Whoa, Luke,' he said softly to himself. 'Who is Felicia Ann Sanders?'

He sat back in his chair, and allowed his thoughts to settle. She could be a wife, a daughter, a sister, even a mother. The last three would be additional information to the case, the first one would make it all worthwhile.

He stood to go and talk to Doris, but was halted by the buzz of the door entry system, and he clicked to allow Tessa and Hannah through.

'It's definitely cosy in here with six of us,' Tessa said. 'Hi, everybody. You have news for me?'

'We hope so.' Mouse looked to Doris. 'Nan, will you take over, this is all down to you and Luke.'

Doris dipped her head in acknowledgement, and Luke spaced out the prints of the photographs they had taken of the man with the wheelie bins.

'You don't need to know all the ins and outs, but mainly by a stroke of luck we ended up sitting at the end of a cul-de-sac in Cromer, checking out a property there. We had been given – no, we acquired – a photograph of a group of seventeen-year-olds at Chester Zoo on a school outing. All the names had been recorded on the back, and they were all friends. Debbie Carter and Nicola Armstrong were on the picture, as was Adam. We began investigating everybody, looking for anything that would link Adam and his escape plan to any of his prior friends. It was a long shot, we knew that, but one of the friends was Ethan King. His business, and it's a massive one, is KingPress. We initially thought it was handy to have a friend in the printing business if you needed a new identity, but it was about so much more than that.'

Tessa and Hannah nodded to show they were listening, but said nothing. They knew the thoroughness with which these women conducted their investigations. They wouldn't need to ask questions; it would be spelled out for them.

'Ethan King has properties, twenty-six of them, and all in Cromer. We marked them on a map,' Doris was being suitably evasive about methods they had used to gain the information, 'and the one that took longer to track down than the others we figured could be a bolthole for someone wanting to stay under the radar. I must stress this was all supposition, and it was only logic really that got us to this point. Luke?'

He looked startled. Why would Doris bring him into it? He felt the colour rise into his cheeks.

'We, Mrs Lester and I, drove to Cromer on Sunday, and on Monday morning, yesterday, parked at the end of a cul-de-sac where we had a perfect view of the house we were interested in.'

He pointed out the various photos that had been their reward for a full day of observing very little, until the last quarter of an hour had justified their wait.

'Has your client seen these?' Tessa asked. Speaking caused the dryness in her throat to lead to a bout of violent coughing, and Hannah reached across and touched her hand.

'You want some water, boss?'

Tessa nodded. 'Thanks, Hannah.'

Kat stood and took a bottle out of the small fridge. 'Isn't it time you saw a doctor?'

'Saw one this morning,' Tessa confirmed. 'I'm on antibiotics, so I should be feeling better in a couple of days, he said. I hope so, it's exhausting, all this coughing. So where were we. Sorry I interrupted, Luke. Has your client positively identified him?'

Mouse joined in. 'No. We thought it best to let you know first, because we have to give her the address, it's what she's paid for. I think she'll get to Cromer as fast as she can, possibly even today, although we haven't said anything yet so can delay that until tomorrow.'

Doris stood. 'Let me get my map. I'll show you what you will be up against when you go to interview him.'

Doris returned with the colourful map, and spread it on the table. She tapped with her index finger.

'This is his house, and this,' she traced the blue marker pen, 'is his escape route. You'll need to position officers before you knock at the door, because he'll have CCTV everywhere. He'll know it's strangers knocking. It was his job when he lived with Nicola. This,' again Doris pointed, 'is where he'll go when he realises who you are. This alleyway here is where he dragged the wheelie bins, and links to his back garden escape. However, further delving showed us this tenant here in the adjoining semi has been in the house slightly longer than Adam, and this tenant here came just after Adam. He is flanked on both sides, I believe, by protection. You have to work on that assumption anyway. I think they've been put there to help him should Nicola ever turn up. The additional two bins he brought out show the numbers of these two houses. The Man U bin is his own.'

Tessa pulled the map towards her, and stared at it intently.

Hannah leaned closer. 'We can take two cars down, have two lads here,' she pointed to the back garden, 'two here at the front, and we'll knock at the door.'

'I agree. We'll set off early tomorrow morning. Can you hold off telling your client until tomorrow?'

'We can,' Mouse agreed. 'But that's a definite to tell her. Tomorrow. Debbie and Simon are paying us, so it's our contractual duty to type the report as soon as possible, to present to them. End of job. It will take me to the end of today though,' Mouse added with a smile, 'so I'll ask her to call in here tomorrow morning. At that point she will have that address. I don't know what will happen after that, because it will be signed off by us.'

Tessa leaned across the table and once more pulled the photographs towards her. 'He's not changed much in the ten years he's been missing, has he. Is it okay if I take these pictures? I'd like to run them through facial recognition, to double-check.'

'That's fine,' Kat said. 'We have another set printed for Debbie and Simon. We also have it as a file, if you want to send it now so that they can start work on it immediately.'

Luke looked at her with something approaching awe. Sometimes she made statements and got all the right technical words in the right order. She seriously looked as though she knew what she was talking about.

'Thanks, Kat,' Tessa said. 'Can you send it to my phone, please?'

Kat looked at Luke, and he said, 'I'll do it, no problem.'

He went out to reception, and did as Tessa asked before returning to the meeting. Kat mouthed *thank you* at him.

Tessa forwarded the file, and suddenly the tension, the general work feeling, left the room. Hannah gathered up the photographs and Kat handed her an envelope to put them in, before standing and waving the coffee pot around. Everyone said yes, and the chat turned to more general issues.

. . .

It was Hannah who let slip about Martin, and it was Tessa who blushed.

'You kept quiet about that!' Mouse joked. 'How serious is it?'

'I like him,' Tessa admitted.

'That serious? Wow.'

'I had to fight Hannah off though.'

Hannah smiled. 'No you didn't, you really didn't. I let you have him.' Her thoughts, hidden deep inside for so long, weren't the same as her words.

'Mrs Lester, you have a minute?'

'I do, Luke. I'm just checking online how to litter train a kitten. Is yours more important than that?'

'Maybe, maybe not.' He smiled.

'Sit down. You have a problem?'

'I need your thoughts. I've got Vincent's address, confirmed he is the owner of the car, confirmed little bits of his life then found out he's joint owner of his house. His co-owner is Felicia Anne Sanders. If that's his wife, we need to tell Keeley. But I don't just want to put down the bare facts, because it might not be a wife, it could be a sister, a daughter... you know what I mean.'

'I do, and well done on finding that out. You have to dig for that?'

He shrugged. 'A little.'

'Right. No more digging, leave this bit with me. Prepare the rest of your report for Keeley, we'll add the outcome of my search later.'

Luke thanked her and went back to his desk. He stared across the road, watching with a smile as two drivers jostled for the same parking place. Eyam was starting to get busy, each day seemed to have an increase in traffic.

He pulled all the various pieces of paper together, sorted them into an order that made sense, and opened up a file to collate everything.

His mind started to drift; he had liked Keeley, and guessed if Felicia proved to be a wife, Keeley would be pretty upset about it. It had begun as an investigation to protect her money, but it had changed. Vince appeared to be quite well off; nice car, nice house, everything in order. And a woman to account for.

Kat's light on his desk glowed, and he popped his head around her door. 'You want something?'

'Yes, I've just spoken to Debbie and she's coming in at ten tomorrow morning. I need you to put it in the appointments please, Luke. How's it going with Keeley's problem?'

'It's fine, but I'm a bit concerned I might have found a wife. He's co-owner of his house with a Felicia Anne Sanders. Mrs Lester is currently investigating her.'

'Oh no, let's hope not. I think Keeley must be pretty keen on him to go to the trouble of having him checked out. Have you enjoyed the research into this?'

'Are you kidding?' he asked. 'I've loved it. I wasn't sure about researching the woman, so I think Mrs Lester was a bit concerned it would have to go deep to find the information. She's a very clever woman, isn't she?'

'I think she's the smartest woman I know. You'll learn such a lot from her, and to be honest we struggle to remember she is getting on in years. She's so active, mentally and physically. And you seem to hit it off remarkably well considering there's more than fifty years between you.'

'That's because she's like my nan. She's a smart old bird as well. Although she's not a black belt in anything unless it's knitting.'

He closed the door, smiling at the thought of his nan. She was starting to become a little bent, but her sharp wit hadn't lessened by one iota. It seemed to him that the older you got, the more you could get away with, particularly with what was said.

He entered Debbie's ten o'clock visit into the appointments file, then wrote it into the diary. Continuing with Keeley's report took up the next fifteen minutes of his time, and then Doris's light lit up.

'Mrs Lester. You want me?'

'They are married. I can find no evidence of a divorce, although they could have just split up and never bothered. Whatever has happened, Keeley needs to know. We'll take an extra day to try to get something one way or the other, so can you ring Keeley and book us in for Thursday afternoon about one, please?'

'I will. Can I make a suggestion?'

'Of course.' She couldn't help but smile at him.

'I'd like to go and park near his house in the morning, before the day properly begins, and see if there's any sign of a woman. I'll take the camera, and if there's any photos to be had, I'll get them. I'll wait until about one, if that's okay, then give up and come back here.'

'I think that's really sensible. Kat and Mouse can handle things here for a morning, I'll be getting Belle.'

'You're calling your kitten Belle? That's really pretty. I'd forgotten you wouldn't be here. Are you sure it will be okay?'

'Luke, it's an excellent idea. There'll be no work done here tomorrow, the girls will sit and chat and laugh all morning. And while I'm thinking about it, go and see if Mouse wants to start building furniture. You two might as well be getting on with that. Have you finished Keeley's report?'

'Apart from the random woman, yes. You want to see it?'

'Is it accurate?'

'Certainly is.'

'Then no, I'll give it a quick read through when we have as many facts as we can get. Leave it for now, I'm sure it's fine.'

He saluted. 'I'll let you know if Beth and I are going. She may be busy.'

Mouse was playing solitaire.

. . .

Cardboard was everywhere, white panels likewise. Luke studied the instructions, and set to work. It didn't take long to finish the basic frame, and once that was done, Mouse supplied him with a glass of shandy and the offer of cheese on toast.

'Your nan said if I got the offer of cheese on toast to take it, because you never have anything else in.'

'True story,' Mouse said, not the slightest bit concerned by this slur on her character. 'You want some?'

'Yes, please. I'll just text Mum and let her know I'm dining out, then they'll not wait for me.'

The cheese and toast went down very well, and they talked about Doris.

'It was like talking to a friend,' he said. 'We sat in that car all day Monday and chatted, and laughed. She's not old-fashioned, knows exactly what I'm talking about when I spout my rubbish, and she's funny, very dry sense of humour.'

'In her younger days she was a civil servant. Very hush hush, she won't talk about it but I know she left home to work wherever she worked. She was hog-tied by the Official Secrets Act, and to my knowledge has never said a word about what she did. She married another civil servant, agent I suppose, and they had my mum. She was their only child, but then she ended up with me because I lost my parents. Nan isn't a secretive person, except about what she and my granddad worked on. I adore her, and can't bear to think of a future without her. I suppose everybody starts to think about their mortality when they reach their allotted three score years and ten, but I hate it when she talks about not being here one day.'

Luke carried his plate and glass to the sink, and returned to remaining piles of whiteboards. 'Where is this going to go?'

Mouse looked around. 'I think next to the other one. If I leave my full wardrobe where it is, shuffle my chest of drawers up a couple of feet and then put this one next to it, I'm pretty sure the other wardrobe, the empty one, will fit in at the side of it. It'll look quite smart if I have a complete wall of furniture.'

'You want to get me a tape measure before we start second guessing measurements?'

'Haven't got one. Let's move the chests of drawers into position, and then we'll have a better idea.'

Apart from the new chest having no assembled drawers, everything fitted perfectly. There was a whole two inches to spare.

Luke dropped back to the floor and began to stick and screw drawers together, and half an hour later it was complete.

'It looks absolutely lovely,' Mouse said. 'Thank you so much, Luke. It took hours to build the damn wardrobe, I felt suicidal by the end.'

'Glad to help. It wouldn't have been a fun weekend if you'd had to be building furniture before Joel could unpack, would it. I'll head off home now. Thank you for my food. I'll call at Mrs Lester's to get the camera, I've an early start tomorrow, and I don't think she'll appreciate being woken at six just for that.'

Mouse laughed. 'She'll be awake at six tomorrow anyway, preparing for the kitten. She's really giddy about it. She went home with Kat tonight to make sure she'd got the carrier to fetch it from the vets.'

He sighed. 'And it's yet another female...'

Tessa and Hannah, along with their handpicked team of four, left before dawn and reached Cromer by half past eight. Tessa, in the lead car, drove to the spot Doris had advised, and parked, indicating to the following car that the driver should pass her, and park up fifty yards further on.

There was a dull leaden feeling in the air, as if a storm was brewing and was about to unleash energy on the place, energy that Tessa could have done with bottling.

Her phone rang.

'Parked up, boss.'

'Okay, you know where your positions are. Don't go yet. Wait until you see the two of us almost at his door, then get in place. I don't want him spotting you. I want him to think we're Jehovah's Witnesses or something, I don't want him imagining he's about to be discovered. Okay?'

'Okay, boss.'

Tessa and Hannah got out of the car, picked up their handbags and walked across to the house, hoping they looked like innocent middle-aged ladies going about their business.

Tessa rang the bell. There was no response so she rang it

again. This time she heard movement and she gave a slight nod towards Hannah.

The door opened, then stopped as the chain prevented it opening any further. Tessa took out her ID.

'Mr Owen? DI Tessa Marsden and DS Hannah Granger. Can you remove the chain, please? We'd like to talk to you. As you can see, there are two officers positioned at the front, and a further two officers are in your back garden.'

He didn't speak. The door closed, the chain was removed, and it reopened. He stood there, still without speaking.

'Mr Owen? Or should we be saying Mr Armstrong?'

He tried to make a move, to push them aside, but the sudden and imposing presence of Ray Charlton and PC Dave Irwin stopped him. He looked at them all then simply turned his back and walked away from them, down his hallway. Tessa and Hannah followed, with Tessa indicating to Ray that they should remain outside the door.

They entered the kitchen and Adam sat down at the table. He indicated that the two women should join him, then finally he spoke.

'How did you find me? Why did you find me? She's dead, isn't she?'

'Your wife? Yes, I'm afraid she is.'

'Thank God,' he said. 'My son and I have lived under this massive dark cloud for over ten years. No rainbows in our lives, I can assure you.'

'You have never once been in touch with her since you and Daniel left?'

'No!' It was almost a shout. 'Two days before we left she threw Danny, my five-year-old son, down the stairs. He had a broken arm and a huge lump on his head. I was still in considerable pain from the beating she had inflicted on me with a baseball bat, and I was peeing blood.'

'You could have gone to the police.'

He gave a short bark of a laugh. 'She would have probably been locked up, but maybe for only a couple of years. Then she would have found us again. DI Marshall…'

'Marsden,' Tessa corrected him.

'Sorry. The day after she threw our son down the stairs like a rag doll, she held a knife to my throat and said she would never kill me, she wanted me alive to remember seeing my son cut up into little bits while he was still alive. I had been taking money out of our account because I knew one day we would have to go. We left with around five thousand pounds, one suitcase between us, and a friend who I knew would help.'

Luke was out of the house by seven, and twenty minutes later, parked within twenty-five metres of the house where Vincent Sanders lived. He checked the camera was good to go, and laid it on the passenger seat.

The church was to his right, and although he had been a couple of times when he was a child, primarily to see Little John's grave, he knew nothing of the history of the building. He took out his phone, typed in the name of the church and settled back to add further knowledge about Derbyshire into his brain. If he was going to work in the county, he had to be as familiar with it as he was with the plague history of Eyam.

The door of the house opened, and he shut down his phone and picked up the camera. Vincent Sanders came out, then leaned back in to speak to someone before closing the door and walking down the front garden path. Luke crouched as low as he could and grabbed as many pictures as possible.

Seconds later the front door opened again and a woman ran down the path calling some instructions to the man. He acknowledged he understood with a thumbs up sign, she returned inside and he continued to wherever he was going.

Luke photographed them until eventually there was no-one

to be his subject. He put the camera on to the seat again, and pursed his lips. Was the woman Felicia Sanders? If she was, it explained the lack of divorce papers; they were still together.

Luke continued to watch, sinking lower into his seat, as Sanders returned, holding a plastic carrier bag with a newspaper sticking out of the top. Luke raised the camera and took photographs until Sanders disappeared back inside his home.

The next two hours passed slowly and then the woman came out of the front door and walked down the hill towards the main Hathersage road. Luke locked the car and with the camera slung around his neck, followed her, keeping some distance away.

She turned right and headed down into the village. Luke increased his pace, not wanting to lose sight of her. She stopped abruptly and disappeared into a hairdressers.

Luke continued to walk past the shop, and he saw her removing her coat, a stylist standing by to take it from her.

'Time to think, Luke,' he muttered, and crossed the road to sit on some steps. He needed confirmation of who she was.

She was in the shop for almost two hours, but when she eventually came out she looked completely different. Her hair was much shorter, and much lighter in colour. Having taken advantage of a coffee shop, Luke drained his drink and waited until she was out of sight before leaving the warmth of his bolthole and crossing the road towards the hairdressers.

He went into further warmth, and paused as if surprised. One of the hairdressers walked over to him and smiled. 'Can I help you, sir?'

'Yes, I thought Mrs Sanders was here. Her husband rang to ask if I could pick her up as it's looking like rain and she's having her hair done. This is the right hairdressers, isn't it?'

The girl laughed. 'Yes, it is. She left about five minutes ago. But don't worry, she has her umbrella with her. Are you taking them to the airport?'

'Yes, that's the plan.' Luke needed to get out. 'Thank you for your help,' he said, and went to open the door.

'I hope they enjoy their break. Barcelona for a twentieth wedding anniversary is pretty special, isn't it?'

Luke nodded and smiled before leaving the shop. He needed to get her picture now, with the new hairstyle. He jogged up the hill, passing Felicia Sanders walking on the opposite side.

He set the camera to video, and filmed the church and surrounding area, capturing Felicia as she reached her home. Luke knew he wouldn't look out of place; anyone in Hathersage without a camera was viewed as strange.

He got in the car, and pulled away, knowing Felicia had seen him. She wouldn't think anything of the filming, but she would if she saw him sitting in his car for any protracted length of time.

The vet smiled as he handed the tiny kitten to Doris. 'She's a little cracker,' he said. 'All of them are, they'll make lovely adult cats. How somebody could dump them…' He shook his head in disgust.

'She'll be well looked after, I can promise you that.' Doris lifted the kitten up and spoke to her. 'Welcome to my world, Belle.'

Doris headed for the reception and paid all outstanding fees, adding a further fifty pounds to go towards the care of any future dumped cats or dogs, then strapped the carrier onto the back seat.

'Can't take any chances,' she said to the small bundle of fur, who squeaked at her.

She drove to the office, noticing Luke's car was there. She hoped it meant he already had a result.

Carefully transporting the carrier into the office, she introduced everyone to Belle. After much oohing and aahing, she put her away again and turned to Luke.

'You have something to tell us?'

'I do. What's the date on the marriage certificate you found?'

'It's tomorrow. Twenty years ago, but tomorrow is the day. Why?'

'They're spending it in Barcelona, Mr and Mrs Sanders. She's had her hair done today, ready for the trip later this afternoon.'

'Oh no. Poor Keeley. You're absolutely sure?'

'The hairdresser told me.'

Doris thought for a moment. 'Okay, Luke. Ring Keeley and ask her when she is next seeing Vincent. If she's seeing him in the next couple of days, we know we've gone awry somewhere, but if she's not seeing him for a few days...'

'I'll do it now,' he said.

'I'm not seeing him until next Tuesday,' Keeley said. 'He's got to go somewhere with work. But he's booked for us to go for a really nice meal next Tuesday evening. I've organised a babysitter for Henry and I'm really looking forward to it. You two still coming over this afternoon?'

'We are,' Luke said. 'See you later.' He disconnected before she could ask any more questions.

'I'll add this morning's work to the report,' he said. 'Perhaps you'll check it, Mrs Lester, when I've finished it.'

'Of course. Keeley's going to be upset, Luke, but better now than in a year's time.'

He nodded, then moved to his desk to download the pictures he had taken that morning. Kat strolled across and watched what he was doing. He put all the photos in one file labelled Roy/Sanders, then clicked on the file.

Kat watched as the pictures appeared on the screen, then laughed.

'You know him?' Luke asked.

'Not him, but I'd know that Saab anywhere. Leon wanted to buy it for me, but the owner wouldn't sell. It's immaculate, a beautiful car. He told Leon it was a source of his income. We assumed he rented it out for weddings and suchlike, but clearly he uses it to con women.'

'I'll make sure that goes into the report as well. I need to print about half a dozen of these pictures – Keeley needs to see we have evidence to back up everything we've found.'

'You've done well, Luke,' Kat said. 'Thank you.'

Luke felt proud and… pleased.

Tessa took Adam Armstrong to Cromer police station to give his statement, in which he confirmed he hadn't seen his son for around six months. He had spoken to him twice in that time, and he had said he was happy with the fairground people he had chosen to spend the next part of his life with. He wouldn't be returning to school. And Adam wouldn't be returning to Baslow. That part of their life was over.

He was also able to prove his whereabouts on the night his wife was killed; his top-of-the-range CCTV system worked not only to show unwelcome visitors to his home, but also the presence of anyone in that home at any given time. Adam Armstrong was definitely not at Chatsworth.

Tessa felt somewhat cynical as she thought of what would probably happen over the next couple of days when Debbie Carter took possession of Adam Armstrong's address.

3 2

Debbie arrived with Charlie in the pushchair to find only Kat and Mouse in residence at Connection.

'Quiet in here,' Debbie said. 'You must be busy.'

Kat laughed. 'We're always busy. You just get me today; Mouse has some work to do for our Manchester business, dealing with a couple of interviews she's organised. Luke is out on a case, and Doris has a new kitten which is taking precedence over everything else. Come into my office, the coffee's ready. I can make tea if you'd prefer.'

'No, coffee's fine. It will maybe give me some energy. This little monkey had me up three times in the night. You have news for me?'

'We do.' Kat waited until Debbie had settled Charlie before handing her the coffee. 'Sit down, Debbie, and we'll go through it.'

Debbie's hands shook as she clutched the mug. She prayed it was good news and not merely information that Adam had disappeared for good. She shivered as Kat's pale pink nails hovered over the folder.

'First of all, Debbie, I need you to look at these pictures and tell me if you believe it to be Adam.'

Kat thought back to the short but sweet text of half an hour earlier, that simply said **Confirmed and statement taken. More later.**

She removed the photographs from a white envelope and handed them across the desk.

Debbie's breathing became erratic, and she stared at the man she hadn't seen for ten years. She stroked a shaking finger down his face, and tried to collect her thoughts so that she could speak.

She looked up at Kat. 'Of course it's him. Does he know we're looking for him?' She brushed away tears, trying not to show how much the picture had affected her.

Kat shook her head. 'No, he didn't when these photos were taken. We had to assess the situation, because we knew if we approached him he would run and his name would never be cleared. As you know, we are legally bound to advise the police if we know anything at all linking to any crimes, and so we had to tell DI Marsden. She has been to see him this morning...'

'But...'

'Debbie, I know what you're going to say, but by doing it this way, the correct way, he has given a statement which I'm assuming exonerates him, although I'll find more out later.'

'And Danny?'

'I don't know yet. We have tracked down Adam, and, as you can see from the photos, he was actually seen by Doris and Luke, but there was no sighting of Danny. He was possibly inside the house when Adam brought out the wheelie bins. I'm sure we'll get the full story when DI Marsden returns, but until then I can pass on Adam's address. I'll get his phone number when DI Marsden returns. I didn't want to keep you waiting any longer to find out that we'd tracked him down. All incidentals will follow.'

Debbie picked up the pictures once more, and sat and stared at them.

'You want some advice, Debbie? Wait. Don't go tearing off to Cromer. I imagine he's disappeared again anyway, but that will only be temporary. He'll go back to his home; he'll probably want some time out to gather his thoughts. We've just changed his world. The best way you can go about this is to send him a letter, possibly one from you and one from Simon, reassuring him that he'll be welcome back home in Derbyshire. I think all this is going to take time, and if you push too hard he'll do a bit of long-distance selling up, and you'll never get to see him or Danny again. He's gone to a lot of trouble to keep any connection to Baslow out of their lives. What Nicola said or did to him to make him so scared is almost beyond comprehension, but he's been a frightened man for ten years. What's just as concerning is that his friend who helped him has continued to give him his full support for so long, so the threat must have been very real. And if instinct is serving me well, I think the threat was probably against Danny, not Adam.'

'He had a new name?'

'He did. It was James Owen.'

Debbie smiled, while still brushing away tears. 'Michael James Owen, Adam's all-time hero. I should have known.'

'Mine too,' Kat laughed, feeling relieved that the meeting seemed to be going so well, despite not having all the information. 'I was the one that picked up on it, because in my misspent youth I had a poster of him on my wall that had his full name on, and of course, hearing the name James Owen took me straight back to that time. Then Simon confirmed they were both Man U supporters, so Bob's your uncle!'

Kat handed over the second envelope. 'This is the report with all the information we have – there will be more, obviously, once Marsden can comfortably tell us without compromising her investigation, but I suspect he really is in the clear, because she would have said if she had to arrest him. Did you love him?'

The question hung in the air. Kat couldn't believe she'd asked it, but now it was out there, she waited for an answer.

Debbie glanced down at her hands, lying in her lap. 'Yes, I did. We had to split up when Nicola told him she was pregnant. The only way to get over it was to stay away from each other, which we did, until the scars and cuts required medical assistance. That's when he turned to me. I loved him so much. I cared for Rob, but in the end, even with Adam off the scene and possibly dead, it wasn't enough. Rob's happy now, and so am I. That's made so much better by knowing Adam is alive.'

She paused for a moment, sorting out her thoughts. 'I always wondered if he did it on purpose, the complete disappearance bit, in the hope the police and all of us would think Nicola had murdered them. Lots of people knew of her anger issues – in fact, lots of people had been on the receiving end.'

'I'm sure that one day you'll be able to ask him. Just handle it carefully. Don't rush him and Danny, let them return to the house, maybe even on their own the first time, because if he's not coming back here he will need to sell up. Let him set the pace, Debbie. I'll give you every bit of information I can get from DI Marsden, then we'll send you our final account. Is that okay?'

'It's fine, Kat. I'll pass all the info I have on to Simon; he'll be chuffed that his best mate is alive, but I imagine he'll feel some antagonism towards him too. He would have helped in a heartbeat, and Adam knew that.' She stood. 'I'll wait to hear from you, and thank you for all you've done so far. I knew if anybody could do it, you could. The police were never really interested. I loved him so much, Kat. We would have been perfect together but the so-called pregnancy made us realise we couldn't be partners.'

Luke and Doris sat in Keeley's kitchen watching her face crumple.

'Married? He's married? But...'

Doris reached across the table and grasped her hand. 'It's better you know now, rather than a year down the line. Everything we've found out is in this envelope. Luke has worked really hard on it, so I want you to read it all carefully. I haven't brought you a final bill, in case there is anything else we can help you with. Take time to digest it all, and Luke will give you a call in the morning, to make sure you have everything in there that you need to know.'

Keeley clutched the envelope in her left hand, and stood. 'I'm not going to read it until Henry is in bed. I have to get him from school in a few minutes, so I'll have to go now. Thank you, especially you, Luke, for this. I'll speak to you tomorrow, I promise, when I've had time to think things through.'

She walked them to the door, waved as they set off, then allowed the tears to fall.

Married? Fecking married? She grabbed some kitchen roll and dried her tears. That piece of gob-shite gigolo was going to find out what it was like to be caught out in a lie, a hefty lie at that. Tonight, plans would be made that would rock Vincent Sanders's world to the very core.

Tessa and Hannah discussed events all the way back, both recognising what a massive part Connection had played in finding Adam Armstrong. Neither of them thought Adam would return that night to his Cromer home, he had been shaken to the depth of his being by their arrival.

The miles disappeared underneath them, and eventually they pulled into Chesterfield headquarters, tired, yet knowing they wouldn't sleep. It had been a good day for clearing one mystery, but Adam had been unable to help with the murder of his wife. He had admitted to feeling relieved that it was all now in the open, and Danny was safe, but he couldn't begin to imagine how his life would pan out. He wasn't convinced he would ever set foot in Baslow again; the memories were too overwhelming. Somewhere in that village was every bit of confidence he had ever possessed, destroyed by Nicola.

Tessa thanked Hannah for doing all the driving.

Hannah simply smiled. 'I hoped you would close your eyes for a bit, get some rest, but no, there's too much running round your head, isn't there?'

'There is. Anybody on the outside of this, looking in at what we're doing, what information we have, would say Adam Armstrong is the one who has killed Nicola. Now, I know he is clever with security, it's what he does, but our tech lads will soon be able to suss if there's any tampering on that tape, with either date or times. He'll know that, so I believe him, damn it. And I also think he really struggles with being away from his home. He was in a panic when we said he had to go to Cromer police station, not because it was a police station, but because it meant he had to go out. How can anybody destroy a person, because that's what she did. I think he's had ten years of not daring to go out in case she had tracked him down.'

'She must have been a nightmare to live with. Why would you want to go home after work if you never knew what was waiting for you?' Hannah mused. 'I understand he had no choice, not once she started hurting Danny, but what a bloody awful life he must have had. She's messed with his mind, and in some ways that's worse than the physical attacks.'

'Let's get in and report to the DCI, then we'll head off home. It's been a long day.'

'You… erm… you don't fancy going for a drink or anything?'

Tessa smiled at her sergeant. 'No thanks, Hannah. I think Martin's at my place, so I'd best get home. He'll have cooked something delicious, best not keep it waiting.'

Tessa didn't see the look on Hannah's face, a look that spoke of disappointment. And something else.

33

The phone was ringing as Luke entered the office next morning. He grabbed at the receiver. 'Connection. Can I help you?'

'I hope so. I've been up all night planning this.'

'Keeley?'

'Oh, sorry. Yes it is. I'm not thinking straight, I'm so blazing mad. Have you time to call round today?'

'Of course. You need Doris as well?'

'Is she any good at decimating people? No, I don't mean people, I mean men.'

Luke thought of the video of Doris he had watched. 'I would say so,' he said with a laugh.

'Then in that case, if both of you can spare me ten minutes at some point today, I'll be very grateful.'

'I'll book you in for ten. Does that suit you?'

'Fine. Thank you, Luke. See you later.'

Doris was sitting with the sleeping kitten on her knee, reluctant to move. 'Belle,' she whispered, 'I have to go to work now. Try not to destroy anything, play with your ball and your teddy.' The tiny cat ignored her.

Doris stroked the top of Belle's head with one finger. 'Five minutes more, then we really have to move.'

She wanted to be early this morning – she had a feeling Tessa and Hannah would call in at some point to fill them in on their trip to Cromer. She hoped it had progressed the investigation, but thought they would have heard by now if it had.

Belle moved slightly, and Doris scooped her up into her arms and carried her through to the kitchen. She placed her on the cat bed, and stroked her. 'Now remember what we discussed, little one. If you want to poo or wee you use this tray with the grey stuff in. We practised, remember? And you did very well. I've left you some food and water down, so be a good girl. I'll come back at lunchtime to check on you.'

Doris glanced around the kitchen to make sure there was nothing Belle could wrap herself around, into, or swallow, then quietly closed the door.

Belle opened one eye, surveyed her domain, and drifted off to sleep once more.

'Simon? You got ten minutes?' Debbie felt and sounded stressed.

'About that, yes, then I've got to go. I'm working in Matlock today.'

'Then I'll make it quick. I have Adam's address.'

'What? But...'

'But what, Simon? Did you know he was still alive? Just how much did you know?'

'Hang on a minute, Debs, of course I didn't know. I didn't believe he could be alive, not after all this time and no word from him.'

'I'm remembering how you didn't want me to ask Kat to track him down. Why was that, Simon?'

There was anger in her voice, an anger reminiscent of Nicola's underlying tone whenever she spoke.

'Because I felt we were throwing money away, and Connection won't be cheap. You know I always thought Adam and Danny were dead. So tell me what we now know.'

'I thought you had to go to work.' The anger had been replaced by sarcasm.

'Debs…'

'Okay. He's been living in Cromer for years, possibly since he went. There's a lot more to the story that we don't know yet, but Connection found him. Because he's a person of interest in Nicola's murder, they had to tell the DI who's investigating it, and the police went to see him yesterday. Kat is going to be speaking with them, and she'll pass on any further information as and when she can, but we've got a starting point with his address. She suggests we both write him a letter, keeping it light. If we start with heavy-handedness, she says he'll disappear.'

'Okay,' Simon said.

'Okay what? You're being very strange.'

'Feeling a bit angry, if the truth be known.'

'Angry that he's alive?'

'In a way. He could have let us know; he knew we were on his side. Do you really expect him to come back to Derbyshire, after everything he went through? And how's Dan? You've not mentioned him.'

'That's because they only saw Adam, putting bins out of all things. I'm hoping we'll have news of him soon.'

'Can I go now?'

'You can. I'll keep you informed.' Debbie knew her words sounded stiff, but she couldn't help it.

The briefing room went quiet as Tessa walked to the board. 'Good morning, everybody. Good day, yesterday. Thank you everybody who took part, and we had no problems. Apart from a very scared man. We found Adam Armstrong, talked to him and took him to Cromer HQ to make a statement. We have CCTV from his home to check, and I want it checking to the nth degree, please. This CCTV is his alibi. He says he very rarely goes beyond his front gate; he has something of a phobia brought on by fear that his ex-wife would find him. However, he is something of an expert in CCTV and everything related to it, so we need to make sure that the recording didn't mysteriously stop working, and it wasn't tampered with in any way. If it's spot on, Adam Armstrong is in the clear.'

'Any information on the lad, boss?' Ray Charlton's voice rose above the general hubbub.

'Not much. It seems a few months ago Adam and Danny had a fall-out because Danny was hanging around with a gang of lads from the fair. They were dabbling in drugs, generally being a nuisance. Anyway, he said when they moved on, Danny disappeared overnight and went with them. He's apparently rung home a couple of times, and says he's all right, so I'd like somebody to try to track that fair down. Adam said it was around last June when it was in Cromer.'

'Do we have a photo for the board, boss?'

'No. If you saw the inside of the house, you'd understand why. It takes minimalism to a whole new level. There was nothing in the way of ornaments, no pictures on walls, no photographs, not even cushions on the two armchairs. It felt like an empty house when we walked in, as if an estate agent was going to show us around, that sort of feeling. I asked him for a picture of Danny to help us identify him once we've tracked down the fair, and he just looked at me. He said there was nothing. No pictures, no mobile phones, an ex-directory landline for emergencies and business only, no Facebook, nothing. He did say that it was probably the reason Danny left, he wanted to be part of the world the fair lads had, with their phones, and their texts and stuff. Adam even had his groceries collected by the tenant next door, which is something that's happened ever since Adam and Danny arrived there. I had a brief chat with the adjoining neighbour – we may or may not have to talk more, but for now he said he paid a much-subsidised rent to Mr King to keep an eye on Adam and Danny, and help them get away if ever it became necessary. In Adam's pantry there's a door, a low one, that leads straight through to the next door. It's all been well thought out, I can tell you, but I'm also sure it was set up well in advance of the great escape. He was planning to leave for months, but had to go quickly in the end because the violence dramatically escalated. I've interviewed many many people in this job,' she said, her mind drifting to the most recent one with Adam, 'and I have never seen such a scared man before. He knows she's dead, but there's more than that. Whatever's still wrong, he needs psychiatric help to work through it. Now, is everybody clear on what they're doing? Priority is the CCTV; I need to know beyond any doubt that it's genuine.'

She returned to her desk, and pulled Adam's statement towards her. She reread it, and then once more. They drove away from Baslow in his car. Car. Tax, insurance, MOT. She opened her computer and went into the DVLA site. Two minutes of clicking showed her that Adam did still own a car, an eleven-year-old car, albeit under his new name of James Owen, and it was fully legal compliant. It would be; he couldn't risk ever being stopped. The transfer of ownership had taken place two weeks after Adam had driven away. All his new life had been ready and waiting for him, new name and everything that went with it. Ethan King was a powerful friend to have. Powerful enough to arrange a murder?

Tessa drove for the first time in a few days, and they went to Connection. Luke and Doris had just returned from talking to

Keeley; they said nothing to Kat and Mouse, just that it was sorted.

They all greeted each other and moved into Kat's office. Two plates of biscuits were placed in the middle of the table, and Luke handed out drinks.

'You're feeling better, DI Marsden?' he asked.

'Much better, thanks, Luke. I'm starting to feel I might actually survive.'

'You had a good result yesterday?' Doris asked.

'We certainly did. That's one reason we're here, to say thank you. I think we've almost ruled him out as a suspect, because if his CCTV is genuine, he was in Cromer on the night Nicola died. We're checking it to really tighten up that alibi though, in view of that being his job. It seems he runs his business from home, does detailed drawings for security systems, and employs others to do the actual fitting. I'm not convinced he's totally agoraphobic, but he's pretty close. We got him to the police station without him collapsing in a heap, but he wasn't happy. That's another reason why he's not a suspect. I don't think he could have got to Baslow and out into Chatsworth. He could have had somebody drive him here, but he's still not top of my list.'

'Who is?'

'At the moment, in the absence of any other bugger, I'm leaning towards Hannah.'

They all laughed, and Hannah said, 'Thanks, boss. But I've got an alibi, I was in bed under the duvet praying that the snow wouldn't be as bad as it looked as though it was going to be. Is that good enough?'

'Maybe. I'll think about it. Just a minute while I grab a chocolate biscuit, and I'll fill you in on everything we know. I know you held back with your client, and I'm grateful. She could have cocked everything up with one wrong move.'

Tessa took off her coat and grabbed two biscuits. 'Okay, here goes. We have a list.'

'Do we?' Hannah looked surprised.

'We do. I do, anyway. I believe, quite firmly, that Nicola Armstrong was killed because of something that happened ten years ago. I don't know whether it was the damage she caused to Adam and Danny, or simply the fact that she drove them away, or even that somebody believes she killed them. But whatever the reason, it's somebody who knew her, was close to her, knew her routine. So, my list.'

She reached into her pocket and pulled out her notebook. Opening at a page tucked under the elastic, she put the small pad on the table. 'Okay, this is my list. If anybody thinks anyone else qualifies to be on it, let me know. Debbie Carter, Simon Vicars, Harry Hardy, Neil Ireland, Paula Ireland.'

'Who's Harry Hardy?' Mouse asked.

'He's an employee at Chatsworth, found both bodies. He's not seriously on my list, but he lives alone so nobody to alibi him. He knows the estate better than he knows his own garden, so would know where to stash bodies, and he's a brooding sort of chap. Doesn't talk much, and from what I've gathered he doesn't sleep much. He starts work at around six every morning, his own choice, and finishes in the evening. It seems he's hardly ever away from Chatsworth. Having said all that, he actually comes fifth on a list of five, so don't read too much into him being on it. Before I joked Hannah was my top suspect, I had actually decided Simon Vicars kind of qualified. He has no alibi; his partner is somewhere abroad so he's in the house on his own. I shall be digging deeper into his background.'

34

'I've known Simon for some time,' Kat said. 'He's quite a gentle man, and while he doesn't have an alibi, I'd be really shocked if he needed one. I just don't see him hitting her over the head then strangling her. He's no murderer.'

'Somebody is, Kat. And I don't think it's a random drunk out for an evening walk. It's a person known to Olivia, and I suspect known to Nicola because I believe that phone call to Neil Ireland was because she was scared. If he'd taken that call, we would have solved this the following day.'

'So what's next? Reinterviews?'

'I think so. We'll start with Simon. I have nothing that will place him at the scene, and according to him and Debbie, he had nothing to do with the initial disappearance of Adam, despite being what Simon considered his closest friend. It almost feels as if we're going through the motions, and then something will erupt and put us on the right track.'

'You don't think you'll get anything else out of Adam Armstrong?'

'Not without using extreme torture, no. He's a strange one. When I was interviewing him at the station, I was aware he was out of his comfort zone. It wasn't that he didn't co-operate, because he did. It was clearly that he wanted to be back home, but he was a major person of interest and I had to do everything by the book. As soon as he'd finished his statement, he stood up and looked towards the door. He asked if he could go home, so we took him back. His friend from the adjoining house was standing outside Adam's, waiting for him. And if I wasn't a bit brain dead at the moment I could even tell you his name.' Tessa paused, trying to grasp at something to remind her.

'Trevor Coleman,' Hannah said quietly.

'That's it! Trevor Coleman. He came straight over to our car, and didn't even wait for Adam to get out before asking him if he was okay. Very protective, he was. He took Adam inside, after giving us such an evil glare I thought we might melt into the paving slabs, and we left. But thinking about it, I should have questioned him, he's the one there before Adam arrived. In fact…' Tessa was aware she was starting to ramble, but that was why she always ended up at Connection, 'we need to go back to Norfolk and interview Mr Coleman first, then hopefully that will give us more questions for Adam.'

'Tomorrow?' Hannah asked. 'Do we need to take anyone else with us?'

'No, I don't think we'll be arresting anybody, but if we do I'll handcuff them to you.'

'Thanks, boss, you're all heart.'

Tessa smiled at her DS, and reached across for another biscuit. 'I know.'

'So,' Kat said, 'is there anything you can tell us, now that we've finished with the lovey-dovey bit? We have a client, remember, who is currently itching to contact Adam, but at the moment is wary of stepping on your toes. She has Adam's address, but that's all. If we don't throw her a titbit soon, she'll head off to Norfolk.'

'Would his phone number help?'

'Massively. It's probably the one thing that will stop her shooting off down there.'

'I'll text it to you, as soon as we get back to Chatsworth. Is there any more coffee?'

Chesterfield HQ rang Tessa less than a minute after they had left the Connection office. Tessa took the call, closing her eyes to the speed Hannah was taking the corners.

'Two men? They have names?'

Hannah slowed down, in case it meant they had to turn around.

Tessa listened to the response. 'Okay, many thanks. We'll be there in about twenty minutes. And tell the one that doesn't need to give his name because he's only the driver, that if he hasn't given his name by the time I get there, he won't be driving back home again until he does. Can you put them in separate interview rooms, please?'

She disconnected. 'Bloody men. I'll show him who's boss. Won't leave his name, huh.'

'Boss?' Hannah was trying not to laugh. Whoever hadn't left their name was clearly in some sort of trouble.

'Hannah, pull into that lay-by, can you? I need to think.'

Hannah indicated and slowed down before bumping over the rough surface and coming to a stop. 'Something wrong?'

'Guess who's at Chesterfield.'

'No idea.'

'If I said I won't need to handcuff you to him, would that be a clue?'

Hannah widened her eyes. 'No... Adam Armstrong?'

'Spot on. It seems Trevor Coleman has driven him here, but has chosen not to give his name because he's not here to be questioned, he's just the driver. Oh boy, has he got a surprise coming. However, does this mean Adam has something else to tell us? I still don't see him as the murderer though, do you? It would mean he stayed up here for a few nights, because the same person definitely killed both females. He's not capable of having stayed in this area, away from his home in Cromer, even if he's capable of murder. Okay, we'll head off to Chatsworth, pick up anything we might need, then go to Chesterfield. I might have said twenty minutes, but they can both sweat for a bit.'

Trevor Coleman rose to his feet as they walked into the interview room. The PC moved towards him, and Tessa spoke.

'Sit down, Mr Coleman. You really don't want to cross swords with our young PC here, and you definitely don't want to cross them with either of us two.'

They sat at the table, and slowly Trevor sank down onto his seat.

'Why am I in here?'

'Because you are a personal friend and next-door neighbour of a man wanted in connection with the death of his wife. He is a person of interest, Mr Coleman, and you've brought him to us. Now does it make sense?'

She logged them all into the room for the recorder, and opened the file she had carried in. 'Okay, Mr Coleman. Tell me how you came to be living where you do.'

'Why?'

'Because I'm a DI, and I'm asking.'

His thought processes were clear; he'd done nothing wrong, so he didn't really have a problem. And she was a DI and she was asking.

'I rent the property from KingPress. I had an accident at work which meant I couldn't do my job, so Mr King offered me a house on the coast, minimal rent. He's taken care of me ever since.'

'Whose fault was it?'

He laughed. 'It was definitely mine. Don't ever think it was his guilty conscience that made him offer me the house, far from it. He's just a good bloke, and I'd been there at KingPress for twenty years or so when the accident happened. I got cocky, I suppose, didn't turn a machine off when I should have done. It took half my arm off.' He waved a prosthetic hand in the air, and Tessa nodded.

'I'd been in the house about a year, learnt to manage with only one hand, and he rang me one day to say somebody was moving in next door with a little lad, and behind the fridge-freezer in my pantry was a door. He needed me to move the fridge-freezer and keep that door clear at all times. We had a long chat about helping this chap if he ever needed it, and to keep Mr King informed if things started to go wrong for either the chap or the little 'un.

'Although I don't know if I'm right with this, about a month before this chap arrived, Mr King sent me to a place in Scotland to be fitted with a better prosthesis. I was away a week. When I got back he'd taken out the worktop size fridge, and a smaller freezer, and replaced them with an all-singing all-dancing model. I thought nothing of it, just thanked him, and said it was easier because the fridge was now at waist level. I knew nothing of the work that had been done to connect the two houses, because it was all hidden behind the fridge-freezer.'

He took a sip from the bottle of water Hannah handed to him, and then carried on. From vowing to not say a word, he had become quite voluble.

'The day they arrived they had nothing. One suitcase between them, and a car. That was it. Over the months we said the odd hello, and I really took to the kid. My wife walked away with our little girl after the accident. She said I was no good to her if I couldn't work. One day James showed me a newspaper cutting, and that's when I found out he wasn't James at all, he was Adam. He said Danny wasn't taking to his new name at all, but that name was just for any legalities that might crop up in the future, like going to school, taking his driving test, that sort of thing. We agreed for the sake of the little lad that we would call him Danny. And that's how we've lived, quietly, for nigh on ten years. I've watched Adam deteriorate, especially when Danny went, and I support him as much as I can. I do all his shopping, and he does things that don't panic him like cutting the bit of grass we have out back, and...'

'Putting out the bins,' Tessa said with a smile. 'Whose idea was it to come here today?'

'His. He wants to try to get his life back, but it's mostly about rebuilding his confidence, I reckon. He says he's got things to tell you that he couldn't tell you the other day, because he's had to bury things for too many years. He's not capable of driving all this way, but something else that he does to keep himself as sane as he can, is he keeps that car in immaculate condition. I take it to the test centre every year, and it's never failed yet. He asked me last night if I would bring him to Chesterfield, and of course I said yes. I've told Mr King because this is more than just out of the ordinary, it's totally off the planet.'

'And you haven't heard from Danny?'

'Once. He rang me on my birthday. Said he was good, enjoying what he was doing. I think he said he was in Middlesbrough.'

'We have people tracking down where the fair is, so maybe he'll want to make amends with his dad, see him again. This is a big step Adam has taken, coming here. Is there anything else you can tell us, Mr Coleman?'

'I don't think so. I'll be sorry if he moves back up here, we've been really close for ten years, but with the dragon dead, he has nothing to fear. I know he had half-share in the house, so presumably it's all his. I tell you, DI Marsden, I'm glad she's dead. He deserves some peace in his life, as does Danny. Being thrown down the stairs was imprinted in Danny's mind, you know. At the beginning he used to tell me about it, over and over, but as he grew older he stopped talking about the past, and started to want to become involved in the future. It caused trouble between him and his dad. I'm sure that's why he left. All he wanted was a bloody mobile phone.'

35

Hannah took Trevor a cup of tea. She and Tessa had warmed to him during the interview, and felt they understood Adam Armstrong's years of exile better.

With Trevor's signed statement under their belt, they moved on to Adam. They stood at the two-way mirror watching him, sitting quietly, making no fuss. His designated PC had nothing to do but stand and observe.

'Nice-looking, isn't he,' Tessa said. 'He's forty, and starting to look more mature, but he's not running to fat. When we've caught whoever killed his wife, he could be footloose and fancy free,' she said with a smile, and nudged Hannah. 'Wink wink, yes?'

'Oh my god, you're incorrigible, DI Marsden,' Hannah said. 'The poor man's newly widowed, not buried his wife yet, and you're trying to marry him off. So no, I'm not interested, for a variety of reasons.'

'Really?' Tessa took a sip of her coffee and turned to her DS. 'What reasons?'

'Shall we go in?'

'No! What reasons? You met somebody?'

'Maybe. Now come on, we'll never get home tonight. Let's go and have a chat with our handsome suspect.'

They approached the table, and Adam Armstrong held out his hand and shook theirs. 'I'm sorry to cause all this bother, I couldn't speak yesterday, couldn't focus on anything that was happening. As you've probably realised because it was blatantly obvious, I have some mental issues.'

'Let me log us on to the recording, Mr Armstrong, and then we can talk.' She recited all their names, and then sat down facing him, Hannah to her right.

'Do you need a doctor, Mr Armstrong?' Hannah asked.

He shook his head. 'No, I have all my medication with me, thank you. What I really need is to stop feeling scared all the time. Part of that issue has been solved with the death of my wife.'

'Then can we get you a cup of tea, water, fizzy pop?'

'No, I'm fine. This young man,' he waved towards the PC, 'organised some water for me because I have to take midday medication, so I don't need anything now, thank you, except to talk and to apologise for saying nothing of any value to you yesterday. I spoke at length with Trevor last night after you dropped me off, although he knows very little of the full story; he is fully aware of the events of the last ten years, but not of how my life was prior to that. He has only recently found out that the woman murdered in Chatsworth was my wife.'

'Did he know of the violence suffered by you and Danny?'

'A little. Danny was quite obsessed at one point by the fact that he was thrown downstairs, and he spoke of it to Trevor. I told Trevor a little bit about her temper, but he certainly didn't know how bad it could be.'

'We've seen photographs of the bruises, Mr Armstrong. And a picture of Danny when he was about five with a cast on his arm.'

'That was from hitting every stair on the way down. He had a massive lump on the back of his head as well. That was the day the fear took over and I contacted Ethan. Within two days we had moved in here with just a few clothes and five thousand pounds. Oh, and the trusty car. Only Ethan knew the full story. He has supported the two of us by letting us live here for free until I could build a business and begin to pay him rent. We now pay him the going rate, but he still has Trevor as my go-to aide, and the chap at the other side but not connected to my house as backup. He knows very little, and we have never had to call on him for help. He checks in once a week, just asks how I am, and that is sufficient.'

There was a long pause and it was evident to the two women that he was wondering how to say what had to come next.

'Danny didn't remember everything quite so accurately as he thought. Yes, he saw his mother beating me with that baseball bat, and he screamed and screamed to get her to stop hurting his daddy, but she wasn't satisfied until I was unconscious. When I started to surface, she was all over me, couldn't apologise enough. I think initially she thought she had killed me. She bathed the wounds, dressed them where she had broken the skin, was goodness personified. But it was too late. Danny had seen it all. He wouldn't go near her.'

Again Adam showed reluctance to carry on.

'I'm scared. I thought I was scared before, but it's nothing like this. Two days after the hammering that almost killed me, Debbie came around to have a go at Nicola. There'd always been bad blood between them, both had mega problems with their tempers, but it was more or less under control with Debbie. Until that day. I had been round to her house in the morning. I couldn't move, and one part of my back was particularly painful. I was peeing blood, and my face looked like I'd done fifteen rounds with Muhammad Ali. Her anger erupted. She stormed around to our house, and stuffed Bridie into my arms.'

He stopped again, and they knew something was about to happen, something momentous. Tessa called a temporary halt. She stopped the recording, and Hannah went to get drinks for them all. The atmosphere in the room was electric, and Adam sat, his head bowed.

'Thank you,' he said. 'It's bringing everything back, and I'm struggling.'

They resumed fifteen minutes later. Adam had recovered slightly, but wanted to get everything off his chest.

'Debbie stormed upstairs to find Nicola, and I was at the bottom, still holding Bridie in my arms. There was some significant shouting going off, and I looked everywhere downstairs for Danny, but I couldn't find him. Then suddenly, as I was about to tackle going upstairs carrying the baby despite the pain in my back, I saw Danny come out of his bedroom. He was shouting for his mummy, and could hear all the crashes and bangs coming from our bedroom. One of them was screaming, Nicola I think, and then there was a huge bang as the door was thrown open. Debbie came out, absolutely livid, and still yelling at Nicola. She saw Danny, picked him up and threw him down the stairs.'

Tessa held up her hand. 'Whoa. Can we backtrack, Adam? You're saying it was Debbie Carter who threw Danny down the stairs.'

'I am. Don't get me wrong, Nicola was capable of it, but it was Debbie who did it. I rushed towards Danny, who was unconscious, and I had to put the baby on the floor at the bottom of the stairs so that I could see to Danny.'

He took a deep breath. 'This next bit is going to tell you exactly why I've been hidden away for ten years. I had a very brief affair with Debbie. We'd always had feelings for each other, but life wasn't easy with Nicola, and when the bullying and physical beatings became too much, I turned to Debbie. Stupidly. We slept together twice, that was all. Then she became demanding, wanting me to leave Nicola. I couldn't do that, I had Danny. I told her it would never happen, and she told me she was pregnant. I said no way, and she said she hadn't been sleeping with Rob, they were going through a difficult time themselves. When Bridie was born we found out for definite, although I have to say she never doubted that Bridie was mine.'

He stopped to gather his thoughts. 'After throwing Danny down the stairs, she followed his route and stood beside me. Her words that day put so much fear into me, I actually rang Ethan from the hospital while they were fixing Danny's arm. She said she hoped Danny would die, because then she could have me, but she also said that if I told the police the truth about Danny's fall, she would make sure Bridie suffered the same fate. Only Ethan knows the story, the full story. He wanted to get me out of there the next day, but they kept Danny overnight, so it had to be the day after. Nicola went to the hairdressers, and we drove away. Ethan met us at the house, introduced us to Trevor, and we've been there ever since.'

'So why do you think Debbie is trying to find you? And why does Danny think it was his mother who threw him down the stairs?'

'I couldn't let Danny think it was Debbie; if he'd ever said anything to anybody in authority, there was nothing to stop Debbie carrying through her threat to get rid of my other child, Bridie. And I think Debbie is trying to find me to kill me. It's as simple as that. She attempted to murder Danny. I'm a witness, the only witness because I brainwashed Danny into believing it was his mother who threw him. You think I'm soft, unmanly, for not sticking up for myself?'

'Not at all,' Tessa reassured him. She could see he was

becoming distressed. 'You're not the first man I've interviewed who has suffered domestic violence from their wife, and you won't be the last. It's just not talked about in the way it is when the positions are reversed. So let me get this straight in my mind. Debbie threw Danny down the stairs, intending to kill him and punish you, because you wouldn't leave Nicola. Then she threatened to kill your daughter if ever you spoke of what she had done. Where was Nicola while all this was happening?'

'She was still in the bedroom. I handed Bridie back to Debbie, and Debbie went home. Her words as she went out of our door were, "Sorry for the accident. Let me know if there's anything I can do".'

'Was Nicola injured?'

'Her pride certainly was. Debbie had gone for her with a pair of scissors, not to stab her, but to chop off her hair. That was why she was at the hairdressers when we left. She had scratches all down her arms and the beginnings of a black eye, but nothing to compare with either mine or Danny's injuries.'

'And Danny has never queried why his mother threw him down the stairs?'

'He didn't at first, it was only when he reached about eight or nine that he started to mention it, and ask why it had happened. I said Mummy was poorly and didn't know what she was doing, and that's why we left. He seemed to accept it. He never queried where Aunty Debbie and Uncle Rob were, in fact he seemed to forget our previous life very quickly, unlike me. It's as clear today as it was ten years ago. I actually thought, hoped, that the police would think Nicola had killed us, and she would be arrested for murder. I know there have been cases of successful prosecutions when there is no body. But it didn't happen, and we continued to live in Cromer, hearing nothing, or very little, until Ethan rang to tell me that Nicola was dead.'

'And what will you do now? Will you go back to Cromer, or move into your home in Baslow?'

'The first thing I have to do is find Danny. Once I've spoken to him, we can make decisions together. I'm certainly going to need his help, I struggle with going out, as you know, and if Danny won't come home, I would be better off staying in Cromer where I have Trevor.'

36

Tessa turned to Hannah. 'Contact social services – I want those two children cared for while we bring her in for questioning. And I want a safe house setting up tonight for Adam and Trevor. Adam, thank you for this. I need to check in with my team at Chatsworth, I've had them tracing that fair where we're hoping Danny is, so I'll be back in a few minutes. Would you like a drink?'

'Water will be fine, DI Marsden, and thank you. Is Trevor okay?'

She smiled. 'He's good. And a brilliant friend. We've fed and watered him, so he's probably asleep in reception, waiting for you. I'll find him and tell him about arrangements for tonight.'

They stopped the tape and Hannah disappeared to follow Tessa's instructions. They had certainly been fooled by Debbie Carter, but it was retribution time.

Tessa took out her phone and rang Ray at Chesterfield.

He answered immediately. 'Was just texting you, boss, to say we've tracked down that fair to Sunderland. I asked the local coppers to pay a visit and get Danny for us, but according to the owners he's not been with them for a couple of months. Told them he was going home to his dad.'

'Unless Adam Armstrong is bullshitting us, he didn't go anywhere near his dad. Okay, thanks, Ray. I'll see what Adam has to say in response to this bit of knowledge. I've got an urgent job for you. I want you to go to Debbie Carter's house in Eyam, and bring her in for questioning to Chesterfield. Social services have been advised. She has two children. If they don't get there in time, leave Fiona and Penny there to wait with the children.'

Tessa's mind was reeling as she walked back down to the interview room. She paused to look through the one-way mirror, and Adam was sitting with his head forward on his arms, which were resting on top of the table. She delayed going back in, and went to grab a coffee, while she waited for Hannah to get back to her.

'Done all that, boss,' Hannah said, and Tessa turned around, a coffee in each hand.

'Let's have these before we go back in. It seems Danny left the fair a couple of months ago to go home to his dad. Think he did? Think Adam's been lying to us?'

'No I don't. I can tell when people are lying, especially when you're asking the questions, and whatever he's said today, he believes it to be the truth. Everything he's done for the last ten years has been done to protect not only Danny, but Bridie as well. I suspect Danny just got fed up with the fairground life in winter, and took himself off to find something else.'

'Thank heavens you've said that, because I don't believe he's lied either. I think he forced himself to come here today to tell the truth. He's afraid for Bridie because he knows everything is likely to come out and Debbie could continue with her threat.'

'Social services said they would get the necessary paperwork and go round there. I said it had to be now, one of the children in particular was in grave danger. I also said social services in Chesterfield would be plastered across every newspaper, on every television station, and on every Facebook account if anything happened to Bridie Carter. I think it was the Facebook account bit that swung it. They're on their way. I've told them to ring me when they've got the children.'

'Brilliant. Thanks, Hannah.'

'You're welcome, boss. I gave your name as the authorising officer.' Hannah grinned.

Hannah logged them back in, and immediately began to speak of Danny. 'We've tracked down the whereabouts of the fair, it's currently in Sunderland.'

'Is he safe?' Concern was reflected in Adam's face and his tone of voice.

'We don't know. He's no longer with them, left a couple of months ago. Can you think of anyone in that area where Danny would be? Any relatives? Friends?'

'We don't have friends. We can't have friends, and I don't believe we have anyone north of here. All our relatives think we're dead anyway.'

'We've sent someone to bring Debbie Carter in for questioning, so her children will be temporarily in the care of social services. I believe we need to make sure Danny is safe, and that's a priority. We'll use the media, see if that will bring him forward. When you changed your names, I know Danny didn't like it so you stuck to Danny, but what name is on his documents, his birth certificate and suchlike that I'm sure you've no idea how you obtained?'

'I do know how I got them. I bought them from a bloke in a pub.'

'I'm glad to know it was nothing to do with Ethan King, because forgery is a crime, you know.' Tessa's voice was dry, but she received no response from Adam.

'All his stuff for starting school, taking exams, everything like that, is in the name of Davy Owen. He's never used it though. Told everybody at school his dad called him Danny, and that's how he wanted to be known. I called him Davy, because it was the closest I could get to Danny, but he wouldn't have it.'

Tessa opened her file and flicked through it. She ran her finger down one page, and looked up at Adam.

'He's using it now, Adam. DI Marsden and DS Granger leaving the room.' She switched off the recorder. 'Adam, in view of this news, I'll have to ask you to remain in this room. We'll let you know what's happening as soon as we can.'

Hannah's foot was pressed hard down on the accelerator all the way to Chatsworth.

PC Kurt Wentworth had been sent to the kitchen where the estate workers took their breaks to check on Davy's whereabouts, and found he had been in the glasshouses all day, transplanting. Kurt was currently pretending to look at the plants already in the vegetable gardens, but keeping a much closer eye on the young man inside the glasshouse. Harry Hardy was with him, although he seemed to have adopted a supervisory role as he hadn't done anything to any plants as far as Kurt could see.

Marsden and Granger walked through the entrance way towards

the glasshouses and the young PC met them. 'He's still in there, boss, along with Harry Hardy. You need me there as well?'

'Yes please, Kurt, in case he tries to run.'

Tessa led the way into the glasshouse, taking the left-hand path towards where Davy and Harry were standing at the central plant bench. Hannah went up the right-hand side, and Kurt stood in the doorway.

Davy looked up and grabbed hold of the slim almost-pointed tool he had been using to help with the transplanting.

'Daniel Armstrong? I am arresting you on suspicion of the murders of Nicola Armstrong and Olivia Fletcher. You do not have to say anything. But it may harm your defence if you do not mention when questioned something which you later rely on in court. Anything you do say may be given in evidence.'

Danny lunged with the dibber towards Harry, but it wasn't sharp enough to pierce the heavy waterproof coat he was wearing. Harry stepped backwards to avoid the thrust and his weight sent Tessa and himself crashing to the floor. Danny jumped up onto the plant bench and ran, heading for the door. He didn't make it anywhere once he reached it; Kurt Wentworth wasn't moving at all, and he held Danny while Hannah locked on the handcuffs.

Tessa dusted herself down, helped Harry get back to his feet, and went down the glasshouse towards Danny. 'You may live to regret that,' she said in the quiet tone she always used to great effect when she really meant what she was saying.

'Let's get him back to the station. We'll sort out a responsible adult and a solicitor when we get there.'

Tessa broke the news to Adam first. He looked grey. He couldn't look at her, until she said his name, forcing him to respond.

'I've worked it out,' he said. 'It's Danny, isn't it? It's Danny who killed his mother.'

'Not just his mother, Adam,' she said, trying her best to break the news gently to a broken man. 'He also killed Olivia Fletcher to stop her going to the police. I'm going to leave you with Hannah to give your statement, then we're going to take you and Trevor to the safe house. I'm not convinced you'll need it, but it's organised so we'll make use of it. Danny has a responsible adult with him, and a solicitor is on the way.'

'And this is all because I told him a lie. I told him his mother had thrown him down the stairs, which has left him with pain ever since. His arm never healed properly, and that's partly because I couldn't take him to the hospital. By the time I could, it was too late, there was too much nerve damage.'

'Whatever the reasons, Adam, murder doesn't solve them.'

Danny denied everything until Tessa showed him a picture of Olivia Fletcher. He had, up to that point, said *no comment* to every question, but when he saw Olivia lying on the ground in the glasshouse, he looked at his solicitor and said, without flinching, 'I shouldn't have done it, not to Liv.'

Two hours later he was formally charged with both murders, his statement had been taken, and he was locked in a cell until transport could be arranged to take him somewhere more secure, and suitable.

Adam and Trevor had their request to see him denied, and it was as they were leaving to be taken to the safe house that Debbie arrived, escorted by Ray Charlton and Fiona Ainsworth.

They stared at each other, then Debbie held up her hand as if to touch him. He flinched and moved away from her. Adam couldn't speak, not even to Trevor. The child he had done everything to protect was in police custody charged with murder, with matricide. And until Adam had seen DI Marsden's face when he said Davy Owen, he hadn't considered the possibility for one minute.

He watched as Debbie disappeared down the corridor to the cells, where he knew she would have to wait until DI Marsden had finished interviewing Danny. He guessed she would be there for some time.

The whole team went out for a drink, and Tessa and Hannah clinked glasses. 'We done good, boss,' Hannah said, and smiled.

'We certainly have, my nurse extraordinaire. Without you bullying me into taking time out to get better, we'd still be searching for answers. Thank you, Hannah.'

'No problem, boss. Any time.' *Any time*, she thought, meaning something entirely different.

37

Doris and Luke arrived at Keeley's house before eight, and she looked beautiful in the wedding dress she had bought from a charity shop in Bakewell. The bouquet of flowers was created from some plastic ones that looked a bit past their sell by date, but the excitement of what she was about to do shone out of Keeley's face.

She climbed into Doris's car and they were at Manchester airport in plenty of time to meet the flight arriving from Barcelona. Luke, dressed impeccably in a dark blue suit, held a board that said Vincent and Felicia Sanders.

They waited patiently outside the arrivals hall, and when the board announced the plane had landed, Doris and Keeley moved to one side, out of sight of people heading their way.

As travellers started to drift through, Luke held up his board.

He spotted Vincent and Felicia at the same moment they spotted him. Felicia still looked good with her new hairstyle, but she also looked puzzled by her name being on a board. He saw her speak to Vincent and point to him, so they headed towards him.

Keeley swung out from her hiding place as Luke held the

board higher, the signal to her that the Sanders were heading towards him.

She ran up to Vincent, and planted a huge kiss on his lips. 'Darling,' she said loudly, 'the answer is yes! Of course I'll marry you. I love you!'

The entire crowd in the arrivals hall cheered and clapped and Vincent looked around, clearly panicked. His wife, however, wasn't panicked, just pissed off.

'I thought you said she would never find out you were married until it was too late. Can you ever get anything right, Vincent? And now we've spent all this on this bloody holiday, we'll be broke.'

Keeley's acting was something to behold. 'What does this woman mean, my darling? Why is she saying such nasty things? I thought we would be married very quickly, now that the baby is on its way. Vincent, my love, who is she?'

Despite the large crowd, the silence was deafening in its magnitude.

'Baby?' Vincent's eyes were huge.

Keeley approached Felicia. She poked her in her chest. 'Who. Are. You? What are you doing with my fiancé?'

'He's not your fiancé.' Felicia's face was bright red, and it was nothing to do with any sunshine they had experienced in Barcelona. It was pure anger. 'He's my husband.'

'Your husband?' Keeley turned around and allowed the tears to fall down her cheeks.

Doris walked up to Sanders, sporting the camera around her neck, and shook his hand. '*Sheffield Star*, sir. May I congratulate you on your engagement to this beautiful young woman. We're doing a feature on unusual proposals, and Miss Roy invited us along to take photographs.' She held up the camera and began to shoot pictures, until Vincent came to his senses and held up his hand in front of his face.

'Get the fuck away from me,' he snapped. 'And if I see one picture in that newspaper, I'll sue.'

'It's already all over Facebook, sir,' Doris said, the sweetest smile showing on her face.

He grabbed Felicia's hand, pushed Keeley to one side, and then ran for the exit, both dragging suitcases behind them that couldn't cope with the speed of their owners.

Keeley collapsed laughing into Luke's arms. 'Fun over, everybody,' he said to the people who had gathered around to comfort the weeping bride. 'If anybody took photos of the idiot who's just run out of the airport, please post them on Facebook. Make it go big. He tried to cheat this young lady out of money, but he'll try it again with some other woman. Make him visible, will you? His name is Vincent Sanders. Thank you everybody!' and he led Keeley and Doris back to the car.

There was much laughter at Connection when Doris and Luke told the story of their morning's excursion.

'Keeley actually threw the bouquet of flowers over her shoulder for someone to catch? I so wish I'd been there,' Mouse said. 'Since I've been concentrating solely on the Manchester work, I miss out on all the fun stuff we used to do.'

'You mean like finding bodies? I know we haven't found one this year, but it is only March, you know.' Kat smiled at her friend.

'We felt it wound that little case up remarkably well. Felicia was obviously in on it just as much as Vincent was, and Keeley gave an outstanding performance. It was actually nothing to do with us, it was all her idea, but we couldn't say no, could we, Luke? I think he's handled the whole case brilliantly, so well done.' Doris smiled with some affection at their young receptionist.

· · ·

Luke didn't know how to react. He was starting to feel as though he belonged in this business, but didn't know how to let them know. His ladies, coupled with his ladies at home, formed a huge part of his waking and sleeping, and he made a silent vow that he would always do his best by them, no matter what he was working on. His pride when Doris had offered the simple little case to him had been huge, and when it had taken a more sinister turn with the discovery of a wife in Vincent's life he knew he had to step up to the mark and think for himself.

The surveillance had been so damn good. The camera was superb, and it made him smile when he thought of Doris's face that morning. 'Take care of it, Mrs Lester, we don't want it damaging, do we?'

The scuff around the back of his neck told him what she thought of his comment.

And now it was over. He would write up the report, insert it into the folder and put it behind him, taking it out to savour every once in a while, his first real case.

They were still in a laughing and joking mood when Tessa and Hannah arrived. The mood became more sombre the instant they walked through the door.

'Coffee?' Luke asked, and was surprised when they refused, saying they only had a few minutes.

'We just want to fill you in on everything that happened yesterday. Adam was driven to Chesterfield by his next-door neighbour, and finally told us the whole story, not the bits and pieces he came out with when we took him to Cromer police station. It turned out that it was Debbie who threw little Danny down the stairs, although for several different reasons Adam thought it better if Danny accepted it was his mother who did it. Danny has not only lived with this incorrect knowledge for ten years, he has also lived with considerable pain that will be there for the rest of his life. When he left his father some six months ago, he reverted to using the name he is registered everywhere with, Davy Owen.'

Tessa paused and looked around. Nobody spoke.

'We've now arrested Debbie Carter, and I imagine we will be charging her. We're not at that stage yet though. She's watched too many crime shows on tv, her answer to everything is no comment. It doesn't really matter, we have Adam's statement, and I'm going to drag the elusive Ethan King into the station to give his version of events. I'm sure I can't get him on providing fraudulent papers, because Adam has already stated he got them from a man in a pub. This man in a pub is definitely a friend to anyone who needs to disappear, or live outside the law. He's in every pub there is.'

She coughed, and Hannah went to get her a glass of water.

'Thank you, Hannah. But to get to the main point, Davy was holding off extremely well with his own no comments, but then I showed him the photo of Olivia's body. He caved almost immediately. We've now got his full statement, and he'll be transferred from Chesterfield very shortly.'

She sipped from the water and looked around at the faces, expectantly waiting for anything else she might want to share.

'And that's it, really. We'll be charging Debbie, as I said, and her children are currently with social services, but I suspect Adam may try for custody of one of them, possibly both to prevent them being split up.'

'Why would Adam do that? Oh...' Kat experienced a light bulb moment.

Tessa grinned at her. 'Got it in one, Kat. Bridie is Adam's child. She was part of the hold Debbie had over Adam, which drove Adam away in the first place. I'm pretty sure he'll get custody. I'm not convinced he'll stay in Baslow though; I think it holds too many sad memories for him. And then, of course, we have the issue of Simon Vicars. He's currently residing at the station, about to be charged with withholding information pertaining to a case. Danny has been staying with him since he left the fair.'

'Oh, for goodness' sake,' Mouse said. 'I've booked him for some electrical work, to start next week.'

Tessa laughed. 'Only you, Mouse, only you. The poor man is looking at a prison sentence for harbouring his nephew and not telling us, and you're concerned about your electrics.'

Hannah looked at her watch. 'Boss, it's time we weren't here.'

Tessa nodded. 'We'll call for a coffee later in the week when everything isn't so frantic. We've a meeting with the DCI, so have to get off. You gave us the biggest lead of all with this case, so thank you, ladies, and Luke. We're seeing the DCI to give our report, and it will be mentioned.'

Nobody said anything else about the case until the police officers had driven away, but then Kat spoke first. 'I'm finding it hard to believe. He's not even sixteen yet, and he's killed twice. And Debbie and Simon... it beggars belief, doesn't it? It's like Debbie has two personalities. The Debbie I saw every time I was in her presence wasn't the Debbie who would throw a five-year-old down the stairs. Sorry ladies, I need to have five minutes in church. I'll see you in a bit.'

She didn't even stop long enough to put on a coat, simply ran across the road and up the hill towards the place in which she felt most comfortable.

'It must be wonderful to have a faith like that,' Luke mused. 'My mum pops in all the time, she gets so much comfort from it.'

'Not you?' Doris asked.

'Nah, and I do think it's because it never crops up at school these days. My mum used to have assemblies where they sang hymns, and said prayers. She also went to Sunday school. I've never done anything like that, but I see Kat with her total faith and it makes me wonder what I'm missing. Maybe one day I'll find out. Not today though,' he finished, and moved across to his computer. 'I'm writing up the report for this morning's activities – you know, the activities where I impersonated a taxi driver, Mrs Lester impersonated a journalist, and Keeley impersonated a bride. I wonder what Kat's god would have thought to all of that,' he said with a smile.

'He'd probably say it's okay, as long as you didn't hurt anybody. But if you ever want to know what He would say or think, you ask Kat. She'll definitely tell you. The Reverend Kat Lowe is one person God will have a lot of respect for.'

ACKNOWLEDGMENTS

As always my thanks begin with my publishers, Bloodhound Books. They gave me my start back in 2015, and the book you have just read is my twelfth publication with this amazing company.

Bloodhound is the sum of its parts, and those parts are Sumaira Wilson, Tara Lyons, Heather Fitt and Alexina Golding, all prepared to go the extra mile for their authors – thank you, we appreciate the work you do for us.

Morgen (with an E) Bailey is my editor, my long-suffering editor. She guides me through every tiny part of my manuscript, and without her, my writing life would be so much more diffi-cult. Thank you, Morgen, you're such a star.

Just as long-suffering is my beta reader (yes, I only have one!), my lovely friend Sarah Hodgson. She reads the first twenty thou-sand or so words for me, and, just like me, has no idea what will follow those words, yet she still manages to make sense of them, and points out any potential plotlines that may be starting to appear. Thank you, Sarah.

During a conversation on Facebook one day, a phrase was used – negative nellies. This really tickled me, and so I have

Suzanne Lambert to thank for the comment that led to it being included in this book.

Debbie Carter, you have played a major part in this book, and I hope you enjoyed the role I allotted to you. Thank you for lending me your name in this final Kat and Mouse story.

And now I must thank my group of ARC readers, who read early versions of my books and leave reviews on publication day. Massive thanks, you do me proud.

I will miss Kat, Mouse and Doris. Doris, everybody's favourite nan, arrived accidentally, and definitely wasn't in my head when I started this series. I'm so glad she came to see me.

And a final thank you to Derbyshire, the stunning county full of picturesque villages, outstandingly beautiful scenery, lambs in the fields, Blue John in the caves, Winnats Pass – and the odd murder or two. You have served me well.

Anita Waller
Sheffield, 2019

Printed in Great Britain
by Amazon

65146663R00163